The Garden of the World

WEST WORD FICTION

LAWRENCE COATES

The Garden of the World

UNIVERSITY OF NEVADA PRESS

RENO & LAS VEGAS

cheers!
Lawrence

S

WEST WORD FICTION

University of Nevada Press, Reno, Nevada 89557 USA

Copyright © 2012 by Lawrence Coates

All rights reserved

Manufactured in the United States of America

Design by Kathleen Szawiola

Library of Congress Cataloging-in-Publication Data

Coates, Lawrence, 1956–

The garden of the world / Lawrence Coates.

p.   cm. — (West word fiction)

ISBN 978-0-87417-870-8 (pbk. : alk. paper)

ISBN 978-0-87417-877-7 (ebook)

I. Title.

PS3553.O153G37 2012

813'.54—dc23   2011039043

The paper used in this book is a recycled stock made from 30 percent post-consumer waste materials, certified by FSC, and meets the requirements of American National Standard for Information Sciences—Permanence of Paper for Printed Library Materials, ANSI/NISO Z39.48-1992 (R2002). Binding materials were selected for strength and durability.

FIRST PRINTING

21 20   19   18   17   16   15   14   13   12

5   4   3   2   1

The following chapters were previously published in somewhat different form: "Eye of the Mountain" originally appeared in *Long Story* 21 (2003); "The Beautiful Country" originally appeared under the title "The Garden of the World" in the *Greensboro Review* 74 (2003); and a small section of "Monster" originally appeared in *Ascent* 31, no. 1 (2007) as part of the short story "Belmont."

In memory of

JAMES BYRON HALL

and

JAMES D. HOUSTON

Writers, teachers, guides

We shifted our place of residence to the Pueblo (which is about 80 miles distant) for obvious reasons; one is, that it is much more convenient to the gold mines; and another is, that the principal part of the lands we own are in and about this place— the garden of the world.

—*From* Letter from California,
written in 1849 by Joseph Aram

Vedremo in cento anni.

—*Italian proverb spoken
when a new vineyard is planted*

CONTENTS

The Garden of the World

ONE · *The Beautiful Country*

Paul Tourneau's first wife, Pascale, died in that fall when the vineyards were torn out on the west side of the Santa Clara Valley, 1907. Phylloxera had been spreading slowly through the valley for years, galling the roots and withering the leaves of grapevines before killing them in the third year, and growers on the east side had planted plum and apricot trees between the dying vines, then uprooted the vines when the fruit trees began to bear. But Tourneau's land climbed steep and rocky into the wall of the Coast Range, close to the ocean-laden air, unsuitable for tree fruit. He had helped break the land for grapes, with horse and roller and fire, and he kept it in vines even as the yield dropped, until a new rootstock was found that promised resistance.

After a last miserable harvest, the vineyard looked tattered, exhausted. The grape leaves were papery and pale, and the year's fruiting canes draped untended in the dirt. Tourneau walked through the October dawn to the stables, where he met Augusto Corvo, his foreman, and together they harnessed the two big Percheron horses. Then he walked back to the house for his son. Gilbert was eight now, old enough.

"Gill!" he called. "Come on."

Pascale's voice answered. "He doesn't want to come."

Tourneau found them in the front parlor. Pascale sat on the black horsehair sofa, still dressed in her white nightgown, and she held Gill standing between her thin knees. Her hair was dark and glossy and long, and it fell uncombed down either side of her sharp and hollowed face. Gill had already put on his overalls and chambray shirt, and he looked soberly from his father to his mother and back again.

Pascale grasped the boy's shoulders with her long-fingered hands. "He's too young," she said.

Tourneau laughed at her. He was a large man, with a black beard fanning over his chest, and he always seemed outsized in any room he was in, as though the chairs and tables had been built for someone smaller than him.

"You're just afraid to be alone," he said. "Afraid he's growing up."

She lowered her head so that her hair fell over Gill. "You want to take away my only comfort."

Tourneau leaned over and pulled the boy easily from her. "It's almost daylight," he said. "No time to waste."

Together, they walked out to the front porch. Tourneau took a deep breath and smiled. In the house behind them, Pascale sobbed quietly. She had long been withdrawing into a world shaped by illness. As she found herself needing to rest every afternoon, unable to cook or tend the kitchen garden, her illness undiagnosed and therefore real only to her, she discovered that she'd been abandoned by her husband. And she understood that he didn't love her, had never loved her, had only married her because she was an only daughter and he wanted the land her father had first claimed after the timber companies cleared it of redwoods.

Her son alone cared for her, she thought. And now Paul Tourneau had taken this last solace from her, even though he owed all of his land to her, and all of himself to her.

A crew of harvesters had stayed on to help clear the vineyard, mostly Mexicans who came north every season. The work proceeded in the old way, with ropes and chains and horses, because the land was too steep for a tractor. A good oak tree on the edge of the cleared land was chosen to anchor a double purchase block and tackle, and the rope's end was then harnessed to the horses. The running block had two chains attached to it that were tied with half hitches high on two separate vines, one taut, the other with two feet of slack. When the horses pulled, first one vine was snaked out of the ground, and then the second chain grew taut and snaked out the other vine. After they had pulled all they could reach from one anchor tree, they moved down to another, or used four or five of the vines themselves as an anchor.

The rhythm of the work built long and steady, Tourneau or Augusto running the horses, the crew tying and untying the chain from vines and grubbing out deep roots with mattocks and spades, and building a great pile of twisted and decaying roots. Tourneau kept Gill busy helping move the chain, and at times he picked up a gnarled root and called his son over to inspect the damage. They never saw the phylloxera infestation itself—the insects had already moved on to younger, living roots.

At midday, they remained in the field, eating the same handmade tortillas as the crew, made from masa harina and lard and brought out by two silent older women dressed in widow's black who accompanied the men. After an hour's rest to let the day's hottest time pass, they worked again into the evening. Then Tourneau had Augusto bring out a barrel of sugar wine, *piquette* it was called in France, and they built a bonfire out of the uprooted vines, and drank to the day's work, drank death and damnation to the old and diseased, health to the young and vital.

When Gill asked his father when they were going to go back to the house, Tourneau shook his head.

"We're going to sleep out with our workers," he said, "sleep with the new vineyard."

"But what if Mama doesn't feel good?"

Tourneau looked back at the bonfire. One of the workers had brought out a guitar, and he sang *corridos* while the dead roots and vines burned.

"She's fine," he said. "There's nothing wrong with her."

They spent the next night there as well, and the night after, leaving the house to Pascale. Every night, a bonfire was lit and a barrel of wine tapped. Tourneau sent Augusto's sixteen-year-old daughter, Sophia, for his accordion, and he pumped and fingered the accordion in time with the guitar and sang hugely, his black beard tangled across his broad chest. He called on Gill to join him within the circle of men, join in and sing near the fire. But Gill stayed out in the half-light and turned his face to the darkness and worried about his mother.

On one of those nights, when bonfires brushed the sky, the two old women saw a white figure, like a ghost or an angel, around the edge of the firelight. The old women greeted it by making a cross of their fingers and kissing them. The angel disappeared. They told their sons about it the following morning and urged them to tell the *patrón,* and one young man who spoke some English shyly approached Tourneau. Not looking him in the eyes, he told him what had visited his fields. Tourneau listened carefully at first. Then he said that if it was an angel, they had nothing to fear. Perhaps it was coming to watch over them because they were doing God's work. And if it was a soul in pain, it would be laid to rest no doubt when all the vines were laid to rest, banished when the new rootstock was planted.

The two women saw the figure again the following night. It appeared when the bonfire was full ablaze, and the music had started, and men were throwing fibrous branches with rusty leaves into the flames. It seemed to agonize on the light's verge, hovering to and fro, and the widows kissed their fingers and bowed toward it.

When a song ended, Gill turned his head and noticed the old women looking toward the uplands, toward the end of the scoured land, and he saw what looked like a white gown at the end of the firelight's reach. It flitted in the sinking light, pale as moth wings, fading in and out of vision, into the light and back out into darkness.

Gill took two steps toward it and called out. He called out for his mother, and the gown slipped away into the folds of night.

Then he ran into the midst of the fire circle and yanked at his father's sleeve. Tourneau laughed and picked him up high, swung him high into the firelight and blew laughter from his cheeks as the music played. Gill shouted and struggled in his father's grip, and his father smiled large, delighted that Gill had come in from the dark. Gill began to beat his father about the shoulders with small fists until he was lowered to the ground, and he shouted again.

"Mama," he shouted. "She's out there."

He pointed to the two old women still gazing at the forest's edge, the backs of their widow's habits painted reddish by the fire.

Tourneau followed Gill away from the fire, and they stood and watched. At first there was only darkness, the trunks of oak and redwood standing out from the blackness between them. Then Gill saw the white figure, faint and wavering and barely earthbound, the hem of the garment swaying free above the ground.

"That's her," Gill said. "That's her."

Tourneau took a step in the direction Gill pointed, and it vanished. He peered toward the wood, waiting for a white flicker from the dark uplands to reveal itself, waiting for some sign of white from within the trees. There was nothing. He gazed for several minutes with Gill at his side, then patted his son's shoulder.

"It's nothing," he said. Behind them, the bonfire was falling in on itself, spent for the night.

"But Mama . . ."

"She's fine. Don't worry, she's fine."

It was cool the next morning in the uplands of the Santa Clara, but the sky was clear to the east, and on that plot of scratched and vacant land, the sun would blast the crew finishing off their angry work. One of the old widows, up before the rest to cook, first noticed the angel in the tree at the edge of the field, still and watchful. She kissed her crossed fingers for the angel. When it did not move, she woke up her youngest son, and she told him to rise and see and witness. But when he saw, he went to where the *patrón* slept, in the same blankets as his workers yet apart from them, and spoke to him: *Allá. En el roble. El Ángel.*

From a great distance Tourneau could see it was she, it was Pascale, still and quiet, leaning against the trunk of an oak. He could recognize the long white gown that hung down in embroidered hems. As he scrambled across the blank dirt field, she waited before him, propped up by one of the lower branches, her arms raised over her head as though she had fallen into that place. Behind him he heard the murmured worries grow tall, but he did not turn. She seemed to watch him cross the newly cleared land, her eyes clotted with flies but open and unblinking, and the face with which she met him was stricken, accusing.

He lifted her easily from the tree. She was light as sticks and straw, and so limp that he knew her death was recent, and he folded her over his shoulder and caught the backs of her knees with his elbow. He turned toward his workers, all awake now, standing silently in ranks and regarding him with careful eyes.

Augusto Corvo took off his hat slowly and held it to his chest. Before Augusto could ask what had happened, Tourneau spoke. "Keep the men working, keep going, keep the horses driving."

Then Gill woke from his boy's deep slumber, and he saw his father walking crookedly, large and misshapen by his burden, one shoulder higher than the other. His father slanted away from him, toward the barn and farm wagon, and then Gill saw clearly.

He ran after his father and saw his mother's long black hair hanging slack down his father's back, her arms swaying with every heavy step, her hands veined and brittle reaching out from the frilled sleeves of her gown. Those were the hands he wanted, those and no others, and when he reached them he grasped them and tried to pull his mother away. His father held her fast and whirled terribly toward him, and Gill fell back but still shouted at him.

"What did you do to Mama?"

Tourneau took his son by the collar and shook him once, then told him to follow. There were no telephone lines on the hill then, and the fastest way to let anyone know of a death was to take a wagon into San Natoma. Tourneau laid out the body of Pascale in the wagon bed with a rare gentleness, so that her gown floated about her. Then Gill jumped into the bed with his mother, sure that he cared for her more than his father could, sure that if he left her side, he would never see her again. Tourneau picked him up under the shoulders and put him to the ground. But Gill scrambled back up over the wall of the wagon bed, and Tourneau had to mount into the bed himself to pull him free. He wrapped his son up in his arms and carried him to the stable to bring out the horses.

They rode the narrow dirt road together, down the steep hill and sharp turns, and onto the town's graveled roads. Gill turned to watch his mother in the back of the wagon. Her eyes were still open, and when her head turned right and left with the wagon's motion, it looked as if she were scanning the heavens. And Gill imagined her as yet alive, her head rolling right and left, unstill and searching for a way out of the wagon her husband was driving down into the valley.

Tourneau stopped before the constable's office, which shared a building with the blacksmith's shop. The constable was Cap Andersen, who stumped around on a peg leg but was always reelected because he claimed he had lost his leg aboard ship during the Spanish-American War. Cap pegged out of the shop and looked into the back of the wagon and took off his hat and asked what happened in a raspy, kindly voice. Pascale had been a young woman still, but everyone in town knew about her obscure illness, her pallid skin and unworldly thinness. Tourneau didn't answer right away. He would never in his life say that he had found her in a tree. Cap reached out to Pascale's face to close her eyes and discreetly check her neck for bruises, and Gill, who was standing at the constable's side, kicked at his good leg and knocked him to the ground.

They finished tearing vines out two days later, grubbing out the last of the diseased roots by hand. The bonfire of that night was enormous. Tourneau brought out smoked hams, and rounds of Jack cheese three feet across, and bread, and barrels of wine. The mountains of vines and canes were soaked in kerosene, and Tourneau himself touched match to it.

Gill did not join them round the fire that night. He haunted the edge of the newly cleared fields, out in the half-warmth and half-light. He wandered as his mother had done, but he was dressed darkly and wandered darkly. He witnessed his father dance with Augusto's daughter, Sophia, watched him drink wine and make boastful music with his accordion. Tourneau called to him once to come in where it was warm, to come and eat, come and drink. But Gill kept his distance, small and dark and bitter, while his father turned back to the music.

No one blamed Tourneau for continuing to clear the land. The tree and vine growers in the area understood that work did not pause for grief, and none would have suggested that he halt tearing out the phylloxera-stricken vines. They knew that there followed the precise placing of lines of redwood stakes, just far enough apart so that a harrow could run between them, and that new rootstock had been ordered for the next February. They knew that each new vine would be planted by hand, and weeded by hand, and that Tourneau and Augusto would do most of the work themselves. It would be three years with the best of luck until the first harvest, and they knew how much he would be in debt by then. Some admired him for working without pause for the death of his wife, because a farmer should be willing to do what's necessary, even neglect his family, in order to keep the land. When the local newspaper editor, Bill Finney, wrote about the restored vineyard, he praised it and did not mention Pascale.

But word came out about the mysterious circumstances of Pascale's death, and about the celebration two days later—through Cap talking around the forge while the blacksmith spit tobacco juice and hammered metal, or through the two old widows who bought supplies in town and spoke low in Spanish to women working on other ranches, until the stories leaked into English and became known to all. People talked about how Tourneau had married into the land, talked in knowing tones of how confidently Tourneau had courted Pascale twelve years earlier, when he was working for wages and she was the thin and fragile only child of George Du Maurier. The talk spread when Tourneau married again, scarce six months later, with Sophia Corvo. There was, it seemed, too much of a coincidence. It was clear he had already chosen Sophia before the death of Pascale.

Tourneau worked through the talk to finish his vineyard, nicking off flower clusters by hand in the first year so that all the energy of the young vines would go to root and leaf, field-grafting the shy-bearing Pinot to his new rootstock, choosing a cane from each plant to train up as the main trunk. In that time, he renamed the vineyard Beau Pays, the beautiful country. When he came at last to harvest, he no longer sold wine in bulk to San Francisco merchants but instead bottled and labeled his own, as had been done in Burgundy. He began to fill the large and dark cellars cut back into the earth with tall redwood barrels for fermentation, and smaller barrels of French oak for aging, and riddling racks for sparkling wine, and rows of bottled still wine sold by subscription only. And he had a second son, with Sophia, whom he doted on.

During those years, if he looked at Gill and saw Pascale's accusing eyes, his response was always the same: to set his son at some task that would keep him with his face to the earth.

Tourneau wanted to imagine himself the first man, the man who had been called to the hillside to work in the garden of God. And the past might have been forgotten, all debts paid, if Gill had not enlisted to fight in the Great War and never come home. Everyone knew that Gill had not been killed. His name didn't appear in the local paper's list of boys who gave their lives, and one doughboy from Campbell said that he had seen Gill after the Armistice had been signed, perfectly alive, though half his face had been horribly scarred by a tree burst. But he did not return after the war, and his absence was an invisible crack in the rightness and wholeness of man, woman, child, living together in the beautiful country.

✳ *Loyalty Day*

Gill left the vineyard in 1917, the year the United States entered the war. He'd begun to work in the fields with his father the year the vineyard was replanted, worked through his father's new marriage to a woman only eight years older than himself, worked through the birth of a half brother, Louis, whom his father took into his arms at the end of every day. He remembered when he was first brought in to see Louis, brought in to the same room where he himself had been born. Sophia was sitting up in the bed, and she was dressed in white, and the loose white curtains in the bedroom bulged with light as though the sunlight had weight and density. She held Louis in her arms, also wrapped in white, his red face squinting and wrinkling at the world. Gill was twelve then, and awkward, and he faced what seemed a picture of perfected grace.

He worked those years sullen and joyless. Summers, walking the allées, stripping off a shoot that wasn't going to bear well, clipping a sucker that would steal nourishment from the main trunk, pruning just enough to let the sun in to ripen the berries. Autumns, during the crush, missing school and then feeling stupid and snubbed when he finally rejoined classes. Every day he worked, he thought that he was helping to create the vineyard for the benefit of the small child who had taken his place, and he told himself that the vineyard, by rights, half belonged to him.

When Sophia tried to mother Gill some, he always pushed her away. Though he was jealous of the bond between her and Louis, he preferred his own resentment to any affection she might offer. Even before the war, he was thinking of leaving the vineyard, breaking out of his trapped life, and returning proud to claim what was his own.

When the first call for volunteers for the army didn't bring enough enlistments, a national draft was instituted, and a single day, June 5, 1917, was designated for all men between the ages of twenty-one and thirty-one to register. In some parts of the country it was called Patriotism Day, in others it was Call to the Colors Day, and in others it was Loyalty Day. Most of the men who worked at the vineyard, including those born in France and Italy who were not yet citizens, had to register, and Gill had been hearing for weeks the registration debated, the chances of actually being drafted discussed. One worker named Tullio rushed to complete his naturalization so he would be eligible to serve. Another who had emigrated from France said that two of his younger brothers had been killed at the front, and that his parents were glad he was far away, in California.

All schools and government offices were closed that day, and most of the fruit packing plants and canneries closed as well. At seven a.m., factory whistles blew, and church bells rang, and police sirens raced throughout the valley. Registration booths were set up in every small town, and in every neighborhood of the city of San Jose. Some men had lined up at the booths at five in the morning, wanting the honor of being among the first.

Paul Tourneau gave his workers a half day off, and Gill was glad to be working the southern end of the vineyard, far from the house, far from his father's eyes. He was seventeen, and didn't have to register, but he'd decided to sneak away and join the men going to town. At noon, when he heard someone slap the dust out of a cap against a thigh, and someone else snap shut a pair of pruning shears, he crouched down and let the others filter out of the vineyard.

Gill looked at the shadow of a curling green tendril cross a clod of broken dirt and waited. He knew that Sophia would be placing lunch on the table, a big lunch with pasta and soup and fresh bread. His father would praise the food and smile on Louis, dirty only with play. And Louis would embrace Sophia around the thighs, bunch her skirt up over her rump. Louis could do that, he did that every day.

After a few minutes, Gill stood up and walked the fenceline until he could cut north between sections and meet the road. When he saw the vineyard truck, pluming yellow dust behind it, he stepped from among the vines and held up his right hand. The driver laughed and pulled to the side, and Gill climbed up into the crowded truck bed, fitting himself in among the other men sitting with their knees close to their chins. The truck bounced forward, and the men fell against each other before settling in once again. Tullio was sitting across from Gill, and he nudged him with his foot.

"Does your father know you're here?" he asked.

"No," Gill said. "But I don't care."

Tullio raised his eyebrows. "You care," he said. "You care more than you think."

After the truck dropped everybody off at the town square, Gill walked to the Interurban train station and waited for the train into San Jose. He didn't want to stay in San Natoma and have his father come down after him, or have somebody else ask him what he was doing in town. The station was a simple frame building on the north side of town, with broad overhanging eaves sheltering three wooden benches. Above the eaves, a small sign read SAN NATOMA—ELEVATION 557 FEET. Gill waited back in the shadows until he heard the single-car train rattling into town, a long black trolley pole canting back from the roof and connecting the car to the electrical wires overhead.

On the train, Gill found a seat across from two women dressed for shopping on South First Street, with light woolen coats and hats, white gloves, and long dresses with raised embroidery around the high necklines. One of the women wore a string of pearls, and they both smelled of rose water. Gill suddenly felt self-conscious about going into San Jose in his work overalls and his dirty boots. But the women smiled at him approvingly, and as the train's electric engine hummed, one of them leaned forward.

"Are you going to register in San Jose?" she asked. She wore oval-shaped eyeglasses that made her eyes look huge.

"Yes, ma'am," Gill said.

"Well, bless you, dear boy."

"Yes, God bless you," said the other woman. "Have you heard the things the Kaiser does? Even to babies?"

"Awful," the woman in glasses said.

"Horrid."

"Terrible."

They clucked in agreement with each other, then turned back to Gill.

"You're doing a good thing," the woman in glasses declared.

Downtown San Jose was decorated as though it were the Fourth of July. Flags waved from the light poles, and red and white bunting swung across the streets. Most of the stores were open, displaying flags in their windows, draped over the shoulders of well-dressed mannequins. Gill walked the crowded sidewalks, and everywhere he saw men just a few years older than him wearing red buttons pinned to their lapels. The buttons read: REGISTERED—UNITED STATES MILITARY SERVICE. The young men were dressed up for a holiday, in pressed shirts and ties and coats, and they walked with their chests puffed out, showing off the buttons. Gill watched the older men congratulate them and clap them on the shoulder, and the women shine with admiration. The same women looked at his empty chest and work clothes, and turned away.

He found a registration booth outside the courthouse and joined the line of young men winding down the sidewalk. They all seemed anxious and ready, nervously jostling each other, eager to pass through the booth and get it over with. Two of them near the front of the line were dressed in tweed jackets that they had obviously outgrown, their bony wrists sticking out from the arms of the jackets. More men fell in line behind Gill. Most of them had come with friends, or had sisters or girlfriends watching them and encouraging them. Gill was alone, but it didn't seem to matter. He felt good to be among these men, good to be part of something larger than himself, and the words of fellowship and love spoken to others seemed also to include him.

At the head of the line, Gill stood before a man dressed in a suit and tie and sitting at small wooden desk. A deep wedge of black hair pointed at the center of his forehead, fingers of baldness above his temples, and Gill noticed small flakes of dandruff at his hairline. At the man's right elbow, a stack of completed registration forms was weighted down by a heavy stone.

He looked up at Gill, dressed in a blue shirt and overalls, and he fingered his tie.

"What year were you born?" He kept a hand over a blank registration form.

"1900," Gill answered truthfully.

The man shook his head, disgusted. "Wrong answer."

"What?"

"Can't register if you're only seventeen, kid." He looked past Gill. "Next."

Gill found himself shunted aside, forced to leave the line without a registration button. He heard laughter and jibing voices, and he turned his back and quickly left the milling crowds of downtown.

He struck The Alameda, the broad avenue running between San Jose and Santa Clara, and he caught one of the trolleys that passed by every eight minutes. The street was shaded by poplar trees, the same trees that had shaded the route between the city and old Mission Santa Clara, and trolleys ran on two parallel tracks in the center of the street. Santa Clara had also put out its flags and draped the overhangs above the wooden sidewalks with bunting. The central district was smaller than San Jose's, a few blocks of one- or two-story business buildings with sidewalks shaded by awnings and the trolley line now a single pair of tracks down the street center.

Gill got off the trolley and saw a line of men on the sidewalk outside the brick post office. One group of men shuffling in line were all dressed identically, and he walked closer until an attendant in a white uniform held up his hand.

"You don't want to get too close and frighten them," he said.

The men in line were dressed in canvas straitjackets, the sleeves long and sewn shut and belted together behind their back, so that each one seemed to be embracing himself. Their hands were wholly contained within the sleeves, not free to grab or poke at anything, and they all wore light leg irons so that they could only move slowly, bent forward and rocking back and forth. Gill realized that they must be inmates from the asylum for the insane, at Agnews Station, and he looked down the line. One of them had a large, lumpy body but a tiny head, smooth-cheeked like a baby. Another was muttering to himself, dark-eyed and gaunt, and he looked at Gill suspiciously. A third seemed to be missing his nose—there was only a hole where his nose ought to be, dark and shiny with mucus, and his mouth wouldn't close all the way, so he always seemed to be smiling. There were people in the line only three feet tall, others who were giants, and some who simply stared ahead at something nobody else could see.

The attendant in the white uniform coughed. He was thin and had red blotches on his face, and he carried a cane to tap the inmates and move them along.

"They have to register too?" Gill asked.

"Everybody between twenty-one and thirty," the man said. "Uncle Sam doesn't want anybody hiding from the draft in the asylum, though God knows why you'd want to. Shit, if I were young enough, I'd sign up myself. Anything to get out of here."

He coughed into his fist and poked his cane into the leg of the dark-eyed man. The line moved forward with the slow jingle of chains.

Gill fell in behind the last of the straitjacketed men. Several other men soon joined in behind him. Inside the post office, he saw another man in a white uniform filling out the forms for the inmates.

When it was his turn, he stepped up to a small desk where a balding man with glasses pushed a form at him. He filled it out, birthplace, citizenship, next of kin, and added four years to his age. The man looked at it, then printed Gill's name, the date, and the place on a bluish green registration card embossed with an eagle. He signed it and handed it to Gill along with a red button.

"Does this mean I'm going to be called?" Gill asked.

"Only if your date comes up in the lottery."

"If you want to volunteer, what do you do?"

The man pushed his glasses up his nose and leaned back. "I'll tell you how," he said.

A few minutes later, Gill stepped out into the street, pinning his button to his shirt. He blinked in the sun and found himself standing among the inmates. They also had buttons pinned to their straitjackets by the men in white uniforms, and they stood in ragged formation.

"We've done our part too," said the attendant with the cane, and he laughed and coughed.

Gill caught the trolley back to San Jose, clutching his registration card during the entire trip. There was a parade late in the afternoon, headed by the San Jose Cornet Band, and Gill joined the good-natured crowd of young men wearing red buttons behind the band. Traffic was blocked off, and they strolled in a large and friendly herd, listening to the brassy music, passing beneath the striped and swaying bunting. Those on the sidewalk smiled and applauded.

The vineyard house glowed that evening as Gill walked up toward it, the windows lighted under the purpled sky. On the broad verandah, backlit and shadowy, he saw Tourneau's bearish outline, standing and waiting. Gill knew that his father had already heard what he'd done. One of the workers would have told him.

Gill was sure he had done the thing that would most anger his father. It was the first decision he'd made about his life independently, and it was one that would take him away from the vineyard. He walked up the broad steps, touching the red button still pinned to his chest, holding close the praise he'd received down in San Jose.

Tourneau turned toward Gill, his black beard broad across his chest. "So you were down in town for Loyalty Day." It was a statement, not a question.

"Yes, Papa. I was."

"And what did you do?"

"I signed up." Gill spoke both proud and diffident, trying out how it felt to act free from his father's will. "I'm going to join the army. I'm going to fight."

"You didn't ask me."

"No."

"Why not?"

"I didn't have to. I wanted to do it on my own."

"You thought I would say no," Tourneau said. "I don't like you doing it without telling me, but I won't say no. Come in."

In the front parlor, a bottle of sparkling wine iced in a silver bucket sat on the sideboard, and a sponge cake topped with sliced fresh strawberries was on a salver beside it ready to cut. Sophia and Louis were waiting, along with Augusto Corvo, Sophia's father. When Gill came through the door, Augusto went to him and clapped a strong hand on his shoulder.

"You're off to your adventures." He looked at the button, read what it said, and nodded knowingly.

Sophia, slender in a long blue dress, came to Gill and hugged him and tried to smile, though she could not hide her sadness. Louis was beside her, curly-headed in tiny overalls, and he looked up at Gill.

"Shake your brother's hand," Sophia said. "Wish him well on his journeys."

Gill bent down and took Louis's small hand in his.

At the sideboard, Augusto untwisted the agraffe from the bottle and sent the cork into the rafters. He poured flutes full of sparkling wine and handed them around. Tourneau lifted his glass to Gill and smiled broadly.

"Gill will go out, and fight courageously, and come back a full man, *un homme entier.* And his place at the vineyard will always be waiting for him."

Gill touched glasses with his father, his stepmother, Augusto. He looked at his glass, the bubbles crawling up the sides in tiny chains, and he felt surprised, tricked somehow, that his defiance was being celebrated. He felt as though his leaving had been foreknown, foreordained, not an act of freedom at all.

But his father looked at him with merry eyes, and Gill knew it was impossible now to change his mind. He lifted the glass to his lips and drank, the wine dry but keeping a savor of the grapes from which it had been crushed.

In the fall of that year, he caught a train to camp, and his father, stepmother, and half brother came to the platform to see him off. He waved at them from the window when the whistle blew. They waved back to him, a tight grouping of father, mother, son, and as the train left the station, they seemed to meld together in his vision.

The trench near Chateau-Thierry, the darkness before dawn, Henry Fresher screaming on the wire. Henry Fresher had been the best on the prowl, probing the pocked and wire-strung land between the two lines. He liked to go every night, with a well-oiled pair of wire cutters, and snip the barbed wire near the German trenches. He always said nights on the prowl were the only times he could get over the feeling of being buried alive that came from weeks in the trenches, and he could laugh for hours the next day, imagining the Germans swearing when they saw how close he had come to their lines. He would sit, sharpening his clippers on a whetstone, and imitate the angry German accent he had heard on the farms in Wisconsin.

Fresher had only one eyebrow. The other had been sheared off by a flying piece of shrapnel, and he felt he led a charmed life after that. The platoon had a new lieutenant then, a shavetail, who agreed with him and let him go out every night, while the others rotated in and out of patrol duty.

Gill had been out with Fresher many times, as had every other soldier in the platoon, and had seen how easily and confidently he moved across the dark ground between the lines, and how peacefully he slept during the days. Even when a signal shell went up, a floating red flare that could catch prowlers in its dim and bloody light and make them targets, he was able to freeze absolutely in whatever posture he'd been caught, and had even trained himself to close his eyes until the signal flare burned out. Open eyes, he claimed, could give off a shine to German gunners. And what did you need to be looking at while a flare was up? Seeing yourself get shot wouldn't get you any less shot.

But now Fresher had gotten himself shot, and shot well, and he was screaming on the ground thirty feet from the Germans. He'd been screaming for three hours. The other two boys he'd gone out with, Rue Tane Downey and Bill Toms, were silent beside him. Patrols were in threes, so that if one man were wounded, the other two could carry him back. But Fresher's voice and the silence beside him made it seem like all three had been hit. Gill watched the shavetail pace back and forth as the narrow sky above the trench turned pale, checking again that the other two men had not come back, listening to Fresher scream. Gill knew that the Germans would not go ahead and toss a grenade and kill Fresher. They would use him to lure more soldiers out. It had happened before. And Gill knew that the new lieutenant, in some part of him, had been hoping that the screaming would stop before dawn, so that he wouldn't have to ask for volunteers. But as the sky lightened, the lieutenant called back to the artillery on the hills behind them, and turned to the men who were already waiting for him to speak. Gill and five others raised their hands.

The artillery laid down a box barrage around the wounded men, a curtain of falling shells holding off the enemy. The gunners had their field pieces calibrated, and they could roll a barrage forward toward the enemy lines so that the infantry, at least in theory, could advance behind it. That morning, the guns hit the ground in a line beyond Fresher's patrol and also on either side of them, and after the ground around them was falling upward in explosions, the six men carrying three stretchers went over the top.

There was only one tree still standing in the cratered earth between the two trenches, a stumpy, unidentifiable tree, with most of its branches and leaves blown off, more like the memory of where a tree had been than anything yet living. They ran by the tree on their way to where the men lay, running in a crouch through some of the same cuts in the wire that Fresher had probably made the night before. In the midst of the barrage, they found the two men dead and Fresher alive and bleeding. Shells were falling in a pattern around them, spiking the earth and blowing dirt upward. The air was thick with grit and noise, a noise that forbade speech and shoved them all into a tight huddle around the fallen men, rolling Toms and Downey roughly onto stretchers, and lifting Fresher onto his with care.

It was only when they started back that the Germans began taking potshots at them, shooting at the dead and the bearers of the dead. The artillery fire had kept most of the Germans belowground, but some rifle fire and return artillery had begun. Gill saw the tree again, running as lead man on Fresher's stretcher, saw its lumpy and awkward shape through the smoke and sound and crazed earth, pointing like a swollen finger.

Then, suddenly, the tree was lit from within, a great tower of light from in the heart of it, illuminating it to the tip of its crippled branches. Gill remembered very clearly that sudden light.

The tree burst open from an artillery charge and shot wood chunks in all directions. Gill heard his jawbone break inside his head and his cheek crunch in, heard the wood crash through him before he felt it in any other way, and then he was on the ground. He rose up from the awful ground, took the front of the stretcher, and ran Fresher back to the lines before passing out.

Some weeks later, as he recovered in a hospital, he learned that Henry Fresher had died from his wounds.

Gill didn't return to San Natoma after the war. Whatever notion he'd had of coming home feeling greater than when he'd left was sapped every time he looked into a mirror, every time he saw men recoil when they saw the bad side of his face, every time he saw a woman shiver and turn away. The right side of his face was smooth and regular. The left side, crushed by the exploding tree, was thick with drippings of scar tissue, so that his skin resembled melting wax. And his left eye hung down and looked a little inwards, toward his nose, because of a shattered orbital poorly knit.

He felt shamed by the way he looked, and angry that he felt shamed. He was angry at himself for joining the herd, for stupidly thinking he would find a greater self in the war, and angry at his father's unexpected celebration of his departure, which now felt like a betrayal. His father's words mocked him. He didn't feel an entire man. If his mother still lived, he told himself, he would have returned to the vineyard. Without her, whatever place he could have had there would be the same place he'd had before, marginal and secondary, but worse because he was wounded.

He stayed away, didn't come back in uniform with his medals on his chest, didn't take part in the big Armistice Day parades held in San Jose every year, refused all ceremony of return that would let others either gape at him or treat him as though he were invisible. Instead, he worked dead-end jobs, mining for a time in Red Mountain, building levees in the Central Valley, haying near Salinas, blowing months of pay in a week's time in Rio Dell or Scarlet Row or Poverty Hill, and then hiring himself out again. Seasons passed, and he moved restlessly, like a ghost, belonging nowhere, and nowhere finding anyone who would see him as his mother would have, whole and beautiful.

THREE

Eye of the Mountain

*I*t was in Salinas in 1926 that Gill met Lupita, and because of her began
making whiskey with Big Boy, and because of him began the road back
to the vineyard. Lupita was not the youngest woman at the Golden Staircase,
but with her purpled lips and bruised, purple-looking eyes, she was still able
to look vulnerable. She'd walked right up to him, didn't seem to mind the
thick scar tissue across his cheekbone and his crooked face. He'd liked her
because of that, and because she made him believe that she needed him. She
told him that her father had been a Villista and had been driven north of the
border when the revolution failed, and even today refused to believe that
Villa had been shot dead in his car. Her father sometimes claimed that Villa
visited him at night, and then he was most awful. She had to run away, she
said. Her mother was dead and her father worked her like a beast, kept her
prisoner in whatever shack or common house they found to live in, and beat
her if she even looked at a boy. She didn't really belong working in a saloon,
she said, and she cried on his shoulder the very first night they met.

Gill moved her away from Salinas and found work in the canneries in
San Jose, and they set up in a little flat in Goosetown. In November, the canneries laid off, and he ran into Big Boy while looking for work. They'd been
on the canning line together a few years before, when Gill hooked on there
right after the war. Big Boy had been carrying two hundred and fifty pounds
even then, and so he had never been one of the pretty boys Gill resented.
He'd listened to Gill chip away with his clipped voice at all those men who
had gotten out of serving one way or another, at the women who wouldn't
look at him. Big Boy's weight had kept him out of the war, and Gill seemed
to forgive him this, because he offered an unfailing sympathetic ear.

He found Big Boy in an alleyway beside the Goosetown Saloon, wrestling a ten-gallon barrel of whiskey out of the rear of a Dodge sedan. "Hey, Big Boy," he said.

"Gill!" Big Boy stood up and wiped off his pinkish sweaty forehead with a large bandanna. His face was like a round moon, with a smooth sag under the chin, and his voice, when he spoke, came out high-pitched and scratchy. "How about giving an old pal a hand?"

They rolled barrels together into the speak and hefted them together up behind the bar where the bartender could spigot them. While they worked, Big Boy asked what Gill had been doing, and Gill told him—haying, canneries, warehousing, this and that.

"You should be doing something better, Gill," Big Boy said.

"Don't I know it."

"You interested in making whiskey?"

Gill paused. "I've made wine," he said. "I could learn."

After they finished unloading, they each took a shot of whiskey and sat in one of the booths. Big Boy explained in a low voice that he was setting up a still in a new location, the dry hills back of Coyote, on land owned by a big guy with connections. It was easier when there were two men in on it. One could make deliveries, pick up supplies, while the other could tend the barrels of mash, keep the still running, keep a lookout.

"Sometimes," he said, "a man might have to spend three months or so up in the hills."

"Three months?"

"The last guy I had was a rumdum," Big Boy said. "You can't have a rummy helping you make whiskey."

"I've got a girl. Okay if she comes along?"

"A girl, eh?" Big Boy grinned knowingly. "Sure. Bring her along."

In December, they drove the Dodge on dirt roads into the eastern hills. The track they followed was rutted and overgrown by greening grasses, and they climbed gradually, following the roundness of the land. They were well out of direct sight of Coyote or any of the other valley towns when Big Boy wheeled the Dodge down into a small bowl beside a steep and wooded dry arroyo. Above them, on a knoll, stood a small, rude structure put together from oak beams and concrete, and cracked concrete steps led up to two closed doors about three feet high.

Big Boy set the brake and eased his belly sideways out from behind the steering wheel, while Gill and Lupita got out and stretched from the drive. They both looked at the strange little building above them.

"What's that?" Gill asked.

"That's the tomb of William Kingman, the first white man to own this land—'s why there's a road." Big Boy already had the back door of the Dodge open and was huffing out a sack of rye. "The coil and can are already here. Had to move them from the last place because we used up all the wood. And because that drunk might tell the Prohibition dicks where we were at."

Gill was still staring. "Why did he want to be buried here?"

Big Boy shrugged. "He called this place Ojo de la Montaña. Eye of the mountain. Maybe he just wanted to keep an eye on things here."

"*Ojo* means spring also," Lupita said. "Mountain spring."

"Spring, eye." Big Boy shrugged again. "How about giving me a hand unloading the gear."

They first cleared the brush from the bowl and flattened out a site for the canvas tent Lupita and Gill would live in, a twelve-by-twelve tent with a large single center pole holding up the peak and a wooden smoke hole where a stove chimney could run through. Then Big Boy and Gill dug out a row on a south-facing slope for twenty mash barrels to stand upright and catch the sun, and a fire pit that the can could sit over, and they piped in spring water to cool the coil and condense the steam.

Within three days, they were ready to set the mash. Big Boy explained that he had made sure he got irrigated rye with large, mature kernels, and that the rye had not been salted. Salt kept the mash from working. Lupita heated kettles of water over an open fire while Big Boy and Gill dumped forty pounds of rye into each fifty-gallon barrel. Then they mixed forty pounds of sugar into about twenty gallons of warm water and stirred it into a rich and bubbled syrup, and poured that into each barrel of rye. They topped off the barrels with more warm water to within three inches of the top and added half a cake of dry yeast, the size of a man's hand. Finally, they covered each barrel with canvas torn from the sugar sacks and let the mash warm in the sun through the day, then covered all the barrels with a tarp at sunset to keep in the warmth and let the fermentation work through the night. As a precaution, Big Boy and Gill also rigged up a dry cell battery and a bell mounted on a post, and ran wire a quarter mile down the road, where they installed a switch with a spring trigger held open by a black thread stretched across the road.

The mash quieted down at the end of a week into a clear and sour liquor, and Big Boy told them it was time to run the still. Once it was running, he would leave for a few days and return with more barrels and supplies. Together, Gill and he poured in mash until the still was about three-quarters full, and built a fire with dry smokeless wood under the can. "You've got to get it boiling, and then cut back the fire," Big Boy said. "Otherwise the mash will puke into the coil."

The copper can began to change color slowly over the fire as it heated, growing purer and brighter, as though glowing from within. Big Boy shrewdly poked at the burning logs to dampen the flame, and Gill watched the end of the coil.

"Here it comes," he said. A single drop crawled to the lip of the coil and hung there. Gill stretched out a finger and cropped the cooled and distilled liquid from the coil and tasted it.

"Bitter," he said.

"It'll mellow out on the oak," Big Boy said.

They each had one cup of the bitter, unaged whiskey that night as they sat around the fire burning low under the can. Big Boy wanted them to keep the fire going as long as one of them could tend it, as late into the night as possible. More hours meant more whiskey, and they could set mash again as soon as they had some empty barrels.

Gill held his tin cup up, considered it, and took a sip. "I feel like a man of property."

Big Boy looked at him, then slowly began to chuckle. "If being a man of property is making hooch on someone else's land."

"It's more than I've had for a damned long time." Gill turned to Lupita for confirmation. "Or Lupita either."

Lupita leaned up against him, and Gill stroked her hair.

"Fair enough," Big Boy said. "Your old man had property, though, didn't he?"

"Yeah, that he married into. And then saw my mother into an early grave."

"He still making wine, you think?"

"Sure," Gill said. "I heard, when he saw Prohibition coming, he suddenly got religion and is selling sacramental wines to the church. But I'll bet he's got his best wines still stashed back in those old Chinese caves cut into the hillside."

He looked around, a little dreamy, at the hills disappearing into darkness beyond the firelight.

"I'll bet you could grow good grapes right here, make fine wine right here."

Big Boy laughed. "That won't happen while the Volstead Act is in place."

"Maybe not. But someday." Gill nudged Lupita until she smiled at him.

"Well. It don't hurt to dream, I guess," Big Boy said.

Gill bent down and kissed Lupita's black hair, closing his eyes and thinking of his mother's dark hair, while Big Boy watched with a lewd grin.

The next morning, after Big Boy left, Gill emptied the distilled liquor from the previous night into an aging barrel, then bucketed mash into the can and screwed it shut while Lupita arranged kindling under the can. They built the fire together, Gill handing her larger pieces when she called for them, until the can was hot and the fire had to be flattened out. When the new whiskey began to trickle through the coil, he left camp with an axe and a canvas wood carrier and went up the arroyo to chop wood.

He picked out a live oak and took off his shirt in the cool morning and began to swing his axe into the downhill side of the trunk. He worked steadily—not too fast, so that he would wear out, but fast enough to warm and sweat with the growing sun. He swung top and bottom, chopping out a bird's mouth that wouldn't bind his axe blade and would let the weight of the upper branches help the tree fall. When he was more than halfway through, he heard a creak and groan, and he stood back while the trunk cracked and its branches swished and whispered to the ground. It fell softly, recoiled a little bit before settling, and Gill smiled in satisfaction before he began to trim the branches from the main trunk. This tree would keep him busy a couple of days, and provide wood for a week at least.

He came back with a load of wood rolled in canvas on his back, and he paused by the tomb of William Kingman and looked over the prospect. The smoothed hills of the eastern Santa Clara Valley fell away endlessly before him, leading down to the valley floor that now appeared to him to be of another time and place, utterly remote from where he stood. At the center of the rounded hills, he watched Lupita carefully tending the fire. And he tried to convince himself that he'd found a place, at the eye of the mountain, to be seen by no one but Lupita, whom he'd saved.

He took the wood down and laid it out by Lupita's side. She looked at the wood, approving.

"Are you happy?" he asked. "*¿Contenta?*"

"Yes," she said. "Of course."

"Really?"

She looked up from the wood and the fire.

"Yes," she said.

That night, he took Lupita's body to him as though it were a part of him that had been missing, as though he could see in her eyes his own full and ageless face, made whole again, reflected back to him. He took her to convince himself that this was also a living place, that he didn't miss his father's vineyard, that he was home. It was a lie, because he knew that Lupita did not love him and was only with him because it was better than what she had left, but it was a lie he told himself, and then told himself to forget that it was a lie, so that he could live as though it were the truth.

They worked the still every day, from early morning until late at night. Lupita tended the fire, boiled the syrup when it was time to set new mash, stirred the mash, made sure that the canvas sacking was tight over the barrels to keep out yellow jackets and flies, cooked. Gill cut wood, filled the can and the aging barrels, sealed some barrels with paraffin to store the whiskey in, hauled water. Once, they made charcoal, digging a pit and laying a length of corrugated metal over it, covering it all with dirt except two air holes, then lighting a slow fire.

At least once a day, Gill asked Lupita if she was happy. He didn't know he did this. He didn't know how much he'd come to depend upon her simple affirmation that she was happy, how much of his own thought of himself as her good angel rested upon her telling him yes, she was happy.

After a month, Big Boy arrived in the Dodge, bringing with him more sugar and rye, empty barrels, wheat and lard and beans, canned vegetables and bacon. He tested the whiskey in the barrels that had been aging longest, checking the alcohol content, holding it up to the light to see that it was taking on a reddish cast and that it was free of sediment, and finally tasting it. He declared it good, and they loaded up ten barrels in the back of the Dodge, which had the rear seats removed. He didn't stay the night, but said he would be back in a week or less with some money.

"We'll be able to move all we make when it's this good," he said. "You all want anything special when I come back?"

"No," Gill said. "Got everything we need."

"I guess you do," Big Boy said.

A week later, he returned, with more empty barrels and dry goods, and food of a better kind than he'd brought before. He had some fresh-killed duck, and smoked salmon, and cans of oysters, and a bottle of wine. He also brought up an envelope of cash, which Gill looked at privately, then stuffed inside his shirt.

They feasted together that night on roast duck, sitting around the fire under the still while the liquor continued to trickle into the funnel. Big Boy uncorked the wine and poured it into three short mason jars, and Gill unconsciously swirled it around and looked at how it clung to the side of the glass, smelled it before he took a sip, rolled it around in his mouth before swallowing.

Big Boy watched him, his mouth open. "Is that how you should drink wine?"

"Not this wine," Gill laughed. "It's Alicante Bouschet. Cheap stuff."

"That's all you can find to buy in San Jose," Big Boy said. "Can't find nothing better."

"I'll bet people buying from my father have better," Gill said.

Before they all bedded down, Lupita noticed that the envelope of cash was missing from Gill's shirt. She had tried to keep an eye on him, but at some point he must have managed to hide it.

When Big Boy left the next day and Gill went to cut wood, Lupita searched the tent and the camp. She checked in the pile of empty duffel bags, in Gill's pile of clothes, around the woodpiles. She scouted the perimeter of the camp and looked for any stones that had been overturned. She found nothing. Then she decided to look inside the tomb of William Kingman.

One door of the tomb had been opened recently. Lupita could see a whitish scrape on the dull and broken concrete. She took note of how the doors were shut and latched, so that she could leave them just as she had found them, and then she creaked one open. The opening was less than three feet high, and it was dark inside. She peered in, saw the long oaken box that took up most of the space inside the tomb. The air smelled musty and cool, as though the body had long since turned to dust.

Lupita turned and looked around once more, at the fire under the can, toward the grove of trees fed by the spring. Then she crawled half inside the tomb and reached around the coffin on both sides, groping in the dark for the envelope on the rough concrete floor. When she didn't feel it, she squeezed her body all the way inside and leaned across the top of the coffin, feeling the smooth polished wood against her cheek. There, on top of the box, at about the length of Gill's arm, she found the envelope.

She slipped it carefully off the wood and brought it out into the light. She counted the cash, not disturbing the order of the bills, careful that the envelope didn't crease or tear. When she finished, she counted it again. There was exactly two hundred dollars in the envelope. More than she had ever seen in her life. More than her father could earn in six months, more than she would ever have gained at the Golden Staircase. More than she'd ever thought she'd hold in her hands at one time.

Two hundred dollars. And half of it belonged to her. She did half the work, she tended the fire better than Gill would ever be able to, since she'd been tending woodfires since she was a girl. But she knew Gill would never give her any money, or admit that any of it was hers. She thought she knew Gill better than he knew himself. He wanted to think of himself as her savior, and he would never give her anything that might make her something more than the girl he'd saved from the life. He wanted her to be always grateful, and to love him, because of what she'd been in the past.

She shut the flap of the envelope as it had been before and slipped it back on top of the coffin just where she had found it. Then she closed the doors of the tomb, latched them, and started back down to tend her fire. The still, and the barrels, and the tent nestled among the open and empty hills, now seemed to her like the walled-in room at the top of a tall and lonely tower.

That night, while they ate dinner around the still fire, Gill smiled over at Lupita. "¿*Contenta*?" he asked.

"Gill," she said, "how much did Big Boy give you for the whiskey?"

Gill looked at her mistrustfully.

"What do you want to know for?"

"Well, was it five hundred dollars?"

"Five hundred dollars?" Gill laughed. "You think big. Five hundred bucks."

"Was it four hundred?"

"It was enough. Now why do you want to know?"

"It wasn't even four hundred?"

"Maybe it was, maybe it wasn't."

"Was it enough to buy a car?"

"Ho, ho, ho," Gill said. "Now you're being silly."

"It's not me who isn't getting enough for the whiskey."

"How do you know it wasn't enough?" Gill asked.

"If it was enough you would tell me. And Big Boy has a nice car, and he isn't doing any of the work. Shouldn't we have a big car too?"

"We will."

"How?" Lupita asked. "When you're getting cheated."

Gill covered the left half of his face with his hand. "Why are you so anxious about getting a car?"

"We never talk about going anywhere, Gilberto. We never talk about doing anything. It's as though you want to stay up here forever."

"You're not happy here?"

"You don't really care if I'm happy or not. You only want me to be happy so you can be happy with yourself."

"So everything I did for you doesn't mean anything anymore."

"You want me to care what I was. I don't care what I was. Only what I'm going to be."

"You can't stop carrying around everything you've been and done."

Lupita picked up a bucket of water. "*You* can't. That's why you only care about yourself and your dead mother. But I can."

She threw the bucket of water on the still fire, and sparks spit and hissed. Then she left Gill sitting there and went alone into the tent.

When Big Boy arrived a week later, he brought fresh supplies, and an envelope of money for Gill. He also brought a cheap silver bracelet for Lupita. She instantly tried it on and held it up, flaunting it in the early sunlight.

"It's beautiful," she said loudly. "So beautiful. The most beautiful thing I've ever been given. Thank you, Big Boy, *muchísimas gracias,* for thinking of a poor girl."

Big Boy grinned fatly. "Sure thing, Lupe," he said. "Pretty girl like you deserves pretty things." Gill in the meantime had turned his back on the both of them. He was counting the money in the envelope, finding that there was less this time than the last.

In the grove of oak by the spring, both Gill and Big Boy shucked their coats and shirts to cut wood in just their undershirts. Even though it was still morning, Big Boy was sweating heavily, and his round face was turning pink, and the straps of his white undershirt cut into his softish shoulders. Gill's body was dark and scant, and he didn't perspire at all. They worked in silence except for the sounds of two axes on two separate trees. Gill felled his first, the old tree whispering down into the tall grasses, falling softly on a cushion of its own leafed branches with a *whish*. Then, before he began to trim off the limbs, he turned to Big Boy.

"Why'd you bring the bracelet?" he asked.

Big Boy stopped chopping and leaned on his axe. "She just seemed kind of unhappy last time I was up," he said in a light tone. "I thought it might cheer her up."

"You let me worry about whether she's happy or not. It's got nothing to do with you. Jake?"

"You're getting awful worked up over a little chippie," Big Boy grinned. "You going soft over her?"

Gill scowled and said nothing. He picked up his axe and began to chop at a thick lower limb but stopped after two blows. Big Boy was still resting on his axe handle, wiping his brow with a handkerchief.

"Less dough this time," Gill said.

"You know how it is, Gill. Prices go up and down, and sometimes you got to make payoffs."

"Yeah," Gill said. "I know how it is. But I want to start going on runs with you. Lupita can run the still if we leave her enough wood."

"Oh yeah?"

"Yeah. I've got a right."

"It's risky. You don't know."

"I know I want to do it."

Big Boy whistled between his teeth, thinking. "Okay. Not this run. They're expecting me alone. But next time I'll set up some big deliveries. We've got enough product ready."

"Good deal."

As soon as they got back to camp, Gill told Lupita he'd be heading down the hill next time with Big Boy. He didn't tell her that he would be making more money. He expected her to understand that.

"Good," she said. "That's good, Gill."

She smiled in a way he hadn't seen for some time, and he noticed that she had taken off the bracelet. "I'll buy you something while we're down there," he said. "Something nice. To make you happy."

"Good, Gill," she said.

Two weeks later, Big Boy drove up with a low farm trailer towed behind the Dodge, carrying some bales of hay. They loaded up the Dodge with ten barrels of whiskey and placed eight more in the trailer. Then they piled flakes of hay around and on top of the load in the trailer and tied a tarp over it. As the sun was setting, Gill kissed Lupita and told her he'd be home in a couple of days.

"We're leaving you plenty of wood," Gill told her. "You'll be okay, won't you? You won't get scared?"

"I won't get scared," Lupita said.

"Okay," Big Boy said. "Let's go make some money."

They drove back down the grass-covered road, the grass yellowing into straw, springing back behind the car and trailer. It was the first time Gill had left the mountainside since he and Lupita had arrived there.

He was in a good mood as they reached the gate before the light failed, and he jumped out to open it, let Big Boy ease the Dodge through, closed the gate, then hopped back in the open door. They drove the main ranch road toward the valley floor and were passing slowly through walnut groves just about to come into leaf as twilight ended.

"Know what I'm going to do?" Gill said. "After a few more runs?"

"What's that?" Big Boy asked.

"Get a car. Maybe a Dodge, like yours. This is a real powerhouse."

"That's a good idea. You'll be able to get one before too long, the way we're going."

"Yeah." Gill smiled at the walnut trees they were passing by. "Where'd you get yours?"

Big Boy hesitated a moment, but Gill didn't notice. "Beckwourth Motorcars," he finally said. "Only Dodge dealer in San Jose."

"Good," Gill said.

"Gill, you're packing heat, aren't you?"

"Sure thing."

"Good. The guys we deliver to will be. But say we get caught, dead to rights. The prohi dicks have us with a load of liquor. What do you do?"

"I was in the war," Gill said. "I know what to do."

Big Boy shook his head, keeping his eyes on the road. "You shoot a cop resisting arrest, you go to San Quentin. You kill him, you get the rope. You don't want to do something simple."

"Okay," Gill said. "What should you do?"

"Maybe you talk to them," Big Boy said. "Maybe they know somebody you know, and they'll let you off for a price. At worst, maybe you go to the county pen. You ever done time?"

"No," Gill said.

"Lots of guys have, and they're no worse than me or you. Maybe they floated a bum check, or got caught sleeping with the wrong guy's wife, or got in a fight. Lots of things can get you sent up besides bootlegging. As long as you don't turn rat, you'll make it through okay."

"You've done time, Big Boy?" Gill asked.

"I guess I have," Big Boy said.

Big Boy first drove the Dodge down a dark lane to a high and silent barn.

The car bumped over the waves baked into the uneven earth in front of the barn while Big Boy maneuvered to line up the trailer with the closed barn door. Then they both worked to unhook the trailer and slide open the creaking door, and they rolled the trailer inside the barn. Some horses in their stalls stamped uneasily as they walked by, and a barn owl hooed.

They left the trailer at the end of the building and unloaded the barrels into an empty stall. Then they walked back out quietly and slid the doors shut. Big Boy said he was glad to get that out of the way. Driving with a trailer made him nervous. It was too easy to get noticed.

Once they were back on the main road, Gill asked how they were going to get paid for those eighty gallons.

"Don't worry," Big Boy said. "The owner of that barn belongs to the Elks Club. It's his trailer too. We'll go by the club tomorrow and get paid cash."

They drove into San Jose and made two more deliveries. Five barrels went to a bootlegger near the railroad yards who would break the barrels into bottles and sell it with phony labels showing it to be Scotch. He showed them how he dipped a curling iron into each bottle to make it taste smoky, and where he buried new bottles out back, so that when he dug them up to fill them, they would look at least eight years old. Three more barrels went to a blind pig in Goosetown, like the one where Big Boy had run into Gill five months earlier. Each of these places paid with spot cash. Gill let Big Boy hold the money, but he noted very carefully how much it was each time.

It was near midnight when they were returning to Coyote with two barrels left in the back. Big Boy said that he had one more bootlegger there who would always take product, and that they could flop in Gilroy afterward. They were at the edge of the walnut groves when Big Boy pulled onto the graveled earth in front of a dim building beside the railroad tracks. The building had an overhang covering a wooden porch in front of it, and a single lamp shone in one window. Above the overhang, Gill could read the words COYOTE FEEDLOT on a sign, flanked by the checkerboard squares of Purina.

Big Boy flashed his headlights at the building, two long and one short, and then cut them off. The lamp in the building switched off, then on again. Big Boy nodded.

"Wait here," he said. "They weren't expecting anyone, but they know me."

"Okay," Gill said.

Big Boy got slowly out of the car with his hands in plain view.

As Gill watched, he walked toward the building without speaking. Gill expected him to say his name, call out to the people inside. But he just walked slowly to the porch. In the pale lamplight, Gill saw him turn the doorknob without knocking, open the door, and go in.

Then, from behind where the Dodge sat, the headlights of several cars suddenly flashed on, pinning Gill from three different directions. He leaped out and crouched by the door, but there was no cover. Voices hit from everywhere, telling him freeze, don't move, or we'll blow your damned head off. Then he heard one voice shout clearly.

"Prohibition Service. Sheriff's here too. Now put 'em up."

Prohi dicks. Now Gill understood why Big Boy had told him how to act. Because he'd been set up, and Big Boy didn't want him to pull his gun when he got caught.

Gill stood up, left his pistol in his holster, put his hands in the air. He saw walking toward him between the shafts of headlights large men in uniform, with badges on their chests and guns drawn. Their leather belts and bullets were shining dully in the light, but their faces were still in shadow. Farther back, remaining near the car, he saw a couple of men wearing suits. One of them bent his head to light a cigarette, and Gill noted a gaunt face with high cheekbones, a trim black mustache, a thin-brimmed hat.

Then the officers were on him, and he was turned around and handcuffed. He didn't wonder whether they were going to go into the house, look for Big Boy, arrest anyone there, or whether they would ask where the still was operating. He knew they had exactly what they had come for. He knew Big Boy would be free to head back up to the mountainside tomorrow, find Lupita running the still, maybe take Gill's own place with her. He knew he had been betrayed, again betrayed.

G ilbert Tourneau was released from the county penitentiary in the late spring of 1928, the time of the cherry harvest, a year and a day after he'd gone in for selling whiskey.

The first month of time, Gill had been on the sawdust pile, shoveling sawdust and scrap wood out of boxcars and into bins, and then from the bins into the furnaces and boilers that provided heat and steam power for the jail. He was a fish, a first-timer, and all new prisoners were put on the sawdust pile at the beginning of their time. Later, he was put out on a gun gang to work in the corn and onion fields that surrounded the pen, spending all day in the fields with eleven other men under the eye of two guards with shotguns, and being locked up only at night. In the fall, he helped prune apricot trees after the harvest so they would bear evenly the following year, and he did the work well, though he knew he'd never see the trees come into fruit.

His scarred face kept most at a distance, even those guards and prisoners who were also veterans of the war, and he grew close to no one. One old guard on his block, a man named Casey, looked after him some, even though Gill had never asked him to. Casey had thin white hair and a sagging face red as brick, and it was common knowledge among the cons that he slept and ate every night at the pen, never going outside the walls. It was thought that he had killed a prisoner once, and that there were people outside who would kill him on sight, or else that his wife had died young and beautiful, and that after her death he had never found reason to go out in the world again. Casey did some small favors for Gill, making sure that he was around when Gill came back from the prison store so he wouldn't get jumped for his cigarettes, or seeing to it that he wasn't put on a gang with anyone who would abuse him.

When Gill's time was up, he went to the warden's office to get mustered out. The warden always tried to strike a jovial, optimistic tone with those who were getting out, and he asked Gill what he planned to do now that he was a free man.

"Don't know," Gill said. "Go back to where I came from and see if there are any pieces to be picked up."

"You've got a name in the Valley," the warden said. "Your last name is well known."

"That's got nothing to do with me," Gill said.

"Well, you're young. You can walk out of here with a clean slate and make your own name."

Gill went to Casey to get dressed out and pick up his traveling money. Casey fitted him out as best he could with a suit of the cheap and hard-finished cloth that all prisoners were given at the end of their terms. He also gave him a new dark blue work shirt, the kind called a thousand-miler because it didn't show dirt and wear, a short-billed cap, and stiff-soled shoes with hobnails that were painful to wear, and two pairs of socks. They walked together to the prison doors, and Casey advised him to hop a train to save money right off.

"The cinder bulls expect it. They been seeing releases hop trains forever, and they won't bother you as long as you ride on top of the boxcars and don't try to ride inside."

"Good deal," Gill said.

Casey signaled to the guard in the tower over the main entrance, and a thick barred gate rolled slowly back. Then Casey himself went forward with a key and unlocked a second large door and opened it.

"Did the warden tell you that you were starting with a clean slate?" he asked.

"Yeah," Gill said.

"Says that to everyone. Full of shit as Christmas turkey."

"I didn't believe him," Gill said.

"Good," Casey said. "It's not true. Now there's the road. I don't want to see you back this way."

"You won't if I can help it," Gill said. He struck out toward the train yard and looked back to see Casey, standing at the threshold and waving his hand to him slowly.

From the prison siding, the first stop for the local was in Morgan Hill. Gill climbed off the boxcar and hitched a ride on the back of a farm truck to the foot of the hills below Ojo de la Montaña. He walked the four miles to the spring, stopping to change his socks when they sweated through. He'd had a sergeant in France who told them all how important it was to keep changing socks on a march, and he tucked the wet pair into his belt to sun-dry.

The grasses in the hills were the same height now that they had been the day he'd come down the hill with Big Boy, changing shade from green to straw as they had been then, and the smells of the grass in the sun were unchanged from that day. As he came to the rise overlooking the bowl where they had placed the still, he found himself hoping that he would find the tent still there. The tent flap would stir, and Lupita would come out, walk to the fire, add a couple sticks of wood. Then she would turn back to the tent, where she had something on the stove, and she would see him. See him and call his name, as though a year of his life had not been plucked from him.

But the bowl was empty. The grasses were already growing over the cut in the earth where they'd placed the mash barrels, softening and reclaiming the tent site and the scorched earth beneath where the still had been. The tomb of William Kingman rested above the site, quiet and closed, but other signs of human residence were diminishing. Only the spring ran unchanged, the eye of the mountain, burbling as it had before they arrived, and during their tenure, and after.

Gill walked up to the tomb and scraped open both doors. The simple oak coffin rested still and quiet within the shadows. He felt along the top of the box, searching for the envelope with the money. He scrabbled both hands along the sides, then grabbed the coffin and skidded it halfway out of the tomb. He crawled inside, coughing at the crumbling dirt and the spiders. There was nothing.

He backed out, sat on the sill of the tomb, looked out at the hillside that had never really belonged to him, except in his own pretensions. He didn't know why he'd expected anything different than what he'd found, didn't know why he'd come at all, except that he was like a dog coming back to its own puke.

After a time, he pushed the coffin back into the tomb and closed the doors on the dusty remains of William Kingman.

Gill reached the Coyote Feedlot in the late afternoon. In the daylight, he could see that the store looked neat and prosperous. The sign was freshly painted, and the porch was swept, and the drive was spread with new gravel. In one window, he noticed the signal lamp still sitting.

Inside the store, the air was warm and close, smelling of wet spoiled grain and old manure. Yellowed window shades were rolled down against the west-facing windows, and two men in overalls were leaning against the long wooden counter. They both stopped talking to look Gill over, and he knew they were taking in his prison-issue clothing, and his scarred face. The storekeeper behind the counter wore a white shirt and bow tie, and blinked behind round owlish glasses.

"Help you, mister?" he asked.

"You know anything about the Ojo de la Montaña?"

One of the men in overalls shifted his weight from one foot to the other. "What's that?"

The storekeeper answered. "It's an old name for part of the Chabolla land grant. You got business over there, mister?"

"Just wondered who owns it."

"Why do you need to know?"

Gill looked at the storekeeper, his left eye gazing a little inside what the other focused on. Then he walked over to the lamp in the window and turned it on, then off, then on again.

The two men straightened, watched him carefully, and the storekeeper took from below the counter an axe handle of polished hickory. He tapped it in the palm of his left hand.

"Easy now," he said. "*We* never did nothing to you."

Gill knew that all of these men had drunk whiskey he'd made. Drunk it and made money from it probably. He knew it and they knew it. And he was broken now, just sprung from the pen, and they were respectable men.

"Bet you got a fifth of rye behind the counter," Gill said. "Why don't you pull it out? Toast my release."

The storekeeper hesitated. Then he put down the axe handle and placed a square unmarked bottle on the counter and poured a single shot into a shot glass.

"After this, you're on your way," he said.

Gill walked to the counter. He reached toward the glass, but instead snatched the bottle by its neck and smashed it against the counter.

Whiskey sprayed from the cracked glass, soaked the storekeeper and one of the men, and Gill leaped back with the jagged half bottle in his hand. He held it before him like a weapon.

The man drenched with whiskey moved toward him, and Gill aimed the broken bottle high, at his eyes.

"You like my face? You want one like it?"

"Get the hell out of here," said the storekeeper.

"Who owns the Ojo?" Gill asked.

"We'll call the sheriff. Send you back."

"Who owns it?"

"Beckwourth." The man who hadn't been soaked spoke up. "He sells Dodges in San Jose. But you didn't hear it here."

"Beckwourth. Good." Gill looked at the storekeeper, who had picked up the axe handle again. "Nice place you got here. Shame if it burned down some night."

He threw the half bottle to the floor and walked out.

Beckwourth Motorcars lay several blocks west of downtown San Jose. Gill saw Dodge sedans coming and going from the lot, the same kind of car Big Boy had driven to the still, and he wondered how much of what he saw was bootlegging. How many of those new cars were carrying liquor in the trunk, making pickups and deliveries and payoffs behind the sleek and gleaming facade of chrome bumpers and waxed paint.

Gill ignored a salesman who tried to talk to him and went down a hallway with a long plush runner rug until he found a door with a walnut plaque inscribed WILLIAM BECKWOURTH. A secretary behind a desk guarded the door and slowly inspected him.

Gill looked back at her. She wore a white blouse open at the throat, and he could see her hair was dyed blond. "Could you please tell Mr. Beckwourth that I'd like to see him."

"He's busy right now," she said.

"I'll wait."

"He may be busy all day."

Gill sat down on a settee beside a floor lamp. He hoisted his left shoe over his right knee and settled back.

"I don't have any other appointments," he said.

The secretary sighed.

"Name, please?"

"Gilbert Tourneau."

"Tourneau?" she repeated as though she knew the name, and she raised a black eyebrow.

Gill waited through the afternoon, watching the secretary and the door. Men in fine linen suits came and were admitted and left again, and she answered calls and took messages or buzzed the call through. Once, she leaned in through the door and said his name—Tourneau, Gilbert Tourneau— and the light leaking from inside the office seemed green and watery. When she wasn't busy, she touched up her makeup, ignoring Gill's presence. She shaped her lips with red, painting them high and low in the center like a Kewpie doll, and rouged her cheeks from a silver compact. Later in the afternoon, she lined her eyes with black and applied mascara, so that her eyes seemed dark and hidden. She painted her nails, waved them back and forth above her desk to dry. Near five o'clock, she looked brittle and whorish.

Then the door opened, and she stood up and leaned in, and there was some whispered interchange across the threshold, and she giggled. She turned to Gill and told him Mr. Beckwourth would see him now.

The inside of Beckwourth's office was cool and dark. Heavy plaques from the Lions Club, Rotarians, the Kiwanis Club crowded on the wood-paneled walls, and nickel-plated lamps illuminated the expansive oak desk. Beck-wourth leaned back in a leather armchair behind the desk. His face was lean and sharp, with a trim mustache, and his crow-black hair was slicked down to fit the shape of his skull. He gestured toward a metal case of cigarettes sitting on the desk, and Gill took one and lit it and settled into a squarish leather chair.

Before Gill could say anything, Beckwourth told him that he'd informed himself of the situation. He knew that Gill had been working at the Ojo still before he was arrested for distribution. They had to move the still in case he sang, but that turned out to be unnecessary, since Gill hadn't said a word.

"I like that in a man," Beckwourth said. "Knowing how to keep your mouth shut."

Gill could have reduced his sentence two months if he'd disclosed the still's location, but he hadn't said anything because he wanted to protect Lupita. Now he leaned forward in his chair.

"Do you know what happened to the people I worked with?"

"You worried about that girl you had up there?" Beckwourth smiled.

"Sure I am."

"She shacked up with Big Boy for about three weeks. Made him act simple, then took him for a big wad of cash. Headed south, I imagine."

For a moment, Gill thought that he could hop a train for Southern California and somehow he would find Lupita, waiting for him. A train, and Lupita waiting with all the money he had earned and all the money she had taken from Big Boy. And she would look at his scarred face and prison thinness with love.

Then he heard Beckwourth laugh, a quiet, worldly laugh.

"Is that all you wanted from me, Mr. Tourneau? Someone to tell you what you already knew?"

"I didn't know."

"Then you should have."

"I have another question. Was I set up the night I was arrested?"

"These things happen when you're in the business," Beckwourth said. "You didn't think you were immune just because you had a girl up in the hills, did you?"

"Was it Big Boy?"

"It doesn't matter. You're free. You should be thinking about the future."

Beckwourth stood up and took glasses and a bottle from a liquor cabinet behind his desk. As he poured two shots, he asked whether Gill was related to Paul Tourneau, the vintner.

"You must know I am," Gill said. "Or you wouldn't have asked."

"Good. I have a business proposition for you."

He offered one glass to Gill and sat behind his desk. Gill sipped the whiskey. It tasted like genuine Scotch.

Beckwourth explained that whiskey was everywhere these days. It was so cheap that it was barely worth the smuggling. But champagne and fine aged wines were rare, and there were those who would pay top dollar. Two truckloads of Tourneau champagne, for instance, could bring as much as a hundred thousand dollars. Word had it that the vineyard was booby-trapped. Alarms, tear gas, shotgun traps. Nobody who wasn't trusted by Tourneau got near the cellars. And Tourneau didn't want to do business with anyone.

"Just lead us in one night, when there's enough of a moon to drive. Get us by the traps and to the good bottles of wine. Somebody else will drive the trucks and load the boxes. All you need to do is case it and get us in."

"That simple, is it?"

"And a five percent finder's fee would come to five thousand dollars. Think what you could do with that money. Maybe set yourself up on some land of your own. Maybe find a good woman, not like that girl you were shacked up with. Maybe go someplace brand-new, get a fresh start in life."

"That's a lot of money," Gill said. "People will do a lot of things for that kind of money. Even betray their fathers."

"Mr. Tourneau, the world is a deceitful place." Beckwourth reached forward for another cigarette and lit it with a matchstick. He waved the matchstick out and left a strand of phosphorous smoke in the air. "Think of what you've gained from what you've done. Has any of it matched what you've hoped for? Has any of it matched what you've deserved? Yet you still want to keep believing that you'll be rewarded."

Beckwourth shook his head, shadowed eyes and lean hollow cheeks moving in the dim interior light.

"I wouldn't call it betrayal. I'd call it getting back something of your own. Something from that vineyard you have a claim to. I'd call it being loyal to yourself. Five grand is something you can hold in your hand. You can keep looking to the past, for something you'll never have again. Or you can look to the future."

Gill stood up. "That's why you had me in?"

"I like you, Mr. Tourneau. You've had a raw deal in life. I'd like to help you square things up."

"I'll think about it."

As he walked to the door, he heard Beckwourth's voice hushed and insistent behind him. *Five grand. Come back when you're ready. I'll be waiting for you right here. Five grand. Five grand. Five grand.*

FIVE

☀ *New Chicago*

*B*lossom Hill Road followed a long, curving route through orchard land south of San Jose. The road was much traveled by tourists who came to the valley for the Blossom Festival, in late March, to enjoy the vistas of the tens of thousands of fruit trees in flower. But in June, the fruit was heavy and dropping and ready to be harvested, and the road was traveled by pickers looking for summer work.

La Familia Pulido traveled in a Hudson pickup, coming north for the season from Southern California. The truck was a faded gray, the paint shading off into smooth streaks of rust on the half-moon fenders, and the cab of the truck was squarish, with flat windows. There were wooden stakes rising from the truck bed designed to hold bales of hay, though what they held was bedding, bags of clothing, cooking pots, sacks of food, and three people who couldn't ride up front.

Ana Pulido, in the cab next to her brother Miguel, first spotted the hitchhiker standing with the blue bindle at his feet.

"Stop for him," she said. "Stop for that one."

"That *bolillo*?" Miguel asked. "Why?"

"He looks sad," she said. "Forlorn."

Miguel frowned, ran a finger across his black mustache.

"Look at his face," she said. "If we don't stop for him, nobody will. And if we are kind to him, others will be kind to us."

"Everyone is forlorn," Miguel said. But he downshifted the Hudson and came to a stop beside the hitchhiker.

"Where are you going?" he asked in Spanish.

Gill had been trying to catch a ride for hours. Several times, cars slowed down when they approached, but when drivers saw his face, they sped past.

Gill was used to this, but he didn't pull his cap down to shade and hide himself. He held his face out, and let those who would pass do so. This group in the old Hudson was the first to stop. The man in the cab was small and spare and his skin was leathered by the sun. The woman beside him wore a widow's black shawl, and her round, fleshy cheeks were starred by the darkish pits left by smallpox.

Gill answered the man in Spanish. "Somewhere near San Natoma."

"You speak Spanish," the woman said.

"*Me defiendo, por lo menos.*"

"We're going to New Chicago. Does that suit you?"

"Of course. Thank you."

"*Ándale, pues.*"

Gill climbed up into the back of the pickup after throwing in his bindle. A boy and a girl, both in their midteens, stood by the stakes on the driver's side and looked at him shyly. An older man lying down on the sacks and bags raised his head toward Gill. He had a wispy, goatish beard and no front teeth, and as he looked he explored the gap and shiny gums with his tongue. Then he grunted and lay back down as the truck accelerated and the wind and noise picked up.

After passing through orchards and onion fields, the truck pulled onto a short spur road that ran to New Chicago, four miles north of San Natoma. Early in the century, a section of mud flats had been subdivided and laid out for streets when some had planned to dredge a deepwater port and build shipping piers for the south bay. The port had never been built, and a falling water table had taken most of the subdivision below the tide line half the year, and only a few houses had been constructed and then abandoned when brackish water seeped into their basements every November and pooled there until summer.

The houses spired up from the blank flats, lonely and unoccupied until a migrant family or two found their way into them and stayed while picking cherries, then prunes, apricots, grapes, before heading north for apples or inland for walnuts. Miguel pulled the Hudson in front of a two-story house that tilted like a shipwreck, with the porch sagging and most windows shattered out of their frames by the settling of the foundation.

"The same one as last year," he said to Ana. "*Qué suerte tenemos.*"

Gill helped unload the truck, carried supplies into the various rooms on the house's first floor, walked buckets of creek water over to the two large barrels they set up near the cooking fire. His own bindle he left leaning against the front porch. Late that afternoon, when all stood around the pot of chile and beans bubbling over an open fire, Gill asked Miguel if there was room in New Chicago for one more.

"Only pickers get to live here, *güero*," Miguel said. "Just pickers. Anybody else, we kick out. No *pochos*. No *renegados*. No *gachupines*. Just pickers."

"I'm here to pick."

"It's hard work, picking. Dirty. Hot. Bad pay. That's why they let Mexicans do it."

"I've done hard work."

"Tomorrow, we're going to Jacobsen's ranch for prunes," Miguel said. "Then we'll see."

They gave Gill the second floor of the house, which they had never occupied. As Gill walked up the crooked wooden stairs, Miguel told him to be careful, because the second floor was haunted, a place of ghosts and *pesadillas*.

Gill walked through the upstairs hall. Several doors were frozen in place, trapped in their doorframes by the settling foundation. One bedroom door was open, and he walked in and laid out his blankets on the uneven floor. From the window of the bedroom, he could see the slanting hillside of the vineyard, Beau Pays.

That evening, Gill learned that the two teenagers, Francisco and Rosarita, were Miguel's children. Rosarita was the younger, shy and dark-eyed, and she stayed close to her aunt Ana and helped with cooking. Francisco was tall, with thin shoulders that always seemed to be curving in toward each other. Javier, the old man, was an uncle who was a little simple, always pulling on his beard or exploring the gap in his teeth with his tongue. But, Miguel said, he was the Champion Prune Picker every year.

Before dawn the next day, everyone except Ana got on the truck and rode to the Jacobsens' ranch. Stanley "Bull" Jacobsen, the rancher's son, met all the pickers in the south section of the orchards. Bull was nineteen and had played center for the Los Gatos High School Wildcats, and he was broad and squat and thick. His father was entrusting him with directing the harvesters, and he began by telling everyone that he was now boxing in smokers over in San Jose and had so far knocked out three men. Then he assigned different rows of trees to different groups of pickers. There were some white fruit tramps, working on their own, some young people from the area who picked to earn money for school clothes in the fall, some other groups of Mexicans. Gill knew that some ranches, like Ida Valley, used only white labor, and advertised that their prunes had only been touched by whites. The Jacobsens belonged to the Sunsweet Co-op, which had never put any restrictions on its members, but even here, Bull made sure that the white locals were picking in different rows than the migrants.

Bull came to the Pulidos and pointed to two rows and shouted, "Those two rows." He always shouted at the Mexican pickers, even if they were right in front of him. "What's your letter?"

"Peh." Miguel pronounced it in the Spanish way.

"P?" Bull asked loudly. When Miguel nodded, Bull told them he would lay out boxes for them, and to be sure to pick the ground clean under every tree before they moved on to the next. If he noticed Gill at all, it was as a curiosity, a scar-faced white scarecrow who had somehow fallen in with some Mexicans.

The plums, dusty and silvery, spread out in broad circles beneath each tree. Rosa stayed close to her father and Javier near one tree, while Gill and Francisco began on the tree in the row beside it. They squatted to save the knees of their trousers and swept their arms across the ground, gathering up the plums within their reach and shoveling them into a large bucket. Then they moved, buglike with bent legs, dragged the bucket forward, and again picked all the fruit within their reach. When they filled a bucket, they took the time to stand, stretch their backs and legs, before emptying the bucket into one of the harvest boxes chalked with a P. Pay was eight cents a box, and it took two very full buckets to fill one fifty-pound box.

As they worked into the morning, clean-picking tree by tree, Gill dropped his prunes into the boxes marked P, along with everyone else's. Miguel noticed, saw that Gill picked as fast as he did, and he nodded in recognition and approval.

They had hung glass jars of water from tree branches, so that the water would stay shaded and not grow too hot, though it was still lukewarm by noon. If they hadn't brought their own water, there would have been none to drink, and there was no place to urinate but the irrigation ditch at the edge of the section. They stopped briefly for lunch at the midpoint of their ten-hour day, but returned to picking as soon as they could, since they were paid only by the box.

When they finished for the day, they drove back to New Chicago. Ana was crouched by a fire, peeling fresh tortillas from a reddish ceramic *comal*, and an iron pot of beans and chile sat warm on the fire stones, and she had gathered watercress from Cherry Creek. Miguel and Francisco and Javier each came to the stack of golden tortillas and took several to eat, and Ana stood and smiled at Gill.

"Come, eat. A man is hungry after a long day, don't deny it."

After dinner, resting around the fire, Gill asked where they were from, and Miguel laughed.

"In Mexico, from Michoacán. In this country, from every field that needs to be picked."

"That's not true," Ana said. "We have a house, a brick house, in Milagro Park."

"Milagro Park?"

"It's good there. A real house, not something just for now."

"I'm going to start high school there this year." Francisco spoke in English, and Miguel frowned. "I might try out for the baseball team."

"You think because you can catch a ball, they will forget you're Mexican?" Miguel asked his son.

"No."

"Good. Because they won't. No matter if you play baseball, or speak English, or pretend you have never picked prunes."

Later that night, Ana told Gill not to mind so much what Miguel said. He was just worried about his son and daughter forgetting where they came from. Especially Francisco. "He thinks the world will be hard, and he wants his son to be prepared. But I worry that we're making a mistake by taking the children to harvest every year. They miss school in June and September, and they're always behind."

"You can't stay in Milagro Park?"

"We can't make as much money. So I worry the children will know nothing, will never be able to work anywhere but in the fields unless they go to school. I would like to see them work in an office someday, be teachers . . ."

She smiled beneath her widow's black, as though she'd mentioned crazy, impractical goals.

"And where are you from, Gilberto? You've learned about us, now."

Gill looked down, brushed his fingers against his prison-issue shirt.

"You don't know?"

"I think we know."

"I just got out of prison a few days ago. It's like being from nowhere."

"And we picked you up anyway. And you're welcome to stay with us as long as you like."

"Thanks." Gill took her hand and squeezed it, thinking that this was the first circle that had welcomed him in since the war, since his wound. Then he walked up to the top floor of the house, the haunted one where he slept.

 Gill quickly hardened to the work, and day fell into day, each day scarcely different from the day prior. He rose early but always found Ana already up, building the fire, making coffee and warm food. Then he trucked over to the Jacobsen Ranch with the others, where Bull shouted at them which rows to pick. The trees seemed as endless and identical as the days. Each tree they cleaned yielded another tree, encircled by fresh-fallen fruit purplish and silvery in the dust, each row they finished yielded another row.

He found he was in no hurry to decide about the offer from Beckwourth. He was drawn into the Familia Pulido, made a part of their daily conflicts and conversation at work in the orchards or back in New Chicago. When Francisco wanted to speak English with Gill and asked Gill to call him Frank, Miguel accused him of wanting to *empocharse,* become Americanized. He warned his son that this country would never love him. Then Ana intervened, and Miguel grunted and allowed his son to talk with Gill about baseball and the high school where he'd be going.

Ana, behind her widow's black, was earthy and laughing and always ready to talk. She liked to tell him about their little village in Southern California. It got the name Milagro Park from the reactions of immigrants when they first saw it, with its brick, tin-roofed houses, and front porches, and electrical wires. *¡Qué milagro!* What a miracle! She described the people and households of Milagro Park, setting them before him and gossiping about them so that he could enjoy them with her.

It was from Ana that he learned that Miguel had lost his wife in the flu epidemic of 1919, less than a year after they'd escaped the wars in Mexico. He'd thought they were safe, and then he was left alone with two children.

"So Francisco was only six when he lost his mother," Gill said.

"And Rosarita was five. My husband and I came north soon after, so I could care for them."

"I lost my mother when I was seven."

Ana touched Gill's shoulder. "Sad," she said. "Sad to lose your mother."

"And I didn't have anyone like you to take care of me," Gill said.

 They worked through the orchard once, then began the second picking for the fruit that had fallen since their first pass. Several times each day, Bull came over and shouted at them for no reason. Miguel always nodded stoically, agreeing with whatever was being shouted, until he finally went away. Once, after he assigned them two new rows to pick, Miguel nudged Gill. "*Fíjate*," he said. "That bull always gives the Imperial prunes to the white kids."

Imperial prunes were three times larger than the petite prunes, and pickers on groves of Imperials filled buckets and boxes quickly and took home more money at the end of the day.

"It's true," Gill said. "I didn't notice."

"We notice every year," Miguel said.

"That's not right."

"Like many things we notice, that you don't, that keep us down."

As they clean-picked tree by tree, Gill began to think about how much difference five thousand dollars would make to the life of the family. Five grand. Money enough to keep the children in school until they finished, keep the family at home and away from the broken houses of New Chicago.

One night, he asked how much the family could make for a season in the fields. Miguel laughed and said three or four hundred dollars, though one year they'd had engine troubles and spent so much on repairs that they returned home with only twenty-one dollars and fifty-seven cents more than they'd left with.

"What would you do if you had a lot of money?" Gill asked. "Say five thousand dollars."

"First thing, buy a pig to roast. And invite all my friends to eat."

"And then?"

Miguel shook his head. "I don't like talking about fantasies."

In late June, when they were low on food, Gill volunteered to drive Ana to town. He told Miguel that if he went with her to the store, she would not be cheated, and Miguel agreed.

The next day, after noon, Gill left Jacobsen's orchard and picked up Ana in New Chicago. They drove together with the windows down, enjoying the breeze on a hot day. Gill wore his suit jacket of cheap cloth and his snap-brim cap, and Ana still wore her black scarf tightly fastened about her head. As they passed through the orchards and saw workers beneath the trees, she laughed and said she felt like it was a holiday.

They passed through Crossroads, where Highway 9 and Stevens Creek Boulevard met, and where there was a garage, a post office, a feed store, and a church. Ana asked if they shouldn't stop at the Union Home Store, where she usually bought supplies.

"Let's go to the Cash Store in San Natoma," Gill said. "That's where I grew up."

"Really? Do you still have people there?"

"I don't know," Gill said. "I haven't been back for a long time. I don't know if anyone will recognize me."

The road into San Natoma crossed the Southern Pacific tracks and a deep ravine before bumping into the iron-fenced town square, green with chestnut trees and stone pines. Gill turned right onto Lumber Street, past the blacksmith's shop and constable's office and the local bank built of yellow brick, and parked the truck at an angle in front of the Cash Store.

McCarty's store served the town as a grocery with delivery, drugstore, post office, soda fountain, and bakery agency. It had high, plate-glass windows all along the street, and double doors recessed in from the wooden walkway. The soda fountain and red stools were right near one window, so that people on the street might see someone they knew having a soda and stop in. On the other side of the store, the fresh fruit and vegetables were displayed in wooden shipping boxes tipped forward, with pretty labels of orchards and green fields on the ends of the boxes and the prices chalked on the walls above. Farther back were shelves of canned goods and the tall wood and glass apothecary's cabinets and the brass cash register.

Gill held the door open and let Ana walk in as little brass bells announced a customer.

Mr. McCarty wore a white apron and carried a pencil stub behind one ear and a notepad in one of the apron's pockets. When he was nervous or pensive, he would rub one of his whitening eyebrows with an index finger and bite his lower lip. Mr. McCarty had lost two sons in one morning when their car had gone off the road and hit a tree, and he carried his grief around with him every day. He was the manager of the town's baseball team, and after the accident, the town thought that he wouldn't want to do it anymore. But he refused to even discuss giving up coaching, and every year he renewed the team with young men about the same age his own two boys had been when they died. Gill saw, on the high shelf behind the fountain, the baseball trophies carefully polished, more now than when he had last been here.

Mr. McCarty stared at Gill's face for a moment when he joined Ana, then he turned away when Gill looked straight at him. The girl behind the soda fountain counter looked as well, but when he turned to her she smiled without embarrassment, not shy about having been caught with her eyes on him. Gill smiled back and turned to Mr. McCarty.

"Can you fill an order for us?"

Ana ordered everything in bulk, the largest possible sacks and bags and tubs. Gill translated, and Mr. McCarty listened to each item on the list and either brought out unopened sacks from the back or measured out what was desired into one of the various scales hanging from the ceiling, each with a white dial face and a broad, silvery, scoop-shaped basin. He avoided looking again at Gill and shrank back when Gill leaned in to look at the figures being toted up on the spiral notepad.

Gill wasn't surprised that Mr. McCarty hadn't recognized him. His reaction was one that Gill had been through many times, first staring and then turning away and deliberately not seeing. Gill had been one of many boys and young men coming through the store from time to time, and he'd been away more than a decade, but even if McCarty had known him well, he could not recognize him if he refused to look.

When they finished, Ana paid for everything, taking the money from the purse she hid in her skirt.

"Shall we go?" she asked in Spanish.

Gill looked around. Two women quickly turned away and studied the tall glass jars of penny candy on the back counter, and Mr. McCarty busied himself with a brush and dustpan near the barrels. He wasn't ready to leave. Being seen and not seen gave him a foul pleasure and confirmed something for him about the welcome he would have received in town after the war.

"Let's have a cherry soda," he said

"No, thank you."

"Why not? My treat."

"Gilberto, Mexicans don't have sodas here."

The girl behind the soda counter was still watching. Gill took Ana by the arm and walked her toward the counter. "Two cherry sodas," he announced loudly in English. "Two cherry sodas for me and my friend."

Ana took a seat on a red upholstered stool and readjusted her black widow's scarf. She sat stiffly and formally, and hid her open and laughing face behind an impassive mask. After she was served, she didn't place her elbows on the counter and lean down to drink. Instead, she brought the glass up and took short, quiet sips from the straw.

Gill paid for the sodas with a dollar bill from the traveling money he got from the penitentiary and leaned against the counter, ostentatiously at ease.

The girl counted out his change, and Gill looked at her name embroidered on the apron while putting his wallet back in his pocket.

"You worked here long, Janet?"

"I'm Nancy," she replied.

Gill looked at the name on the apron again, then looked up at her face, waiting some further answer.

"Janet's my sister," she said. "She worked here before, until she got married. And we haven't got around to ordering a new apron." She said this last loud enough for Mr. McCarty to hear in the back of the store.

"Did you have another sister who worked here?"

"Helen," Nancy said. "This job has been passed down among the Finney girls for years."

"Oh, yeah." Gill remembered Helen Finney now. She had been a year older than him in high school, treated the soda fountain as if it were a throne and she were a queen. Her father ran the town's weekly newspaper, and she tended to like the boys who came from landowning families, though she'd looked down on Gill because he labored like a hired hand and never had spending money and had never been on any sports teams.

Gill thought Nancy Finney resembled her older sister. But the same features, the blond hair and blue eyes and upturned nose, fell just short of being pretty like Helen. Everything seemed a little broader in Nancy, a little more common, a little more plain.

"Did you know my sisters?" Nancy asked.

Before Gill could answer, the door to the store opened and a man dressed in a mechanic's overalls came in the door.

"Hi, Nancy," he said.

"Hi, Joey," she said flatly.

Joey stood back and looked at Gill. He had a thin, unshaven face, and a sloppy, too-wide smile. "Gilbert? Gill? That you?"

Gill nodded. "Yeah, it's me, Joey."

"I'll be damned, after all these years. What you doing?" He looked at Ana as though she were wallpaper. Ana returned his look, tilted her head slightly to the right, and her eyes were dark shields. Joey turned back to Gill.

"You running Mexicans for someone?"

"Just picking fruit at Jacobsen's. Staying in New Chicago."

"No." Joey let his mouth hang open, as though he couldn't believe it. "That's too bad. You come down some since the war. Hurt pretty bad in it too, I guess."

"You guess right."

"Well, guess what I'm doing."

"Imagine you're working at a garage."

"I *own* the Standard gas station in town." He paused, to let that sink in. "And I'm married to Nancy's sister."

Gill looked at Nancy. "Which one?"

"The stuck-up one." Joey laughed at Nancy's frown. "She doesn't like it when I say that."

Mr. McCarty came forward in the store, wiping his hands on his apron. "It's good to see you, Gilbert. Good to see you. I'm sorry . . ." He paused. "I'm sorry I didn't recognize you." He said, "You playing any baseball?"

"Do I look like I've been playing baseball?" Gill pushed his half-finished soda back across the counter. "We have to be going," he said. "Have to get back to work."

He offered his arm to Ana, and they stood up together. "Glad you're doing well, Joey."

"Drop by and see me, Gill," Joey said. "At least when you need to buy some gas."

"I'll do that." Gill held the door open for Ana and then let it shut behind them as the little bells on it tinkled.

"Who was that?" Nancy asked as the truck backed out onto Lumber Street.

Mr. McCarty looked sadly out the window. "I didn't even recognize him."

"But who *is* he?"

"That's the brother of your hot stuff boyfriend," Joey said.

"Louis's brother?" she asked. "I thought he was dead."

"Is that what he told you?" Joey asked. "Is that what they been telling him?"

Gill drove the Hudson past Joey's Standard station and north toward the bay. They needed gas, but he was sure they could make it back to Crossroads. He didn't intend to let Joey take any more smug pleasure in how much better his life was turning out. Joey was the same age as Gill, but he hadn't volunteered and obviously didn't regret not serving.

As he drove, Ana was quiet beside him. He had expected her to be very reserved when they were in the store, and he'd seen her put on her expressionless mask there. But now she was wearing the same mask with him, and he realized he had used her. He'd used her to get noticed, allowed her to be insulted so that he could prove something to himself about how he would be seen in San Natoma.

They pulled in at Crossroads Garage, and a fifteen-year-old, dressed in stained and faded blue overalls that slanted on his skinny frame, came out to pump their gas. He gawked for a moment at the two of them, the scarred man sitting beside the Mexican woman in black, and Gill scowled at him.

"Are you staring at my wife?" he growled.

"Oh, no sir." The boy ducked his head and went to the rear of the truck to unscrew the gas cap.

On the road again, Gill began to laugh, and Ana laughed with him, the deep and mellow laugh she shared with him when talking about her friends in Milagro Park.

"If he had left his mouth open any longer," Gill said, "the flies would have laid eggs in it."

"*Sí, ¿verdad?*"

The black scarf she always wore around her head loosened in the wind from the open truck window. Underneath the scarf, Gill noticed, her hair was black and glossy, and the skin of her face, though pitted with little dark marks, was fresh and unlined. She wasn't as old as the scarf made her look, not much older than Gill himself.

After she retied the scarf, she turned to Gill. "You wanted that to happen," she said.

"I know. I'm sorry."

"You wanted to find no kindness. My husband was like that, too. He was at odds with the world."

Ana had never mentioned her husband before to Gill, and he hadn't wanted to ask. He paused as the truck passed through orchards thick with fruit, white braces propping up the most heavily laden boughs.

"How long ago did he die?" he asked.

"Eight years ago. We never had children."

She put her hand out the window, cupped the oncoming air in her palm.

"He blamed me for that, though he was over fifty. He said if I had truly loved him, I would have been able to have children. He said I made his life bitter."

The Hudson bumped over some railroad tracks and settled on the Bayshore Highway toward New Chicago.

"Let me tell you how he died," Ana said. "He was on a tract-pull in a melon field near Calipatria, sitting on the disks to give them more weight, and he fell off and the disks ran over his right arm and broke it in so many places that they had to cut it off."

"And he died from that?" Gill asked.

"Not exactly," Ana said. "He was so angry that he had only one arm that he decided to kill himself. He found some rope in the barn of the ranch where we were working and he tried to hang himself. But he couldn't tie a proper knot with only one hand. He went into the loft and tied a loose loop around his neck and the other end to a post. But when he jumped, his head slipped out of the loop, and he fell to the floor and broke his left leg. They found him two hours later."

"Then what?" Gill asked.

"Then the foreman told him not to come back. And he was back home with me, but I wasn't enough for him. He said I didn't love him. He swallowed all his pain pills, then blocked the exhaust pipe of the truck, locked himself in, and let the engine run. But he passed out, and the truck stalled, and he lived anyway."

"So what happened next?"

"He decided to make the driver of the tract-pull kill him the rest of the way. So he limped over to Juan Bautista's house and banged on his door with his crutches. It was late at night, and he knew that Juan Bautista had a shotgun, and he thought he might shoot him. But Juan Bautista recognized him outside the door and refused. Then my husband asked for the gun so he could shoot himself, but Juan Bautista refused that as well. So he walked off, and Juan said he could hear him cursing God."

"So how did he finally die?"

"He was run over by a truck driver later that night. The driver had some insurance money, so we were able to leave the Imperial Valley, my brother's family and me, and buy a house in Milagro Park for four hundred dollars. It's a little funny, no?"

"Yes and no," Gill said.

"He helped us in the end, even though he didn't know it. But I wish he could have known what it was to live in Milagro Park."

"It must be nice, sometimes, to live in Milagro Park," Gill said.

"It is," Ana said.

"So I'm at odds with the world also?"

"I don't know. Are you?"

On the tidal flat at road's end, they saw New Chicago, skewed houses abandoned by those who had imagined in them the beginnings of a great city.

In the late afternoon, Louis Tourneau parked the farm truck at an angle outside the Cash Store. He walked with a tall grace, his chest full as though his heart were light and drawing him upward, and he had dark eyes that tapered down a bit to the sides, sad almond eyes, and black hair that curled naturally into thumb-sized rings.

Nancy had already wiped down the sink and hung up her apron, and she met him at the door. "You have time for a little spin?"

"Sure," Louis said.

On their way out of town, Louis noticed Joey at the Standard station waving at him. "There's your brother-in-law," he said to Nancy.

"Keep driving," she said. "You know he wants to sleep with me."

"What?" Louis said.

"*Show me the ropes* is how he put it."

"You never told me that."

"He lets me know, every now and then, that the offer still stands. Just in case I change my mind."

They were out of town and driving through orchards now, heading toward the bay. Louis began to slow down, looking for a place to turn the car around.

"What are you going to do, Lou?" Nancy asked. "Go back into town and have it out with him? Beat him up for my sake?"

"Well . . ." Louis hesitated. "Don't you want me to?"

"You're so sweet," she said. "What if I just made that story up?"

Louis had slowed the truck to ten miles an hour, and it was almost stalling out.

"Keep going," she said. "Head out to the water. I love these long afternoons that never seem to end, that stay warm and summery as strawberries until midnight."

Louis looked ahead and gave the truck some gas. "Did you make the story up?"

"Would you really have it out with someone just on my say-so?"

"I don't know," Louis said. "I guess I would."

Nancy scooted over next to Louis and leaned against his arm while he drove. "This is the only summer in our lives when we'll be sixteen," she said. "It's special, isn't it?"

"Yes, I guess," Louis said. "I never thought of it that way."

"Joey is just a crumb who thought that when he married my sister, he'd won the lottery. Then he found out that he didn't win the lottery, but he was still married to her."

"So he *did*," Louis said.

"Want to sleep with me?" Nancy asked. "Why wouldn't he? Wouldn't you?"

"I . . ." Louis said, then laughed. "I wouldn't *want* to want to."

"Saint Louis," Nancy smiled. "You're such a choirboy."

They came to the Bayshore Highway, and Nancy told Louis to turn north. The fruit trees stretched their shadows across the entire roadway until the highway grew too close to the salt water for orchards and the fields were low and green with truck crops. Then the slanting houses of New Chicago pushed up into the horizon, the lean and silver trees. Nancy spotted the truck that Gill and Ana had driven in, and she leaned forward. One woman stood by a pot hung over an open fire, and a circle of men squatted and ate a little ways off. Another man ate alone, standing with his back against the side of a porch.

"You ever wonder where they're from?" Nancy asked.

"Somewhere," Louis said. "I don't know. They always seem to show up harvest time. Then they go away."

"I know where one's from. That one, standing up."

Louis looked at the man while they were driving past, puzzling over him. "Who is he?"

Nancy waited until they were just even with the house, just beginning to speed away north. "That's your brother."

Louis craned his neck quick, looked behind him at the man eating beside the failing house.

"Your brother," Nancy repeated.

Louis turned his face forward, driving still northward, and the tires hummed a gray sound that spun around him.

"You aren't going to turn around?"

"My brother's dead," Louis said.

"You don't believe that," Nancy said. "I can see it in your eyes."

Louis kept his gaze down the straight highway. "It's getting late," he said.

Nancy reached over and tugged at the steering wheel, and the truck swerved over to the middle of the road. Louis wrestled the truck straight, and he slowed to a stop along the side of the road.

"How do you know?" he asked.

"Joey recognized him in the store," she said.

The truck's engine chuckled, idling noisily.

"You believe it, don't you," she said. "You believe it's him."

Louis set the brake and got out of the truck, and Nancy joined him. Beyond the road, tidal flats cast out to the northeast, and marsh grass marked where slow creeks crawled the last half mile to join the bay.

"I always hoped he might come back," Louis said. "I was only five when he left, and sometimes when I was a kid, I pretended that he lived in the redwoods, uphill from the vineyard, just hiding out up in the woods. I used to talk to him sometimes."

"Bet you never told your father that."

"No," Louis said. "You know, people said my brother was a hero in the war. Sometimes I talked to him about that. About what it was like to be a hero."

"What did he say?"

"He never answered."

He squeezed Nancy's hand, then opened the door for her. Back in the driver's seat, he put the truck in gear and headed south.

"You stopping?" Nancy asked.

"Not now."

"Are you going to tell your dad?"

"Of course," Louis said.

"He'll tell you your brother's no good."

"You don't know that."

"Your dad's not always perfect, you know."

Louis didn't answer. The sun had tipped over the ridge by the time they passed New Chicago again, and the cooking fire looked bright and lively in the twilight, but they didn't slow down.

*L*ouis walked through the vineyard with his father every morning during growing season. He'd been going with him since he was seven, running on short legs over the tilled and uneven ground to keep up, listening to his father's deep and certain voice. His father seemed to know everything about the daily life of the vineyard. He looked at the condition of the earth, looked at the vines for bloom and set. He looked for threats to the vineyard, from either fungus, or insects, or other pests. And no matter what occurred, he knew what action to take. Tourneau had his men anoint the fence posts around the vineyard with bull's blood to keep deer out, and he paid boys a small bounty for rabbits they killed, and birds as well near harvest. Once, when part of the vineyard was hit by leaf roller, he immediately had it sprayed with fluosilicate, and he had all his workers picking off individual leaves in which the live grubs had rolled themselves and tossing them into a small roasting fire, to sizzle the air with the smell of burning flesh. Although he used a Balling hydrometer in the fields, he knew when to pick grapes from taste alone, already imagining the wine they would become in four or eight years' time.

In the spring once, when Louis was eight, Tourneau had told him to run ahead to the edge of the vineyard, and he would see that bud break had started. Louis went between rows of old, freestanding vines, looking like dwarf trees that had long been dead, with shaggy, stringy bark and five short and tortured branches pointing out. At first, near the fence rails, all seemed still and wintry. Yet when he looked closer at the tip of each branch, he found the small spurs that had been left from the prior year's pruning. On each spur, two buds had been left, and he found tiny, tender green shoots breaking from each. He looked at the next vine, and the next, and he found the same.

He ran back to his father. "It started! Just like you said it would!"

"Good." Tourneau patted him on the shoulder. Louis paused and looked up at his father curiously.

"Did bud break start because you said it would?" he asked.

His father laughed and held up his hand, open-palmed as though bestowing a blessing. "At my word and command, life begins again," he said.

Louis realized later that his father wasn't serious. Yet some of that feeling remained. Every morning, on every walk, he received instruction in the care and maintenance of a vineyard, an addition to his own book of days, inscribed by his father's deep voice. He was taller than his father now, at sixteen, but his father still seemed wise and strong and awesome.

The morning after he saw Gill from a distance, Louis walked with his father down the allées in one of the Pinot noir sections. Tourneau wore a broad-brimmed straw hat and corduroy pants held up with suspenders over a blue work shirt, and he swung a narrow spade in his right hand. Every now and then, he plunged the spade into the soil, checking how the heavy clay was compacting or hacking at an awakening patch of morning glory.

Louis hadn't said anything about seeing his half brother. His father kept a block of silence about Gill. Only once had they spoken of him, on an Armistice Day when Louis was still in elementary school. He'd heard about the end of the Great War from his teacher, and heard about the parade planned in San Jose, and he'd asked his father why Gill didn't come back for the parade.

They were sitting together at the long workbench near the door to the cellars, and Tourneau had been writing in the leather-bound journal, the cellar book, he kept for that vintage. On the shelf above the bench, a line of cellar books stood, one for each year. Tourneau paused in his writing and looked carefully at Louis.

"He's staying away for his own reasons," he said. "He chose to join the army, and now he's chosen to stay away. And his choices add up to the life he's chosen for himself."

He reached down and tousled Louis's curly hair. "And you and I are choosing to make the finest wine in California. *D'accord?*"

"Yes, Papa," Louis said.

"Right." Tourneau turned his heavy head back to the cellar book of the year, and began again to write.

"Or perhaps he's dead," he said quietly, half to himself, his pen still moving. "I don't know why he would stay away."

They never spoke of him again, and with years passing, Gill's absence was accepted as permanent. Louis always felt his place at the vineyard had come at Gill's expense, always felt shadowed by a sense of unearned privilege, but he never told his father. He knew his father would find his unease foolish. Now, he didn't want to announce Gill's return because it brought up those same deep troubles, though he was sure that even if he said nothing, word would soon reach the vineyard.

Tourneau stopped as the sun rose in the east and gazed at the rows of vines above. He held that if powdery mildew were forming anywhere, you could see it best at this hour. Some subtle way that the long horizontal light reflected off the leaves was different if mildew had begun, and when they spotted it, they stopped all other work in the vineyard to apply sulfur.

Louis looked alongside his father. "It looks good to me, Papa," he said.

"It is good," Tourneau said. He bent down to one vine in the middle of the row and turned some leaves aside gently with his large hand, caressing them briefly with his thumb before focusing on the grapes below them. He often stressed to Louis how important foliage was. In the springtime, to protect the young leaves, he even muzzled the horses during plowing. Not enough foliage, he said, and the berries would burn. Too much, though, and the fruit wouldn't ripen.

They could both see that the hard green ovals were picking up water and size rapidly. Now, the danger was overcropping. More than one cluster on a single stem, and the berries would have trouble gaining enough sugar.

"There." Tourneau gestured with his thumb. Louis lifted the smaller cluster on the stem, already noticing the smallish, winged shape typical of Pinot clusters, and sheared it off. Then he stood back and watched his father reposition a few leaves that were too close to the fruit, working tenderly though efficiently.

They walked to the end of the allée, and Tourneau planted his spade in satisfaction. "It just needs some light pruning now, to keep the clusters hanging airy. Your grandfather knows that as well as I do. You and I are going to work in the cellars."

The cellars had been dug in the 1880s by a crew of Chinese laborers who had just finished the tunnels for the South Pacific Coast Railroad. They used dynamite, just as they had done while building the Laurel-Glenwood tunnel, and advanced into the hillside ten feet per day before spreading out into larger, shored-up rooms built up with racks of thick timber for holding barrels and bottles of aging wine. Paul Tourneau had been only sixteen when the cellars had gone in, a recent immigrant, a wage worker for Pascale's father, George Du Maurier. But he helped in their design and construction, recalling what he had seen as a worker in his native Burgundy. He also helped build the three-story winery building, set against the hillside so that horse carts could bring loads of grapes to the upper story for crushing, and then gravity could feed the juice down to fermenting tanks on the second floor and to smaller barrels for racking and fining on the first floor. The building had been sited so that the mouth of the cave leading back to the underground cellars opened into the first floor.

It was always cool in the cellars, and Louis loved the smell of wine working in oak, the heavy, musky air, dense with spice, and cool washed cement floors leading back to where the rows of bottles seemed infinite and the stacks of oval cooperage filled the space from floor to ceiling. Some of his earliest memories came from this cellar, in the days before electricity, when they worked by candlelight because a kerosene or coal oil lamp would taint the wine. His father still liked to use candlelight to look through a glass bottle and see if the sediment was precipitating or whether the wine needed more fining. If the sediment was in grainy bits, like brown sand, it was healthy, but if it looked at all soft or miry, the wine would have to be purified again with protein. Tourneau liked adding egg whites to pick up the sediment, six to twelve for a puncheon, but he told Louis that in Burgundy he had seen ox blood used for fining.

On the second floor, they climbed thirty feet down into one of the massive open fermenting tanks, carrying soda ash and hard brushes. These tanks held twenty thousand gallons each and were open at the top, built of thick redwood staves by the Pacific Lumber Company and bound with bronze hoops, with thick bronze faucets at their base. Metal is the enemy of wine, Tourneau said, along with heat and air, and none is worse than iron. They began to scrub down the sides with hard brushes and soda ash, raising a thin froth before rinsing down with water from a canvas hose. The soda ash neutralized the heady smell of wine-impregnated wood and left the tank smelling fresh and bright.

Louis was on a ladder scrubbing the sides of the tank, while his father attacked the tank floor with a long-handled brush. "I still like to do this myself," Tourneau said. "I like to be in on every step. Control every step. Make sure everything is clean and pure for the juice. But maybe next year, I'll leave this step to you."

"That's what you said last year, Papa," Louis said.

Tourneau laughed. "So I did," he said. "Well, we'll get some help in here after noon, when it's hot for pruning."

They finished one tank and began another. It was dark down in the bottom of the tank. Only a few bare electric lights hung high overhead and the tank sides sloped inward, so that the wooden floor was broader than the open circle above. But at Tourneau's direction, they worked very methodically, scrubbing a section at a time, so that no part of the tank would escape freshening and leave bacteria to attack the wine.

When the men who had been pruning came in from the fields to help, Louis waited for someone to mention Gill. He was certain at least one of the workers would have heard. Tourneau sent a couple of the younger ones up to the redwood tanks to wipe them down with chamois cloths and make sure that no standing water had collected anywhere from the morning's cleaning. The others began to work with the new cooperage, large oval barrels of aged white oak from the Baltic. To make the barrels wine green, they filled each one half full of water mixed with lime, then stood on each side and rolled it back and forth for an hour, to leach out some of the harsher oak qualities. Afterward, it would be rinsed and refilled with hot water and left to stand for at least a day, before being rinsed several more times. Soon, the first floor was filled with the sounds of water sloshing and talk in English and Italian, as pairs of men rocked the barrels back and forth between their knees in the cool shadowy air. Louis listened, but heard only the common talk of men at their tasks.

Augusto Corvo, Louis's grandfather, went to the older barrels. Augusto had a slight stoop, though his body was still thick and powerful, and he walked with his arms flexed in front of him like an old wrestler. A bush of white hair pushed over the collar of his shirt, and nests of whitish hair rested in his ears, but his eyebrows were dark and his eyes black and bright.

Augusto pried open the bung of one old barrel and bent down to smell inside.

"This one's sweet," he said.

"They all should be," Tourneau said. Louis lit a small sulfur candle in a tin lantern, then lowered it carefully on a chain into the barrel that Augusto had checked. The sulfur flame would kill off any impurities that may have infiltrated.

The three worked through the old barrels, smelling them and lighting sulfur candles inside them as a precaution. Tourneau would use the newest barrels for his least-favored wines, and save the oldest barrels for aging his best Pinots and Cabernets. Since Prohibition, the cooperage of many California wineries had been ruined. Some big redwood tanks had been sold in Mexico and were holding water for irrigation. Other barrels had simply been abandoned, and now had the *tourne* so badly they would never be of use again. "The best thing for cooperage is to keep it working," Tourneau said to Louis, "and keep it topped up so that there's never much air in it. And sulfur is a great fix-all."

After an hour, Louis went to the inner cellars to get *piquette* for the workers. He took a key from a hidden hook, opened a small box mounted on the wall, and flipped a switch inside the box to disable the tear gas jets installed at the beginning of Prohibition. Then he gathered up four dark green bottles without labels, all filled with the cheap wine fermented with sugar and water and the pomace left over after pressing. Back on the winery floor, the workers paused in their sloshing and rinsing to take some wine in tumblers and drink to the upcoming harvest.

Tourneau took one bottle and poured a glass. "Augusto?"

Augusto shook his head.

"*Tant pis*," Tourneau said, and drank from the glass he had offered.

Augusto thumped one of the barrelheads with his fist, and it sounded like the hollow body of a guitar. The barrelhead was dark and glossed with age, slightly concave, and the cooper's adze marks that had shaped it could still be seen. "These barrels are like heirlooms," he said. "Something you can pass on."

"And so I will," Tourneau said.

"You have so much to pass on." Augusto's eyes were hard and opaque. "So much. Even more than you think."

"I will pass it on." Tourneau clapped a hand on Louis's shoulder. "Though not for many years."

"Many years?" Augusto briefly caught Louis's eye and half smiled.

Louis sipped from his glass. He'd seen the tinge of a bitterness slip out from time to time, and he wondered if his grandfather had heard about Gill.

Louis was quiet during dinner that evening. They ate in the Great Room of the vineyard house, a large open room framed by redwood ceiling beams, with a twenty-foot-long dining table running down its center and Tiffany glass chandeliers hanging above. Tourneau sat at the head of the table, and Louis sat next to Augusto on one side, while his mother, Sophia, sat at the side nearest the kitchen, bringing in dishes as they were ready.

Normally, Louis felt, they fit this room, filled it. His father alone, with his brute voice and black beard, seemed to demand a great space when he shouldered up from the table and grasped bottles of wine by the neck. But that night, the room appeared large and they small, and the world outside vast and incoherent.

Tourneau noticed that Louis wasn't talking, and he gibed at him about Nancy, the newspaper owner's daughter, telling him that he must be in love, that it was easy to be in love when you were sixteen. When he, Tourneau, was young, he fell in love five times a day. Love was easy, that kind of love. But Louis should be careful, not let her put a ring in his nose before he knew if she could be a vineyard wife.

Then he raised a glass to Sophia, to his own wife. "To your youth, and to your beauty," he said. "To your goodness."

Sophia stood and picked up the serving dishes. "I'm neither young nor beautiful," she said. "As for goodness, that's not for me to say."

"No," he said, "you are like a painting of the Holy Mother. Augusto, don't you agree?"

"Yes," Augusto cackled. "Like the one who will plead for mercy for a sinner or an outcast. The one who will plead before God!"

"Papa," Sophia said, "have you drunk too much again?"

"There's no harm in it," Tourneau said, and filled Augusto's wineglass once more.

Sophia brought in a *ciambelle* from the kitchen, a ring cake filled with strawberry jam and sprinkled with pearl sugar. The recipe had been one of her mother's favorites, and she liked to make it when strawberries were ripe because it reminded her and her father of a happy time when her mother had been alive. At the table, she cut the cake into half-inch slices, warm and steaming, the strawberry heart of each piece shiny and bright.

Augusto sighed at the smell of warm cake and strawberries and he thanked his daughter, while Tourneau left the table to find a dessert wine, something that might be like the Lambruscos of Emilia-Romagna. Louis picked at the cake on his plate and only began to eat it when Sophia looked at him with her eyebrows raised.

"I wish you could have tasted your grandmother's *ciambelle*," she said.

"So do I," Augusto said.

Tourneau returned with a demi of wine made from Muscat grapes. "Try it with this," he said.

After they finished, Louis stacked plates and carried them into the kitchen. His mother leaned against the countertop and watched him place the plates beside the sink. He returned with all the wineglasses, and she was still leaning back, still watching him with her dark eyes.

"Louis," she said. "Something is wrong. What is it?"

He knew it was no use trying to hide from it. She would hold him before her with her deep gaze, and he would look down, unable to meet her eyes until he was ready to speak. It was a power she had. And he suddenly felt relieved, that he wouldn't have to tell his father alone.

"Something I heard in town," he said. "Gilbert is here. And I think I saw him from a distance."

His mother grasped both his hands. She was always beautiful, he knew. He had long noticed how others reacted when she walked into a room, with her long slim waist, and dark-lashed eyes, and lavish black hair, and the smell of lilac water that accompanied her. But now she was transfigured, as though a radiance suddenly framed her person.

"It's true," she said. "I know it's true. I can see in your eyes. And I prayed for this."

She strode back into the Great Room, sweeping Louis along with her. Tourneau and Augusto were sitting before the large stone fireplace, and she stopped before them with Louis one step behind her.

"Paul, I have the most wonderful news," she said.

Augusto laughed, then covered his mouth.

"It's Gilbert," she said. "He's come back at last."

Tourneau leaned back in his chair and turned his large head bearishly, as though trying to hear a distant cry. "Gill? How can that be after all these years."

"Louis heard in town."

Tourneau turned to Louis, waited. He explained uncomfortably how Joey had recognized Gill while Nancy was there, how Nancy told him while they were driving by New Chicago, how he had seen a lone white man standing against a crooked house. At the naming of New Chicago, Sophia murmured in sympathy. When Louis finished, he stood awkwardly, as though he felt he should apologize, but he wasn't sure for what. Tourneau asked him why he hadn't said anything before, and Louis said that he didn't want to say anything unless he was one hundred percent sure.

"Does he have the scars?" Augusto said. "I heard he had scars."

"Nancy said he had scars," Louis said.

"A war hero," Augusto said. "He must have felt he had no home to come to, all these years."

"Augusto, you're drunk," Tourneau stated calmly. "Lou, can you help your grandfather back to the old house?"

"I'm all right," Augusto said. "But maybe Lou would like to come over and sit for a while."

Louis often walked his grandfather back to the old house. He could remember being seven or eight years old, holding his hand, leading him past the kitchen garden and the barn and down the dark pathway. He had walked ahead as a boy, making sure there were no stones to stumble on, leading his grandfather along like a sluggish barge. He had to make sure his grandfather had gotten inside and off his feet, because his mother always asked him if he'd seen him off his feet, sitting or lying down. As Louis grew taller, Augusto sometimes leaned against him as they walked.

That evening, once they were in the fresh air, Augusto didn't seem as drunk as he had in the Great Room. He stretched and yawned and looked up at the sky, then he walked down the path with Louis following.

The old house was the oldest building on the property, the original house that George Du Maurier built while clearing the land for vines in 1885. When Du Maurier built the new vineyard house for himself, Augusto moved into the old one with his wife and Sophia. Augusto came from a family that had worked in the vineyards in Romagna for generations, and Du Maurier was glad to have a foreman with vine-dressing in his blood living at the vineyard. After Sophia married Tourneau, she repeatedly asked him to move into the vineyard house with them, but Augusto always refused. His wife had gotten tuberculosis living in the old house, and he always blamed the house's dampness. If he moved, he felt that he would have been running away from his own guilt.

The old house was made of redwood logs, hewn and squared, and it had settled unevenly over the years into the side of the hill. The roof ridge bent downward, and the porch was now separated from the front door by a gap of several inches. Louis opened the door for his grandfather and let him go in first. The house wasn't wired for electricity, but Augusto could lay his hands on the lamp and matches in the dark.

Inside, Louis saw that his grandfather had been cleaning his pistol again. It was an old cavalry pistol Augusto had brought back after one of his drunks, a Colt .45 Peacemaker with a seven-and-a-half-inch barrel. It lay with its cylinder opened on the room's one table, shiny dark and slick on the light-colored linen tablecloth. A small oil can and a swab on a metal rod lay beside it. Augusto sat down at the table, his face broad and contented, and he picked up the pistol and closed the cylinder slowly and lovingly.

"Think how many men this might have killed," he said. "On the frontier, when the land was there for the taking. The man who sold it to me said it's the same kind of pistol the Seventh Cavalry carried during the Indian Wars."

He lifted it up, admired it in the lamplight, then handed it to Louis.

"Go on," he said. "Aim it."

Louis aimed it at the corners of the old house, where mice might be hiding, to make his grandfather happy.

"Back then," Augusto said, "you had to win land, and be able to defend it." He took the pistol back from Louis and laid it down on the table, pointing away from both of them. "I'm going to leave this to you in my will," he added.

"I don't want it," Louis said. "I just want you to stay well and live."

"I'll want you to have it," Augusto said. He looked down at his hands, scarred and stubbed from decades of work with grapevines. "I have little enough to give. When your mother married, I could give her nothing. It was as though she were giving up herself for me, marrying the landowner so that I would always have a place. And what had I ever done for her except not die of tuberculosis like my wife."

He shook his head.

"A man who has nothing to give his children, who can only be brought things, is to be pitied."

"Grandpa," Louis said, "what do you remember about my brother?"

Augusto picked up the pistol, and though it was heavy as stones, he leveled it steady at the door. "Louis, you think the world ought to be fair, don't you?"

"Sure," Louis said. "Of course."

"God's justice, here on earth. Paul Tourneau, your father, probably thinks the world is fair. He always got what he wanted."

Augusto pulled the trigger of the old pistol, and there was a well-oiled click. "He always got what he wanted. And Gill never did. I remember when his mother died. He blamed your father for that, and he blamed him for forgetting her so completely. Paul Tourneau cared about building the vineyard, and he didn't concern himself much with damage done along the way."

"So Gill left because he never got over his mother's death?"

"That's part of it. I think he went to France because he thought it might make him finally able to stand up to his father. Maybe he even thought it would make his father love him. When Gill joined the army, my Sophia mourned so much you would have thought it was her own son, and he'd already died. She was bent and sad for months, even though she had you, five years old then."

"I remember," Louis said. "She didn't like to watch me play anymore."

"But Paul Tourneau didn't grieve over Gill being gone. Maybe he'd already decided that Gill wasn't the son he wanted."

"But I was," Louis said.

"You're going to go to the university at Davis, aren't you?" his grandfather asked. "To study viticulture?"

"Maybe," Louis said defensively.

"You want Gill to come back," Augusto said. "To be once again a part of the family. No divisions, no jealousies. No memory of the past."

He picked up the pistol again.

"I don't know why he never came back. Maybe because he changed when he was wounded. Maybe he felt shamed by the way he looked. He'll never be able to forget the past."

Aim and click.

"*Poverino*, scarred like that."

Aim and click. Aim and click.

It was full night when Louis stepped outside again. As he walked back to the house, he felt in the midst of something large and changing. Down below him, the land tumbled darkly toward the bay, toward the drowned houses in New Chicago. Above him, the rows of vines angled upward, pointing toward heaven.

SEVEN

Imperial

*I*n the late afternoon, when the hot sun broadened over the Santa Clara Valley, Paul Tourneau drove down from Beau Pays to retrieve his son. As the road passed through the outlying blocks of vines, he automatically looked for signs of trouble in the green foliage. In his mind, the vineyard was always at risk. This time of year, he was watching for the gray blotches on leaves that might mean mildew, or yellow spots caused by leafhoppers, or the red mottling from spider mites, or the metallic brown scabs that could be left by feeding thrips. Even from the cab of the dusty Ford truck, he scanned the mantle of leaves, and turned his full attention to the road only after he'd crossed the bounds of the vineyard.

Tourneau thought that Gill would be returning home just when he was most needed. The vineyard had two mortgages laying over it, and the costs of making fine wines during Prohibition had exceeded income for several years. He found ways to get some wine to market, but the best wines remained unsold, aging in bottles lying on their sides in the cellars blasted deep into the heart of the hill.

The first mortgage dated from the phylloxera outbreak. Tourneau, in the 1907 replanting, had remade the vineyard. He came to look on the diseased and dying vines as a sign that he could begin again, and that the vineyard he envisioned upon the blank fields was in fact new and entirely his. The new vineyard had a specialty in sparkling wines. He planted a dense nursery field from cuttings of Pinot noir and Chardonnay and Cabernet, and when the native rootstock took hold, the nursery field provided the grafts he needed to establish his chosen variety in each section. He was able to pay the mortgage down but not off after he began to sell sparkling wine in 1912.

The first years of Prohibition, the years following 1919, were good for

Tourneau. Home winemaking was still legal. Each household was allowed to make two hundred gallons of wine for home use, and fresh grapes were in demand in Chicago and New York. Prices were strong, rising from ten dollars a ton to one hundred or more a ton in 1923. Tourneau was able to sell his poorest fruit for a profit, and make fine wine from his best grapes. Under the Volstead Act, he could make as much wine as he wanted, but it was illegal to sell except under certain conditions. He sold some to the archdiocese of San Francisco. Monsignor Roig i Verdaguer, a Catalan who could not live without wine at every meal, had helped arrange this. Tourneau also had a license to sell medicinal champagne, and he sold his sparkling wines through pharmacies under doctors' prescriptions.

It was during these years that he began to gaze toward the intermediate hills that strung along to the north, halfway between the cultivated orchard land of the valley floor and the high crest forested with redwood. He named them the *chaine d'or*, the chain of gold, because he knew that each hilltop had the same soil and weather as his own land. And he thought about his son Louis attending the University of California at Davis, studying viticulture, then returning home to help him plant new vineyards there.

The second mortgage came in 1926. Many growers, in Napa or the Central Valley, had grafted their vines over to heavy yielders when Prohibition had come, the big immigrant varietals like Mataro, or Alicante Bouschet, or Aspiran noir. These grapes yielded more than four tons per acre, and had thick skins and shipped well. Some growers even shipped table grapes as wine grapes, because they gave juice and color. Vineyard acreage in California doubled. Prices fell in the glutted market, and Tourneau could find no buyers for his small, late-ripening grapes. But he refused to graft over his vines. He called the immigrant varietals *pagadebitos*, debt-payers, and he said to Louis, "I'd rather put my arm in a fire than graft over my Pinots, or my Chardonnays." Tourneau sold grapes locally, sold champagne and sacramental wine, but he was forced to go again to the bank and encumber the land with more debt.

Some bootleggers approached him, seeking a way to sell his wine, but he refused to deal with them. He felt that once he did business with them, they would have power over him and would extend that power into every aspect of the vineyard. And the agents of the Prohibition Bureau, who had put the bottled wine under bond, would notice any large shipments. He was forced to keep many thousands of bottles of fine wine in his cellars, stacked high in glassy labyrinthine walls, waiting for the end of Prohibition when they might be brought to light.

Tourneau worked longer hours after Gill left, driving himself and allowing Sophia to coddle the five-year-old Louis. When Prohibition began, a year after the war ended, he hoped that Gill might return to help against this new threat. But as harvest followed harvest, Tourneau's thoughts of Gill grew low and dormant, breaking out oddly when he drove down the rutted road that clung to the hillside, or when he looked out over his *chaine d'or*, the land he coveted. And he always ended his thoughts by telling himself what he'd told Louis. Gill had made choices. He didn't think of Pascale, didn't think at all of her death and Gill's reaction to it.

He knew, as soon as Sophia stood in front of him, that he would go to fetch Gill. Sophia always wanted to rescue the bird with the broken wing, or feed the fawn whose mother had been shot. He rose from his chair after Augusto and Louis left, and put his arms around her, and told her of course he would bring Gill back to the vineyard. She praised him with her eyes, as though he had already brought him home in celebration. He loved that look of hers when it came. He felt she had renewed him when she married him, given him a second chance to get things right, and that look told him that all was well.

Tourneau drove through San Natoma, skirting the iron-fenced town square and taking the route north toward Jacobsen's ranch. Several people in town recognized his truck and raised their hands as he passed, and he gave a half wave in return. The truck was new, and he had the winery name stenciled in fancy script on both doors. BEAU PAYS WINERY. He was proud of the truck, proud to have the name painted on the sides. It was a small gesture of defiance toward Prohibition. He didn't deal with bootleggers, he had nothing to hide. During the town's Blossom Festival, earlier that year, he and Louis drove the truck in the parade, and filled the truckbed with barrels of wine draped with flowers.

Every year that Prohibition stayed in force, every vintage that was crippled by the laws, was like a year taken from his life. How many vintages would he know as a winemaker? Thirty? Forty? And already nine had been stunted, their true product hidden and untouchable. Tourneau had recently been diagnosed with fatty liver by Dr. Ribeau, one of the doctors who wrote prescriptions for medicinal champagne. He had complained about an uncomfortable swelling on his upper right abdomen, and the doctor was able to feel that the liver was harder and stiffer than a normal liver would be. The causes for steatosis—fatty liver—were obesity and excessive alcohol consumption, and it could be a step on the way to cirrhosis. Tourneau decided the doctor must be mistaken. Still, he felt his upper abdomen at times when he was all alone, felt the hardening organ, felt that he was fifty-five.

He drove along the edge of Jacobsen's orchard, tried to spot the group his son would be in. Mostly Mexicans, from what Louis said. There were several groups dragging buckets under the low spreading branches, but all he could see were the jeans and shirts of stooped pickers, their faces tilted at the ground. He turned the Ford onto the ranch drive and parked with two wheels in the dirt. Jacobsen hadn't planted cypress along the drive to his house like some. Too cheap. He wanted fruit from fence post to fence post.

Tourneau began to trudge out to the nearest group of pickers. He hated to think of Gill doing this work. In France, Tourneau had done stoop labor, drifting with the harvest after the vineyards in Burgundy were stricken with disease and his own father had abandoned the family, until he stowed away on a ship bound for America. He didn't want his son to have to do the same. He wondered what it would have been like if, while he'd been working under the prune trees near Agen, his own father had reappeared. What if his own father had discovered him bent in the orchard and lifted him up? What if his own father, bright as the sun, had offered him a place, a vineyard, a life? Wouldn't he have thought it a miracle?

The morning after he'd been recognized in San Natoma, Gill stepped up to grab a bucket from Bull Jacobsen, and he felt the younger man's eyes rest on him, distinguish him from the rest, appraise him. The sun was low in the east, and the orchard trees cast cool, long-merging shadows over the plowed earth, and the pickers were anxious to begin before the heat set in. But first they had to gather in a ragged half circle around Bull, who stood above them in the back of the pickup truck and handed out buckets and directed groups to various parts of the orchard. Gill took the bucket from Bull's beefy hand and nodded at him. He knew he was easy to pick out, the only white working with a group of Mexicans, and he was sure the word had gotten around that he was working on Jacobsen's ranch. Joey would tell everyone who came into the gas station.

Gill stepped back and joined Miguel and the others. Bull began shouting out directions, and as a group they walked swiftly out to the day's work.

Every time Bull came by their group, loading up full boxes, dropping off empties, punching cards for credit, Gill noticed him pause. He didn't stop picking to make eye contact. Gill didn't know what Bull might want from him, but he didn't think it would be anything kind.

The day was good. They were finishing the second picking of a section near the edge of the orchard, and the fruit lay scattered on the ground, and they filled their buckets steadily. The first picking of a section could be lean, with only the sun-favored fruit from the tips of the branches ripe and fallen. The second picking was the richest, while the third and fourth grew successively more meager, the fruit scarce on the uneven ground. It was this fact that caused growers to offer a harvest bonus, to keep pickers from jumping to a better-paying field before the last fruit was in boxes.

In the late afternoon, Gill found himself working trees with Miguel, each sweeping the ground on opposite sides of the trunk, meeting at the rough line where the fruit was picked clean, and moving on to the next tree. Gill heard Miguel sing or hum quietly from time to time, a folk song called "El Quelite." Gill knew the song, even though only snatches were audible from Miguel. It was a song of longing for a town and a small plaza and friends left behind.

A truck rumbled by on the road alongside the orchard, and Gill looked up from his work. He saw the words BEAU PAYS WINERY painted on the door of the truck, and he stood to watch. The truck turned left, down the lane that led to the Jacobsens' ranch house.

Gill crouched back down and grabbed at some prunes. "Don't you wish," he said, "that after a day's work you could drive your truck and just be at home?"

"Where?" Miguel continued to grasp three or four prunes at a time with each hand and drop them into his bucket. "Milagro Park?"

"No. Michoacán."

Miguel grunted as he crab-walked forward. "Sometimes I wish that," he said. "Mexico is my country, *güero*."

They both stood up and emptied their buckets into a box marked with a P, just filling it. Then they went back to the unpicked ground.

"Would you go back home if you could?"

"Perhaps," Miguel said. "If I could live in peace."

"Still war in parts of Mexico."

"Yes. We hear about this all the time."

"But even without that," Gill said, "Francisco might still want to stay here."

"I know." Miguel was already picking again, the prunes pinging faintly into the bottom of the galvanized bucket. "I know, and knowing that is like having an arrow pass through my side."

Gill began to pick as well. He heard Miguel again begin to hum "El Quelite."

The first group of pickers that Tourneau came across were teenagers, sons and daughters of families in the area, earning pocket money and school clothes money. Some of them were picking slowly, and others were sitting on upended boxes, having decided that it was late in the day and they had made enough for now. They stopped their chatter when Paul Tourneau neared their circle. He asked them where there was a group of Mexicans with one white man working, and a boy pointed toward the section farthest from the ranch house.

"Way over there," he said.

Tourneau continued walking, and he heard the voices behind him jump excitedly. The group they had pointed out was much more active. The pickers stooped under the trees, elbows pumping as they scrabbled in the dirt, buttocks sometimes level with their heads. They all looked alike, working with their faces to the ground and their shirts and jeans coated with dust. He couldn't tell which one might be Gill.

As he walked over the plowed earth to the row of trees nearest the road, the pickers began to stand up one by one, stretching with palms in the smalls of their backs and elbows flared out. They turned toward him, Mexican faces, except one a little taller than the others. Tourneau stopped for a moment, looking at his son's face, half-scarred, caved in, thickened with waxy tissue and one eye looking a bit inward.

"Hi, Papa," he said.

It was Gilbert's voice, Tourneau was sure, Gill's voice from that broken face.

"Hello, Gill." Tourneau tried to look at that face calmly, tried not to show shock or disgust, but it was impossible. That face, which was half his face, was half-scourged, punished beyond recognition. He began to shake his head.

"Look at you," he said. "Look at you."

"Look at me?" Gill asked.

"What have you done to yourself?" Tourneau spoke with a great gasping sob, in a voice he himself did not recognize.

"Nothing." Gill brushed dirt from the front of his shirt and the knees of his pants. "I haven't done anything to myself."

"Why don't you get your goods together," Tourneau said. "We'll throw it all in the back and drive to Beau Pays."

"Drive to Beau Pays," Gill said. "Just like that."

"Sophia is making dinner for you right now," Tourneau said. "A feast, I'm sure. And we'll open up some Oeil de Perdrix."

He half turned to go. "Come," he said. *"Viens, fiston."*

Javier and Francisco had already gone back to work, clean-picking the next tree in the row, and Gill stood motionless on the naked soil, his half-full bucket at his feet. He'd thought about this moment, thought about Beckwourth's offer, five grand, and how the first step would be to return to the vineyard. But now he saw the pity in his father's face, heard the unbearable sense of magnanimity in his father's voice, and he did not move.

"You haven't changed," Gill said.

Tourneau turned back.

"You really think you can come here and snap your fingers," Gill went on, "and I'll go with you. You must think a hell of a lot of yourself."

"What do you mean?"

"You come like you're doing me a goddamned favor. And I'm supposed to be grateful."

"You don't need to be grateful," Tourneau said. "But you could recognize that I came for you."

"I recognize you, all right. I recognize that you want me to come and work and jump at the sound of your voice. I recognize that you want everything forgiven, everything forgotten."

"What needs to be forgiven?" Tourneau asked. "What needs to be forgotten?"

"Nothing." Gill turned away from Tourneau and picked up his bucket and walked to the next tree. Tourneau followed him, stood over him as he crouched and began to gather fresh-fallen fruit with both hands.

"What needs to be forgotten," he demanded again.

"Nothing. You've already forgotten everything."

"Gill, I'm offering you a place, a home."

"A place in your home, that's nothing of mine."

"It's more than you've got now. It's not my fault you've been gallivanting around."

Gill laughed. "Yes, that's what I've been doing. Gallivanting around. And it's not your fault. Nothing is."

"So you want to stay here, picking prunes off the ground?"

"It's good enough for some."

"You want better for yourself than this," Tourneau said. "I know you do. And I want better for you."

Gill stood and carried his bucket over to a harvest box and poured in his prunes, and evened the pile with his hands so that the box looked nicely full. "Maybe you're right," he said. "Maybe I do want better for myself. But I don't want it to come from you."

"You're making a mistake, Gill."

"Then it's a mistake I make."

He turned back to picking. Tourneau stood silent for a moment, looking at his son's wiry back, the bones and sinews working under blue denim. Then he trudged back to the vineyard truck. The sun was disappearing behind the Coast Range, gradually extending its shadow over the orchard as he opened the door and turned over the engine.

Tourneau knew that Sophia would not understand why he was returning alone. He was sure that she had prepared foods that Gill used to like, dishes he would not have tasted in years. She would have the vineyard house open and glowing, a beacon on the hill. Even though he had done nothing wrong, he wondered what he would say when Sophia came to the door and asked, *Where is he? Where is your son?*

Gill continued to pick furiously until he knew that Paul Tourneau was out of sight. Then he sat back onto the ground, the half-empty bucket between his ankles, and closed his eyes.

Miguel's rough hand squeezed his shoulder. "We're quitting now, Gilberto. All the pickers are finishing up."

Gill started. "Are the boxes topped off?"

"You can top them off with your half bucket," Miguel said. "You're a picker, a good one, one of us."

Back in New Chicago, Gill ate silently and then went up to the ghostly second floor where he had his bed. Ana had asked him what was the matter, but he just shook his head and said nothing. Upstairs, he sat in front of the window that faced south. It was dark night, but he knew the direction in which the vineyard lay. At that moment, he didn't feel like a picker among other pickers, one of the Pulidos. Despite the press of Miguel's hand on his shoulder and his kind words, Gill felt separate and distinct from them, and also separate from his father. Alone in the crooked bedroom, the shapes of haunting and nightmare emerged behind him, red and incendiary, setting piles of tangled vines on fire and casting shadows of monsters.

The next morning, when they again stood in a half circle around the ranch truck for directions, Bull Jacobsen asked them if anyone was going to pick a ton that day. "How about it?" he shouted. "Forty boxes make a ton. Who's going to make it?"

"I can," Miguel said in English.

"Good. Hope so." He pointed to rows of trees near the edge of the orchard. "Just start on those rows."

"Hey, Stanley," Gill said.

"Call me Bull."

"Okay," Gill said. "Bull. How about we work on those rows closer to the house, where the other pickers are? We might could make a ton if we were on those rows."

Bull frowned. "Those rows aren't ready for second picking yet."

"Yeah?" Gill looked over, peering. "Looks like there's plenty of fruit on the ground to me. You wouldn't be saving those rows for somebody else because they're Imperial prunes, would you?"

"What makes you think that?"

"Maybe we're not white enough to pick Imperials?"

Miguel shot a look at Gill. *"No servirá para nada,"* he said.

"Ya lo sé," Gill said. He knew speaking out would do no good. But he knew the world to be unkind, and he wanted now to see it bitterly confirmed.

Bull jumped down from the truck bed in front of Gill. He was taller and broader than Gill, and he was smiling. "Daddy told me to watch out for you. Said that anyone who had fallen in the world was bound to be a troublemaker."

"I'm just asking for a little fairness," Gill said. "If we're good enough to pick your fruit, we're good enough to pick all your fruit."

"Anybody wants to make trouble, I just ask if they want to box."

Bull put his hands up near his face, ducked his head from side to side, and shuffled sideways.

"Come on," he said. "I need to get in some sparring. 'Winner, by a knock-out—Bull Jacobsen.' I heard you're a war hero, how about it?"

"You want to fight a war hero?" Gill put up his hands. "Okay. Good. And if I knock you down, we pick Imperials. Deal?"

"Sure," Bull said. "Sure."

Miguel and Javier and Francisco stood back from the two, forming a small ring. Rosarita walked away and turned her face while the two men began to circle each other.

Gill held his fists up near his forehead, to deflect any shots. Bull out-weighed him by some forty pounds, and had arms several inches longer. He was laughing, shooting left jabs and keeping Gill at a distance.

Gill faked his head left and right, but always found Bull's left fist stand-ing him off. He had training as an infantryman, but he had never boxed. He shuffled right, away from the jab, and protected himself against any head blows.

Bull closed in after a minute of dancing and followed a jab with a right hook to Gill's ribs that staggered him back and blew the breath out of him. Then he stepped back to let Gill recover, wanting to make the fight last longer.

"War hero," he taunted.

Gill felt a knot squeezing against his ribs. He breathed deep, trying to loosen the pain, still shuffling right. He saw Bull in front of him, his broad white face grinning. The favorite son, the one who had his place, the face of all Gill suddenly hated and desired.

When Bull closed again, Gill lunged to the left, inside his guard. Bull tried to tie him up, but Gill shot his right knee up hard, buried it deep into Bull's groin.

The larger man gasped and doubled over. Gill pivoted and caught his cheekbone with a hard right elbow. The skin broke, and blood ran down his cheek. Then Gill plowed into him with his whole body, and Bull went to one knee.

"War hero knocked you down," Gill said.

He turned and left, striding toward the highway.

Miguel and Francisco watched him go, then turned to help Bull up off the ground. Bull winced as he took small steps into the truck and drove off.

Miguel, without a word, led Francisco and Javier and Rosa toward the rows near the road, where Bull first told them to go. He knew that going to pick Imperials was out of the question. Bull's promise that they could pick Imperials if Gill knocked him down meant nothing.

One hour later, the truck roared back into the orchards where they were picking, and Pieter Jacobsen rumbled out and stood, wide-legged, looking around fiercely. He wore overalls, broad and whitened with wear in the seat and knees, and he stood with his hands apart until he spotted the Pulido group and advanced on them.

"Where's Tourneau?" Jacobsen still had a slight accent from Norway. "Where is that bastard?"

Javier stood up and moaned. He walked stiffly toward Jacobsen, moaning and growling deep within his throat.

Jacobsen backed off two paces. "Who is this lunatic? Don't any of you speak English?"

Francisco ran to Javier's side and wrapped an arm around his chest, hugging him and stilling him. "I speak English," Francisco said.

"I speak as well," Miguel said.

Javier moaned and leaned forward against Francisco's arm. Jacobsen looked at him. "By the Christ, what kind of a bughouse is this?"

"Just pickers," Miguel said. "Just pickers, Mr. Jacobsen."

"Well, where's that bastard Tourneau?"

"He left," Francisco said.

"Where did he go? Is he coming back?"

Francisco looked over at his father. Then he said, "We don't know."

"Tell him not to bother coming back," Jacobsen said. "And he don't need to bother trying to find work on any of the other ranches around here. I'm calling and telling them all about him."

He backed up to the door of the truck, watching Javier wave his arms and groan. "You tell him," he said. Then he quickly opened the door, climbed in, and shut the door behind him. Francisco released Javier, who roared at the truck as it drove off.

EIGHT　　*Monster*

When Sophia learned that Gill had come back to the Valley, and that her husband was going to bring him home, she thought that her prayers had been answered. Sophia understood more of the vineyard's financial situation than her husband thought she did, and she was sure that Gill's return was providential.

She remembered the year before the great quake, when her mother had gotten the TB and entered the Belmont Sanatorium for Working Women. Sophia once ran away from home to see her at the sanatorium, and she'd tried to persuade her mother to come home with her. She had only been able to talk to her through a screen door and was not allowed to touch her. When her mother died the following year, she believed that if she had only been able to bring her home, her mother would have lived. She still believed that.

Two years later, when Paul Tourneau offered to marry her, she saw it as a way to restore and repair his broken family, and her own. And Mary had said yes, after all.

Now she prayed her husband would succeed in gathering Gill, the wandering son, back into the fold. She prayed that the vineyard would thrive, and that all at last would be gathered in.

She was in the kitchen when she heard Tourneau arrive, and she knew instantly that he had come alone. There was a false brightness in his voice, a large relieved note indicating that he had done his duty and it was now behind him. She heard him hang up his hat and coat with vigorous satisfaction, then stride across the Great Room.

"What time is dinner?" he asked jovially, pushing open the double-hinged door and leaning into the kitchen.

Sophia looked at the meal spread out on the kitchen counters, a feast for no one. She had made pan-crisped chicken, *pollo a due tempi,* because it could be made and reheated at the last minute. Fresh green beans from the garden, fixed Bolognese style with mortadella. A pasta dish with prosciutto, tomatoes, peas. Fresh-baked bread. Rice pudding.

"Let's wait for Louis," she said.

"Good! I'll get your father. We can all eat together."

Louis came from practice with the town's baseball team half an hour later. Sophia heard the truck that dropped him off, and she walked to the verandah and saw him sprinting up the stairs. She knew he was hoping for a grand reunion. When he saw her, she shook her head and told him to wash up.

At dinner, Augusto asked Tourneau directly if he'd found Gill. Tourneau leaned back in his chair and described exactly what had happened, his own fairness and generosity of spirit, and Gill's pigheaded replies. Augusto probed with skeptical questions, but didn't shake Tourneau's story that he had done all that was just and right.

Afterward, Tourneau insisted that they leave the chandelier lit and the house glowing, as though for a celebration, and move out onto the verandah. There, he planned aloud for what he would do someday on the string of hills that stretched north from his vineyard, the *chaine d'or.* They could be cleared and planted with vines, one by one. And the profit from each would pay for the development of the next. The string of hills would all someday be part of the Beau Pays. Gill's name wasn't again mentioned. Tourneau spoke only of how Louis would have control of a part of the expansion, and have to build his own winery and cellars at some point. After he had graduated from Davis, and after the damned Prohibition was ended. Sophia could see her son's disappointment in the short answers he made to his father's speeches, given more out of duty than enthusiasm.

She left them on the verandah and cleared the table and dumped the stripped bones into the trash can and stacked the empty plates beside the sink. She washed and dried each dish to a shine, and then she held each one up to the light, saw her face reflected in the white porcelain glaze. She saw herself pale and translucent, smoothed of age and pain. Her better self. Her spirit self.

She thought that she could be the one to bring Gilbert home, though she'd failed with her mother. This homecoming feast was fruitless, but another feast would come, surely it would. She would find the hurt in Gill that Tourneau hadn't reached, and soften him, and offer comfort.

As she was finishing, Louis came into the kitchen and picked up a stack of dried plates and carried them to the glassed cupboard. Such a good boy, always helpful. He picked up a wineglass and began to polish it dry, wiping thoughtfully around the stem and base and inside the globe.

"This isn't right," he said in a low voice.

Sophia nodded. "I hope he's still at New Chicago," she said. "God willing, I'm going to bring him home with me."

Louis smiled. "You can do it, Mama."

"If I do, it won't be just my doing," she said.

She washed one more plate, and dried it, and studied her image in the shine.

Gill looked for orchard work after he walked off Jacobsen's ranch, but he found only blank faces and closed gates. Jacobsen had called all his neighbors and told them not to hire him, told them he was trouble. The only work he found was harvesting truck crops for farmers who were selling at the wholesale market in San Jose, a few days' work picking lettuce or rooting out onions. The wages were low, lower than for picking fruit.

When he wasn't working, he helped Ana with the camp chores at New Chicago. He hauled water, collected firewood, aired the bedding daily, drove with her to buy supplies. In those days together, they found that talk came easily for them. Stories gave rise to other stories, and jokes, and observations, and their talk was abundant and effortless and never tedious to them. Ana didn't ask Gill how he had been wounded, for which he was unconsciously grateful—he didn't think about his scarred face while he was with her—and he found himself offering other stories about the war to her that he had never told anyone. He'd seen the faces of dead men, many of them. But he was never sure if he himself had killed anyone. The flesh of troops was so massed and anonymous, the rifle fire so general and random, that he never knew for certain what he'd done when he'd gone over the top.

When Ana spoke, she told him about their years in the Imperial Valley, when they first left Mexico. They lived in a shack along an irrigation ditch, the walls pieced together out of cardboard boxes and the wooden roof taken from broken lettuce crates. They added a lean-to on one side using arrowwood from the ditch banks. The floor was dirt, which was not a problem except during lettuce season, in January and February, when dampness rose through the ground. Then, after two years, the fields played out, growing whitish with alkali, and they moved to a different part of the valley. But the house they had was always the same kind, put together out of the leavings from farmwork and vegetable packing.

She often spoke about Milagro Park, and the streetlamp where you were never lonely. The city had placed only one streetlamp in the neighborhood, but some of the young men had discovered a way to hook up a jukebox to its electricity, so people gathered there in the evenings when the weather was good to listen to music and dance and talk.

She told about the families who kept goats, and who had to walk into the hills every morning and drive the long iron stake into the ground with a sledgehammer so that the goat could graze chained to it. And the Corpus Christi processions, when little altars were set up outside of houses and people would walk from house to house to pray and admire the santos. And the weddings that took place where everybody was invited, and a band would play boleros and cumbias, and they would spread sawdust and powder on the rough floors so that people could slide their feet while they danced.

Gill thought about Ana, wearing widow's black in the midst of all the life she described. He thought about how other men might see her—caring for two children who were nearly grown, a part of her life over with, the black dress marking her as untouchable. He asked her once if she always had to wear black, and she replied that she was a widow, as though that ended the discussion. He found another chance, when they were laughing about the past, to ask her how old she had been when she came to California.

"Twenty-three," she said.

"So that would mean now you would be . . ."

"Thirty-two." She smiled, and her cheeks rounded.

"Could you never get married again?"

"Oh, I don't think of that."

Sophia wasn't able to find an excuse to drive into town for more than a week, until she needed to buy honey at Huntington's Apiary. Beau Pays didn't keep bees, as many orchards did, since bees weren't as necessary for pollinating a vineyard as they were for plum or apricot, and bees could be very destructive to the grapes when they sweetened up just before harvest. And even if the vineyard had bees, Sophia would still have loved the fields of sweet clover Mrs. Huntington grew around her hives, and the wholesome taste it gave honey for baking.

After lunch, she gathered the cleaned and emptied mason jars into a slant-sided harvesting box and placed them in the back of the truck. Then she went to the bedroom and changed into a clean dress, a flower print dress with a white collar, not so fancy that it would make her husband wonder, but nicer than her plain blue housedress. She smoothed the dress down over her hips, and she turned to look sideways at herself in the large oval mirror that stood in an oak frame in one corner of the room. Then she leaned her face close to the mirror. There were some shallow lines etched on either side of her mouth, but they were visible only if looked at from very close. And other lines at the corners of her eyes and thinning across her forehead. A map of years across her face, but still blurred into youthfulness at a distance.

After coming into town, she turned southeast for the apiary first. She didn't want to drive straight to New Chicago, past Joey's gas station and the drugstore. People would be sitting, watching from the windows, wondering where she was going. She could drive to New Chicago afterward, by a route that avoided San Natoma.

Mrs. Huntington was always called a witch by the children of the grammar school, because she was gray-haired, and lived alone, and kept cats, and had women who visited her, older women like herself. But the prune and cherry growers who lived nearby loved her, because their trees were always well pollinated by her honeybees. Her husband had left thirty years earlier, because, he said, they couldn't have children. He left her with an orchard that she didn't think she'd be able to keep up herself, and she already knew she would never marry again. So she had the orchard plowed under, except for a few cherry trees near the house, and dedicated herself to beekeeping.

Mrs. Huntington had never seemed to change in the years Sophia had known her. She was straight and tall and lean and in perfect health. Her hair was shortish and gray, and she always wore comfortable men's pants and long-sleeved blouses and a kerchief around her neck. Sophia took the box of empty honey jars to her front porch, and she exchanged them for jars newly filled, each carrying a handwritten label specifying the date collected and the predominant flavor, usually clover but sometimes fruit blossom.

Sophia paid Mrs. Huntington with a bank check. She also took a bottle of wine out of her handbag for her, the steely dry white wine in a long green bottle that she knew Mrs. Huntington favored.

Mrs. Huntington held up the bottle and admired it. "Thank you, Sophia. And give my thanks to Paul."

She looked at Sophia.

"You're dressed pretty," she said. "Too pretty just for me."

"I'm going to see somebody I haven't seen for a long, long time."

"Thought so." Mrs. Huntington didn't smile. "You be careful, Sophia. I'd hate to see you get hurt. You already have a lot of regrets in this life."

"I'll be careful," Sophia said.

"Good," she said. "I have regrets too," she said, "but not as many as I'd have had if my husband had stayed."

Sophia drove back northwest, staying to roads that cut through orchards and onion fields. When she turned onto the dirt road that led to New Chicago, she began to smell the tidal flats, and she slowed down. There were the tilting houses, a pot hanging over a fire, a woman in black tending it. Then she saw a man pouring a bucket of water into a large barrel. He was shirtless and olive-skinned, his chest smooth and hairless. As he moved, his body seemed spare and thrifty, without any waste or excess.

She parked and took a jar of honey from the box in the back of the truck. When she walked toward him, she noticed how he held his face straight, so that she could see the whole scarred cheek, the way the smashed bone made his left eye look in a little. She told herself to not let her reaction to his face show, and she walked right up to him and placed a hand on one arm and kissed his right cheek, the smooth one.

"It's good to see you, Gill," she said.

"Is it?" he asked. "Good to *see* me?"

She stepped back, held up the jar of honey. "I brought this. For the camp."

He took the jar from her and handed it to Ana. "A gift from my stepmother," he said. "*Mi madrina.*"

Ana lifted up the jar. "*Gracias.*"

Sophia ignored Ana. "I've thought about you a lot over the years, Gill. I always prayed you'd come back."

"I'm not back anywhere," Gill said. "I'm in New Chicago."

"But you won't be always."

"You don't think so?"

"You're near the end of a great pilgrimage, Gill. I want to take you the rest of the way home."

Ana had turned away and busied herself with the fire. Sophia was speaking as though she weren't present, and she bowed her head and began to poke at the small branches under the pot to liven up the flames.

Gill looked at Ana, then turned back to Sophia. "Why don't you grab a bucket?" He picked up two buckets and pointed to a third. "I've still got to finish filling up that barrel. For Ana. We can talk over there."

They walked a path worn through a field of dried and yellowed grasses toward the green strip that marked the course of Cherry Creek. The creek, which fell into the bay near New Chicago, was sluggish and dull, greened with algae. Its water had been diverted into irrigation channels a dozen times before it reached the bay, run through orchards and strawberry patches and truck farms. From each field, the runoff was diverted back into the creek, thick with salts, fertilizers, pesticides. By the time it reached New Chicago, the creek was a series of still, silty pools, with insects skittering across the opaque surface, and trickles of water muttering between them through short rocky stretches and bending green grass.

Gill kept a little ahead of Sophia, and she had to stumble after. They stopped at an oblong pool overhung by a sickly willow tree, and Gill straddled the water at the upstream end of the pool, where there was a little current. He dipped one of the buckets carefully, trying to fill it without disturbing any of the sediment. Sophia handed him another bucket, and he took it without looking at her.

"Is this what you drink?" she asked.

"Drink, cook with, wash in," Gill said. "We pour it in one of the barrels, and then wait for an hour or two. It settles out clear, as long as you just dip water out from the top. We're downstream from everything here in New Chicago."

He half smiled at Sophia, took the third bucket, and held it down into the slow-moving water.

"So you can't want to stay here," Sophia said.

"Why not?"

"It's awful here."

"It's nice enough for Ana." Gill set the third bucket on the soft ground beside the other two. "It's nice enough for her family."

"That's different."

"Why?" Gill asked. "They're good people. They've been as kind to me as anyone in the past ten years."

"I'm glad," Sophia said.

"Why wouldn't I want to stay with people who are good to me?"

"They have no place better waiting for them."

"They don't?"

"And you do. You have Beau Pays. Your father would welcome you back."

"So he told me."

"But he didn't tell you he needed you."

Gill laughed. "He'll never admit he needs anyone but himself."

"But he does." Sophia's eyes were bright as she spoke. "I'm here to do you good, and to do him good. He needs you more than he knows, and more than he'll ever let on. And the vineyard needs you."

"He doesn't need me," Gill said. "He needs a dog to follow him around and make him feel grand, to work for little pay and no credit, and to get scraps to eat and a rug to sleep on."

"It wouldn't be like that," Sophia said.

"No? Isn't that a little of what Augusto does?"

"He has his home," she said. "He's not a wanderer on the earth."

"I want something different than that."

"You can find what you want there, Gill. In his heart, your father needs you. And in your heart, you need him. And it would do me good as well, to see you home again."

"Of course," Gill said. "I'd be somebody else for you to nurse. Another lame bird on the windowsill. Another way for you to practice charity. You might not know what to do if someone didn't need you."

"I'm trying to bring you peace, Gill."

She reached out, put a hand on his bare chest. Her fingers spread like tree roots over his flesh.

"Feel that," she said.

Gill took her hand in his, warmly for a moment, then yanked it up to the left side of his face, the side layered with scar tissue. He forced her hand against his broken cheek.

She flinched at the touch and pulled back. He let her hand go.

"Not so easy, is it?" he said. "I look like a monster, haven't you noticed?"

"You don't look like a monster." She massaged the palm of her hand.

"And you're beautiful. You haven't changed a bit."

"Yes I have."

"Not a damned bit. Still beautiful. And I'm a monster. I'm what he left in his wake when he built his vineyard. So if I ever do come back, that's how it will be. I'll come as the vineyard's monster."

"You're not a monster," Sophia said. "I don't believe that."

"How would you know?"

Gill stooped down and picked up a bucket of water in each hand.

"Pick up the bucket," he said.

Sophia rubbed her hand once more, then stooped down and grasped the metal bail. They trudged back together toward the house.

"Tell me about Louis," Gill said. "How old is he now?"

"Sixteen. He just turned sixteen. He's a wonderful young man."

"Is he running track?"

"No. But he plays baseball. He's on the town team."

"Yeah? He must be good." Gill smiled, as though proud of his half brother. "Going to play in the big Fourth of July game, then."

"Of course. He plays center field."

"Maybe I'll go watch him play," Gill said. "Does he remember me?"

"He thinks about you. Your father told him you might be dead, but he never believed it."

Sophia saw Ana, dressed in black, watching them carry water along the worn path. She decided then that she wouldn't tell Tourneau what she'd tried to do. Gill led her to the two water barrels, and she watched him empty a bucket of water into one. She was about to empty hers into the other when Gill shook his head.

"That barrel has already settled. Dump it into this one."

"Gill," Sophia asked, "what are you going to do?"

"For now, finish hauling water."

"Whatever you do," she said, "it wasn't just by chance that you came back now. Somehow, your return was meant to be. As a brother, and a son. Not a monster."

He hoisted his other bucket, and they emptied them together into the barrel. The water boiled up, brown and grainy.

After Sophia left in the truck, Gill sat by the fire and Ana stood behind him and rubbed her fingers gently into his temples with warm circular motions.

*W*illiam Beckwourth began selling liquor in 1920 as a business proposition. His brother was district attorney for the county and wanted to maintain control of the alcohol sold, but he needed a middleman to collect payments and keep accounts. Beckwourth's auto dealership was ideal. It had cars coming and going at all times without arousing suspicions, and he could easily manipulate the sales numbers so that all the income looked legitimate. And many bootleggers favored the powerful Dodge sedans he sold, and were already customers.

As he dealt with bootleggers, he found that they didn't really understand capital. No matter how much money they made, it was always gone in a matter of weeks. They could pay cash for a new Dodge one week, then ask to borrow money for a shipment being smuggled into Half Moon Bay the following week. At first, he simply loaned money for smuggling operations, receiving a fifty percent return on the dollar in a few days. Then he began to finance smuggling operations himself, as well as various distilleries in the hills. By 1922, income from alcohol exceeded income from selling cars, though he still depended on his dealership as a cover.

He bought a large mansion on the Alameda for his family, and had several discreet girlfriends among the crowd who worked for him in one way or another. And he began to invest in land. An old Mexican who cleaned his offices claimed from time to time that his people had once owned land from where they stood "all the way to the *malpaís*." That would have been half the city of San Jose, and Beckwourth humored him. He told the story of the janitor whose family had owned the city at a Rotarians meeting once, and another businessman asked him if the janitor's name was Chabolla. If it was, then he was speaking the truth. The Chabolla rancho had been one of the largest in Northern California.

The janitor's name was Enrique Chabolla. Curious, Beckwourth looked into the land of the great rancho that had lain to the east of San Jose. Much of it was undeveloped, with cattle still grazing on it as they had for the previous century, and Beckwourth began to purchase it, piece by piece, as it came on the market. Someday, he thought, San Jose would become a great city and spread to the east. In the meantime, the hills he owned provided a good place to locate distilleries. When the old Mexican muttered about the land his family had owned, Beckwourth could smile, thinking of himself as quietly becoming like a Spanish grandee. The land he held set him apart from bootleggers who made money just to spend it or gamble it away.

By the late twenties, the profit margins on whiskey had declined. So much was made locally that it wasn't smuggled from Canada anymore. And the income Beckwourth made from alcohol no longer seemed a supplement to his dealership, but a necessity. He had taxes to pay on the land he already owned, land that produced income mainly from stills and jackass brandy, and he wanted to be able to buy more land as it became available. The big money now could be made in fine aged wines and champagnes, sold to wealthy customers. And he knew where a store of such wine could be found, without the risk of smuggling—Paul Tourneau's vineyard.

He had once offered to invest in Tourneau's vineyard, and offered to move some of his product for him. He had guaranteed Tourneau that the local law enforcement would turn a blind eye. But he couldn't guarantee that the Prohibition Service wouldn't take action when they found a large quantity of wine that had been under bond was missing. And Tourneau had been suspicious of him, thinking perhaps that if they had done business once, he would be blackmailed into doing business again. He had refused all offers, and Beckwourth left thinking that his fortune was now waiting for him in the cellars of Beau Pays, and it was only Paul Tourneau's stubbornness that kept him from it.

Beckwourth didn't realize that Paul Tourneau's son had been working at a still on his land until his legal name came out at the trial. Gill had been set up. His brother needed to convict people from time to time, and Big Boy didn't say anything about who Gill was. Once Beckwourth knew, he tried to get his brother to have the trial rigged. He thought he could use Gill as a tool to open up the cellars for him at last. But the evidence was clear, and it had been in the newspaper, and his brother said it was too late.

When Gill showed up at his office a year and a day after being sent up, Beckwourth hadn't forgotten about him. He knew a few things about Gill's problems with his father from the people around San Natoma, and he thought he understood why Gill was working at a still, not making wine. He hadn't succeeded in turning Gill when he first talked with him, but he thought he'd planted a seed. Like a good car salesman, he'd given him something to chew on, some reasons why he would benefit from doing what Beckwourth wanted him to do.

A month and a half later, his secretary leaned in and told him that the man with the scarred face, Gilbert Tourneau, was outside the office again. Beckwourth ran a finger over his mustache and told her he would see him in a little while. He didn't need to seem too eager. He was certain that Gill had already made up his mind, whether he knew it or not, and only needed the convincer.

Beckwourth had Gill into his office after an hour, and he immediately noticed that he was wearing the same clothes he had been before. Clean, yes, and any frayed cuffs had been neatly mended, but the same prison-issue work clothes. And even in the cool dim interior, Beckwourth could see that Gill's face had been darkened by the sun, the skin burned over and over again, never really healing. He'd been doing nothing but field work, that was clear.

Gill sat again in the leather chair and took a cigarette from Beckwourth's metal case. He took it without asking, took it as though he hadn't had a pre-rolled cigarette for a while. Beckwourth smiled.

"So how have you been, Mr. Tourneau?" he asked.

"Not so good. I lost my job. And nobody else seems to want to hire me."

"I'm sorry to hear that." Beckwourth leaned back in his chair. "It must hurt to be out of work and be able to look up the hill every day and know there's a vineyard up there with your name on it."

Gill nodded. "It hurts."

"You must feel sometimes as though Paul Tourneau has everything you ought to have."

Beckwourth paused, remembered Gill asking about Lupita.

"A wife, say," he continued. "A family. Do you feel that way sometimes?"

"Maybe sometimes," Gill said.

"Have you thought about my proposal?"

"You want me to case the vineyards. Find out about the booby traps, the alarms, the phone lines. And lead you to the wine."

Beckwourth nodded. "Somebody else will be driving the trucks and loading the boxes. All you need to do is get us in."

"I'll have to get pretty close to people to find out all that."

"I think you can do it. And I think you want to. Just help us get to some of that wine he's got hoarded away—that wine that you yourself have some right to. I know people interested in fine wines. They know Beau Pays's product, and they'll pay top dollar. They can't get enough of it."

"Probably some of the same crowd who stayed as my father's guests before Prohibition," Gill said. "Restaurant people. Two-faced."

"You won't have to deal with them. They won't even know you're involved. Nobody outside a small circle will know."

"Whoever I get close to will know," Gill said.

"Yes. But you won't need to care about them anymore."

"Suppose I do it. How much money might be coming my way?"

"We talked about five thousand dollars. Enough to start over with a clean slate. But you're not really doing it for the money. Are you?"

Beckwourth thought that this line was the convincer. He watched Gill's mouth tighten, and he was sure he'd closed the sale.

"Here." Beckwourth took a fifty-dollar bill from a money clip he kept in his inside coat pocket. "Look at this as a retainer."

Gill sat with his hands in his lap. Beckwourth was certain he would take the money. But he stood up without extending a hand out for it.

"Let me see what I can find out, first."

"All right." Beckwourth stood up as well, putting the bill back into his money clip. "The money will be waiting for you when you decide."

They shook hands across the broad oak desk.

Bill Finney printed the *San Natoma Star* from a small barn in the back of his property, a drafty and weathered building put up in the 1880s for plow horses kept to cultivate a new prune orchard. On raised platforms under hanging electric lights, a flatbed, single-revolution Hoe press turned out large sheets of newspaper printed on one side, which were then fed through a second time for printing on the opposite side. The Hoe press was nicknamed "Snapper" because of the sound it made when the type smacked the paper against the platen, and as a warning to be careful with fingers. Finney also had a Linotype, where he sat high before a keyboard and entered copy to be printed, and a Buffalo folder, which could automatically fold newspapers of four, or eight, or twelve pages. Finney tried to avoid issues of six or ten pages, which had to be folded and cut by hand.

The loft, which had held hay, now held rolls of fresh newsprint, empty and ready for the press, and also stacks of moldering papers from years past, unsold and unread. There was room on the ground floor next to the Hoe for Finney's car to park and load the papers, sheltered from the rain. The walls of the barn near the press were hung with tools and spare parts, and the whole building smelled like oil, and fine-grained metal, and thick black ink, and the fire where metal type was melted down to be reused.

Every Friday at noon, Finney left the office in town and came to the barn to lay out the *Star* and print it, frequently working well past midnight so that he could meet the delivery boys with their bicycles on the covered sidewalk outside the Cash Store on Saturday morning. He sometimes had one or two boys from the high school in to help him run the press, and he always included their names on the masthead as editorial assistants, so that their mothers would see them in print. His two older daughters had never shown much love for words, and had never helped him in the barn. Only Nancy, his youngest, had loved books from an early age and had been fascinated by the flywheels and the rollers and the barrel-sized cylinder of the Hoe, and all the cams and levers and belts of the Linotype. She had understood that this was how the books she loved were given shape. But she grew less interested when she turned sixteen and began to work at the soda counter, and he was afraid he might lose her to an early marriage as he had his other daughters. He wanted her to go to college, read some of the same books he had read, Emerson and Carlyle and Dickens and William Dean Howells. Then, even if she lived far away from San Natoma, he could remain close to her.

It was hot that Friday, July 3, and the air in the barn was still and thick, and tired flies bumbled in a lazy circle around one shaft of sunlight angling in from the west. On days like this, the faint smell of manure still rose from the porous wood of the old stalls in back. Finney sat up at the Linotype, entering in the copy from his community correspondents. These were mostly women who sent in notices of events in their circles, unpaid except for a free newspaper and an allowance for postage. They wrote about relatives visiting from Iowa, and meetings of the Modern Priscillas. A new shipment of linen and cloth for dressmaking in fashionable colors at the general store. An impromptu neighborhood party to listen to a newly purchased radio. Finney depended on these people. He knew he would never be writing as

Howells did, or as Sherwood Anderson did. In his newspaper, he wrote of a community of warmth and connection, a sweet good place where all could live fully good and meaningful lives. His correspondents, who always wrote of meetings that were *convivial*, merchants who were *enterprising*, greetings that were *heartfelt*, brides who were *blushing*, meals that were *sumptuous*, were the essential elements that he blended together to present San Natoma to itself as it wished to imagine itself.

Finney was typing in some copy from Los Gatos—Mrs. Idwal Thomas has girdled her famous Rish Baba grapes and she plans to enter them in the county fair—when the side door scraped open. He was expecting Anthony Weller to come over to help, but not until later in the day. He looked up from the keyboard, surprised to see Nancy leaning against the doorjamb.

"Aren't you supposed to be at the Cash Store?" he asked.

"I'm leaving in a little bit."

"I'm not trying to chase you away," Finney said. "It's good to see you in the print shop. It's been a while."

"I'm just so busy, it seems," she said.

"Of course," Finney smiled. "Being sixteen is a busy time in one's life."

Nancy walked over to where he sat at the Linotype's keyboard, elevated above the floor, and looked up at him. "You always look so high and mighty up there."

He wiggled his fingers like a magician. "I am authoring San Natoma."

"What part are you doing?"

"Community news." He winked at her.

"Oh. Any sewing circle meetings?"

"Lots of them," he said.

She walked away from him, toward the half-open barn door and the monotonous halo of flies. "Are you going to mention anything about Gilbert Tourneau?" she asked with her back turned.

"Do you think I should?" Finney asked.

"It's news, isn't it?"

"It's not what passes for news here."

"Why not? Because it's not *good* news?"

"If I mention Gilbert, it will bring up some unpleasant memories. When his mother died, Paul Tourneau married Sophia only six months later. Sophia was already known as a great beauty, and here she was, at sixteen married to someone twenty years older than her. People didn't like that."

"How did Gill's mother die? She must have been young."

"A couple years older than Tourneau, but still young. I think it was a heart attack. I don't remember."

"So you only print half of what goes on."

"Less than half," Finney said. "Far less than half."

"The part people will like. Not what's true."

Finney unseated himself from the high perch at the Linotype and came down to Nancy's side.

"What's the matter, baby?" he asked.

"Sometimes," she said, "this town feels like a bag over my head."

"And my newspaper's part of the bag?"

"I don't mean that," she said. "Daddy? Why don't you like Lou?"

"Your mother likes him. Isn't that enough?"

"Oh, Mama would like anyone who seems 'serious.'"

Finney laughed. "You know your mother well."

"So why don't you?"

Finney looked away. "Maybe I'm just afraid of it becoming 'serious.' You going to the dance on the Fourth of July with him?"

"Yes."

"That's my next item. Says they'll 'allow' some of the modern dances."

"If they didn't, we'd find a way to dance them anyway."

"I'll bet you would." He kissed Nancy. "Now I've got to get this copy in. And you have to get to work."

He climbed back up to his high seat at the Linotype and watched her walk out of the dark print shop. Then he turned to the keyboard and finished the item about the blue ribbon–sized grapes, and entered the notice of the dance. He paused, looked out the half-open door, listened to the flies.

"Sometimes," he said, "this town is like a bag over my head."

Finney knew stories about San Natoma that he would never print. About the fifteen-year-old sent off to give birth at a home run by the Lutherans, the family telling everyone she was "off visiting relatives." About the church secretary who had embezzled funds and spent the money on gifts for her circle of friends, allowed to resign to avoid scandal, still attending the same church and sitting in the back pew. About the fire deliberately set in a house being built, and the inflated damage award that allowed the merchant builder to bid on land just come to market. The insurance adjustor had been in on that one.

He had lied to his daughter about what he knew of Pascale's death. He'd heard the stories of her ghostly appearance the night before her death. Some tales had her dead for days in the vineyard house, and only her apparition showing up in the evening before she was found. Others had her found high in the branches of a tree, as though she had flown there. Most held Tourneau to be at fault in some way, through neglect or a failing of love's duty if nothing else.

Finney always wondered if Paul Tourneau's harshness toward his first son was a reaction to any guilt he might feel for the death of Pascale. If he kept his son laboring away at the vineyard, distant from fatherly love, he'd never have to face the conflicted emotions he would have if he embraced him. When Gill joined the army in 1917, part of Finney was not surprised. He thought Tourneau had driven him to it.

But Finney had never written any of that. He was diffident, he had faltered, he would never write the book that Sherwood Anderson had written. When he mentioned Beau Pays in the newspaper, it was only to celebrate its renewal, to announce the sale of its first bottles of sparkling wine, to report on the harvest.

Now he looked around the converted barn, smelled the remnants of generations of horses. The space seemed small and tight about him.

He flexed his fingers and placed them on the keys of the Linotype. In the space after the dance, he wrote up a small item about one of the town's war heroes, Gilbert Tourneau, returning to the area. He wrote that Tourneau was San Natoma's second most decorated veteran, after Howard Jackson, and he wrote that the town wished him well in his current pursuits.

The Familia Pulido couldn't work on July 4, a fact that irritated Miguel. He said that their independence day was September 16, or after the last apple was picked. When Gill announced that he was going to hitch into town to watch a baseball game, Francisco wanted to talk all about it with him, speaking insistently in English even though his father looked at him disapprovingly. Francisco talked about who the coach at his high school would be, a *bolillo* who sometimes let Mexican kids on the team, though he said he didn't like to since they always disappeared before the end of the school year. He talked about what positions he could play, and about the games of catch with friends in Milagro Park.

The morning of the Fourth, Miguel noticed how Francisco was moping, and he pushed his son on the shoulder. "It's good to have a day off, eh? To rest in camp."

"Yes, Papa," Francisco said.

"Or would you rather go with Gilberto and watch the game?"

Francisco looked at his father's face for a second, then realized he wasn't serious. "No," he said.

"No, of course not, it would be no fun to just sit and watch. Better to stay here, rest, cut some wood for camp, no?"

"Of course."

"But maybe, if you went, you would get able to play. They would suddenly need a new ballplayer, and they would of course choose the skinny Mexican kid from the crowd. And when they found out that you could play *and* speak English, they would all love you."

Francisco didn't reply. He gazed out at the mud flats under the low layer of clouds.

Gill looked at Miguel over Francisco's slumped shoulders. "He's young," Gill said.

"I know," Miguel said. "That's why he has to learn that people here do not love us. We come here to suffer, and to work, not to have a good time."

Gill caught one ride quickly that took him as far as Crossroads, where he had stopped for gas with Ana. Then he walked a dozen yards along the road toward San Natoma and planted himself to wait for another ride. Several cars passed by his thumb without a pause. One car, a Model A, slowed by him, then sped up again after the driver was close enough to see his face.

When he looked at the gas station across the street, he spotted the same teenager who had pumped his gas standing stupidly with a wrench in his hands and staring at him. Two other boys, about the same age but not dressed in gas station overalls, were staring as well. Gill scowled at them, and they all looked down suddenly.

Bill Finney took his cup of coffee out on the front porch early on that morning and looked at the sky. Then he went back inside and grabbed his stiff blanket-wool coat from the peg, the coat he wore in the print shop late in the evenings during the winter. A low ceiling of gray clouds lay over the valley, a marine layer of moisture that had spilled over the crests and now put a chill in the air. Finney walked toward the print shop, looked to the east for some sign of the sunrise but could find none. Then he looked to the west and saw the Coast Range cut off from view at a thousand feet. It was a thick one, he thought, probably stay foggy at the coast all day long. But it should burn off in the valley in time for the ball game.

In the shop, he began heaving bundles of newspapers, tied with twine, into the front seat of his Chevrolet sedan. When the bundles were at eye level, he began to fill up the backseat. The *Star* was a twelve-page paper this week, because merchants had placed ads to honor the Fourth of July, and there were community events to announce. He had put a drawing of an American flag rippling in the wind in the upper right-hand corner of the front page, with the legend "Happy Independence Day" below it. He used the same drawing for Flag Day and Armistice Day, but nobody seemed to mind. He knew they just wanted a flag on their newspaper during the weeks when a flag ought to be on their newspaper.

Finney's daughters had always complained about how the papers made the car smell for days afterward, all of them except Nancy, and even she had grown a little fussier lately. Finney liked the way the car smelled of ink. He liked Saturday mornings, after a long evening printing, carrying the news into town in black and white, even if it was only half the news.

He pulled up outside McCarty's Cash Store and began to unload bundles of papers onto the covered wooden walkway. One of his paperboys, Benny, rode up on a bicycle as he was still unloading and laid the bike against the raised walk. He was already wearing his canvas harness over his shoulders with large empty pouches front and back for the newspapers.

"We going to need wax paper today, Mr. Finney?"

Finney shook his head. "It's not that wet."

"Okay." Benny cut the twine holding together the bundles with a Ka-Bar pocketknife and began rolling papers.

"Tighter I roll them, the better they throw," he said.

Finney had to fill up the sedan and deliver bundles two more places. He looked up at the sky once more before he drove off. His paper was predicting a warm, sunny, and wonderful Independence Day, a fine day to spend with family and friends, clear skies for the fireworks. He hoped the fog layer would burn off early and not return in the evening.

The night before the game, Louis lay on his bed with his eyes open and watched the square of velvet light from the window move across his wall. He'd been having trouble sleeping since his mother had come back from New Chicago and told him that she couldn't bring Gill back yet, that he was still wandering for now. He wondered whether he should go see Gill himself, what he would say when he saw him, how he could make everything whole. His visions always disintegrated when he found that whatever he imagined himself saying was the wrong thing, whatever he did was wounding.

At times that night, he seemed to be dreaming while he was awake. He saw himself walking down an allée in the vineyard, the leaves high and green with midsummer. In the allée to his right, he saw his father walking, eyes straight ahead, advancing at the same pace as he was. His father carried a spade, as always, and was plunging it into the ground. In the allée to his left, he saw his brother, also walking at the same pace. Gill carried pruning shears and was dressing the vines as he walked. Louis saw that they were all walking parallel lines, they wouldn't meet until they came to the end of the allée, but when he looked up, the vines seemed to continue forever, the lines of cane and leaf disappearing into a vanishing point. As they walked, the season changed to autumn, the leaves grew red and tattered, and the sky lowered and darkened. He could see now, through the empty vines, that the spade his father carried was a weapon, a club of some sort, and his brother's shears had become a spear. He looked down at his own hands, and he saw that he carried his grandfather's cavalry pistol, and it was as heavy as a stone, the weight of it cold and real. He didn't know when they would reach the end of the field and meet, but he knew it couldn't be very far.

Louis woke with a shudder, surprised because he couldn't remember falling asleep. It was the time the sun should be rising, but he immediately knew that his room was darker than normal, and cold. His bedroom was spare and narrow, with straight and unadorned wooden furniture and no mirror and for decoration only a small carved crucifix at the head of his bed. He didn't keep blinds or curtains on his window, following his father's example, because he wanted the vineyard to be able to speak to him.

He sat straight up in his bed and threw back the wool blankets. The window looked back at him, dark and blank.

"Shit," he said. He pulled on shoes and pants quickly and ran out to the front porch.

The vineyard was ghostly and gray, floating in the midst of a thick cloud. The sun was up, Louis could see, but the light was faint and diffuse, not really illuminating anything, only making solid objects seem like shadows. The head-pruned vines closest to the house, standing like little trees and rich with summer foliage, also looked like shadows. The green of leaf was not green but dark above the gray trunks and plowed earth, dark and dripping, and Louis knew that the swelling grapes would be wet and dripping as well. Further up the hillside, the vines grew indistinct to the eye, blunt dark thumbs, and then were swallowed up wholly by the fog.

Louis turned at the heavy step of his father on the porch. Tourneau clapped a hand on his shoulder and looked out with him. "Good," he said, "you felt it too. Run and tell your grandfather and the rest that we'll be strapping on the hurdy-gurdies this morning."

An hour later, Tourneau and Louis and Augusto and three other workers were walking down the parallel allées of the upper vineyard, among the Pinots, with sprayers strapped to their chests and goggles and respirators covering their faces. They ground a small crank on the side of a box and put out a spray of sulfur powder the color of bread flour onto the foliage, to stop the mildew before it began. They walked slowly, with their collars buttoned high on their necks and their sleeves tight around their wrists, tossing the sulfur to the left. Louis had also wrapped a red bandanna around his neck and over his collar, as extra protection. The air was only mildly breezy, but after several rows, they began to whiten in their foreheads and clothes, and some of the sulfur worked its way through the breaks in the clothing to the skin. Gradually, they all grew pale as ghosts, advancing vine by vine, grinding and walking through the misty vineyard.

Louis looked up to the east at the end of each row, trying to judge the time from the position of the sun. The game would begin at one o'clock. But the air was thick and white through midmorning, and the sun's height was impossible to tell. He looked over at his father, spraying in the row next to him. Tourneau's beard was faded with powder, and the hair beneath his hat had grown colorless and aged. But he advanced stoically, pausing by each darkish vine to pump the sulfur that would combat any mildew.

Louis knew better than to ask him about leaving for the game before the vines were protected. He knew that even to ask would seem a failing and weakness in his father's eyes.

When they finished the upper field of Pinot, they refilled the tanks in their knapsacks with sulfur and began on the lower field of Chardonnay. The sun began to show dimly as the fog began to thin, a pale disc that still gave no warmth. Louis thought it must be a little after ten o'clock. He looked at the acres of grapes spreading down below them, then again at his father, part of a line of whitish men trudging indistinctly through these rows, pausing and grinding, then moving on. And he himself was also part of that line.

Bill Finney walked around the berm behind the ball field around noon, a pencil behind his right ear and a small spiral notebook in his left hand, taking notes for the next week's paper. The clouds had almost cleared, as he'd expected, and the sun was warming the field. There was red, white, and blue bunting hanging from the low fence that ran around the diamond. The flag hadn't yet been hoisted from the flagpole behind home plate. The bunting had been a sewing project of the Rebekahs, the flagpole erected by the Oddfellows Lodge—Finney would note both these facts in his story. There were lemonade stands on both sides of the field, a nickel a cup, and each stand had a fifty-pound block of ice behind it, gradually melting away, from which chips could be ice-picked to add to each drink. Finney saw his wife, Gladys, nicknamed Glad, at the hot dog stand set up to earn money for church activities. Glad was lighting a portable gas burner under a black cast-iron pot of water, and their eldest daughter, Rose, was chopping up onions for condiments. Some families had already begun to spread picnic blankets, and Finney strolled down toward them, to say hello and maybe catch an interesting line he could quote.

On the field, Mr. McCarty was having his boys warm up while they waited for the team from Milpitas to show. He called the team his boys, even though some of them were in their late twenties, because he couldn't seem to keep living without that phrase in his mouth, sweet and bitter as it was. His two sons had died twelve years earlier, but every spring and summer, he had a chance to stand on a ball field, where young men ran and played, and say the words *my boys*.

The Independence Day game was a very important one for him, because he knew that players would begin peeling off from the team as work on their home ranches grew more pressing. This game would be the last one for which the whole team, like a whole family, would be together.

As the overcast was lifting, he had the infielders ranged around the dirt between third and first base, and he was rapping out ground balls for them. Each in turn fielded the ground ball and threw it to the first baseman, who then relayed it in to Jimmy Sparks, the catcher.

"Sparky," Mr. McCarty said, "do you know where Louis Tourneau is?"

"I don't know, Mr. McCarty. I was wondering myself."

Mr. McCarty tossed a ball up and expertly cracked a sharp grounder in the direction of the shortstop. Then he turned around to the people beginning to come, looking for Louis, but also looking for Gill. He had read the little item about Gill in the *San Natoma Star* that morning, and he wondered if it signaled some kind of reconciliation.

He didn't see either one. Instead, he saw the team bus from Milpitas approaching and he would need to clear the field to let them warm up.

"Okay, boys," he shouted to his infielders. "Bring this one home."

He sent a ground ball to the third baseman, who fired it home to Sparky and kept running in. Sparky rolled the ball back out toward him as though it were a bunt, and he picked it up barehanded and tossed it in.

"Good going, son," Mr. McCarty said.

Finney noticed that Reverend Walters, the minister of the Congregational Church, was talking with his wife and daughter at the hot dog stand, and so he walked over. The minister was thanking them for volunteering their time.

"It's our pleasure, Reverend Walters," Gladys said.

"Anything in particular the money is earmarked for, Reverend?" Finney asked.

"The young women's group, the New Ruths, needs tablecloths and things," the minister said. "And I thought it fitting that the young men play for the benefit of the young women."

"That's gallant," Finney said. "Chivalric, even. And I'll contribute by buying a hot dog from my own wife."

The minister thanked him and walked away, and Finney passed a dime to Glad while Rose dipped a hot dog out of the steaming water and onto a bun.

"Funny he's never married," Finney nodded after Reverend Walters.

"Maybe he's just waiting for the right one," Gladys said.

"Maybe." Finney slapped some mustard on his hot dog and took a bite, turning to look out at the ball field, where the Milpitas team was now warming up. "So where's our youngest?" he asked.

"At my house, across the way," Rose said. "She wanted to freshen up a little, she said."

"For her own right one, I suppose," Finney said.

"Don't be a spoilsport, Daddy," Rose said.

"All right. For you, I won't." He looked behind home plate and saw people beginning to stand up and face the flagpole. Cap Andersen, retired now from constable, was marching some Boy Scouts up to raise the flag. He stumped along on his wooden leg, helped now by a cane as well, then stood straight and took off his hat while one Scout clipped the flag onto the halyard. Finney took off his hat as well. He would get the names of the boys in the flag detail as soon as they finished.

In her sister's bathroom, Nancy put some powder on her nose so that it wouldn't be shiny, and some light eyeliner around her eyes, since she thought that they disappeared into her face if she didn't run at least a thin line above and below her lashes. She would be much more elaborate for the dance in the evening. Then she quietly began to open and shut all the drawers and the medicine cabinet, shuffling through things carefully so they wouldn't seem disturbed. She stopped once and listened in the still house. When she heard nothing, she began again to run her fingers through her sister's boxes of powder and paint, searching.

Nancy remembered being fourteen, dressing for field hockey at the school, and snickering with the other girls. Chazzie, a girl who was a little overweight and was already getting breasts, was talking. "If you do it," she said, "you have to have a baby."

Sarah made a face. "Yuck," she said. "Why would you want to do it, unless you're married and have to?"

"It feels good to do it," Nancy said. "That's why you do it."

"How do you know?" Chazzie teased.

"My sisters told me. And you don't have to have a baby. Not every time."

"What do you do?" another girl asked. They all leaned in and looked at Nancy. She was the girl with two older sisters married. She would know.

Nancy found them on the upper shelf of the cupboard above the toilet, in a box marked "This product to be used only for prevention of disease." There were lots of them in the box—"sheaths," she and the girls called them. She didn't know how many she could take without it being noticed. She closed her eyes, reached in, and grabbed a fistful.

"That many," she said, looking at the packets filling her hand. It seemed a wonderful and daring thing to be holding them, like a bouquet.

Gill walked through the dirt parking lot, threading his way through the Fords and Hudsons and Jordans parked in crooked lines, and suddenly came to a view of the ball field, spreading green and bright before him. He had not been able to catch a ride from Crossroads. Hitching near a gas station was sometimes a good bet, since drivers who are already making a stop were inclined to pause once more to pick someone up, but everyone who bought gas heading his way simply sailed on by, and he wondered if the kid working there was saying something to them. Other cars went by heedlessly, and Gill finally turned and walked the four miles into San Natoma. It was cool at first, but as the overcast began to break, the way grew hot, and crescents of perspiration were darkening his blue shirt under his arms when he arrived.

The San Natoma Merchants team was standing along the third-base line with their caps at their chests, while the Milpitas team stood the same way along the first-base line. The crowd had settled on the bench seats or along the berm, and everyone was hushed as Reverend Walters was finishing the invocation, thanking God for the beauty of the day, and the well-being of the two communities who would join in sport on this day, and the peace and prosperity of the nation in 1928, born one hundred and fifty-two years ago on this day.

"We are all blessed to be citizens of this country," he said, "and we ask for your blessings on this day. In the name of your son, the Christ, Amen."

Gill walked past the dugout and looked at the San Natoma players one by one, thinking he might recognize Louis. He wanted to talk to him. He wondered whether Louis's relations with their father had been anything like his own, or whether he was still the favored child, the spoiled five-year-old he remembered. He thought about using Louis to find a way into the winery, and so to the money Beckwourth promised that would change his life, his and Ana's and the Pulidos'. But he had not yet convinced himself to use his half brother as a cat's paw.

As he walked, he felt glances dart his way, flashing onto him from right or left, then falling off when he turned his eyes slightly. He was used to this, used to turning his head and seeing men suddenly occupied in reading the paper, or women studiously picking lint from the collar of their dress, as though their eyes hadn't just been fixed on his scarred face. He had heard young children ask their mothers what was wrong with his face, and once, at a harvest dance in Salinas, he had heard one young woman tell another that it gave her the creeps if he looked at her at all.

Gill turned to see the ball being thrown around, and there was some clapping from the crowd and chatter from the infielders. Someone had just struck out.

He walked back down the first-base side of the diamond, around the flag-pole, and up the third-base side. He held his face up as he walked, seeking out the eyes of others, forcing them to choose to look away. He had expected this reaction, and he savored it now, proving to himself that the town did not care for him.

There was a spot open on the benches along third base, and he asked if it was free. A woman in a broad straw hat tied under her chin told him it was without looking up. He squeezed in, people scooting to one side or another to give him space, a little magic circle widening about him within which he was untouchable.

Gill sat alone for two innings. Nobody would meet his eyes. Everyone knew who he was, and nobody would meet his eyes, recognize him and greet him and welcome him. He had expected no benevolence, and he received none.

Mr. McCarty had noticed Gill walking along the lines as the invocation was being given. There was a little ripple through the crowd as he walked past, people not wanting to get too close to him, yet also wanting to turn for a look. They probably had heard Gill was back in town, or read the item in the morning paper. But they were treating him like a ghost, like someone whose name was on the bronze plaque in the town square, among the boys who gave their lives. Mr. McCarty wished that Louis were here, and that he could send Louis out to his brother to shake his hand and welcome him to the Fourth of July game. It pained him to see Gill walking alone, at once known and strange to the people.

Cap Andersen was standing near the team bench when they came in, and Mr. McCarty asked if he had seen him.

"I saw him." Cap knew who was being talked about.

"I wonder where Louis is," Mr. McCarty said. "I can't believe Gill's out of work, with his father owning that big vineyard."

"I can believe it," Cap said. "That Paul Tourneau is a tough nut to crack."

"I'm going to offer him work at the Cash Store," Mr. McCarty said. "We can't have our boys turn into strays."

As the teams were running in and out, Gill spotted Nancy Finney walking among the people with picnic baskets. She looked fresh and flushed, excited about something. When she looked his way, he raised his hand in a small greeting, and she smiled and walked toward him, the only person there who had acknowledged him. She squeezed past several people and made him move over so that she could sit next to him.

"Enjoying the game?" she asked.

"Sure." The third inning had begun, and Milpitas was ahead two to one. They watched the pitcher wind up and hurl a fastball that bounced past the catcher and went to the backstop. "I was hoping to see Louis play, though."

"I don't know why he's not here, the stinker," Nancy said. "He's always on time. *Saint Louis*."

"That's what you call him?"

"Just because he's so good about everything. You'd think butter wouldn't melt in his mouth."

"Is that right?"

"Hey, you hungry?"

"Sure," Gill said.

"My mother's running the hot dog stand." Nancy was already getting up. "I'll get us a couple."

She walked down to the stand where her mother and sister were working, pleased that people had noticed her sitting with Gill. She walked tall and proud, sure that she was being looked at, sure that nobody knew that she had sheaths hidden in her purse, nobody but her.

Louis arrived on a bicycle during the sixth inning, already wearing his uniform, and Mr. McCarty immediately sent him into the game. He'd worked at sulfuring until all the blocks of grapes had been treated, marching through the Chardonnay with his father on one side of him and his grandfather on the other side of him. The fog was just beginning to thin when they finished at the corner of grapes farthest from the house. Louis tore off his mask and looked up at the angle of the sun. His face was pressed with red, sweat-soaked circles, ruddy around the nose and upper cheeks that the mask had covered, whitened with sulfur everywhere else.

Beside him, his father took off his mask and looked up as well. "It's after one," he said. "We'll clean up the equipment this time, if you want to run off and take your bike to the game."

"Really?" Louis asked. "It's okay?"

"I'll get there if I can," Tourneau said.

"Thanks, Papa!" Louis unstrapped the hurdy-gurdy and ran in his heavy boots through the grapes, hearing his father call after him to be careful, not to brush against the foliage.

At the house, Sophia came to the door of his room while he was shucking his work clothes. "I stink of sulfur," he said, slapping at his hair and arms. "No time to clean up."

She watched while he yanked his uniform pants onto his legs and let the unbuttoned shirt drop over his head and arms.

"Is Papa still going to go?"

"He says he'll try."

"Then I'll be there with him," she said.

Louis grabbed his glove and cap from the closet and threw them on the bed, and he stuffed his shirt into his pants. Then he slung his spikes, tied together by the shoelaces, over his shoulder.

"I've got to go, Mama. See you there."

He kissed her quickly on the cheek as he went through the door.

"Right," she said. The smell of sulfur smudged her nose.

Outside, Louis jammed his glove on the left handlebar above the bell. As he came down off the chill, whitish hillcrest, the sun warmed the colors around him. The greens of leaves grew bright and live. He hadn't ridden the bike much since he began driving, but the road was still familiar to him. He knew where to look for potholes that could warp the wheels, where to slow down because the curves were sharp, where he could let off the brake and feel the bike pick up speed on a straight downhill. The wind from the bike's speed was cutting, but he could sense the air softening around him. When he reached the valley floor, the sun was bright and the sky cloudless, and he turned southeast for the ball field.

He heard the game before he actually arrived. The sharp chatter of the infielders and the furry sound of the crowd carried toward him, and when he saw that there were still cars and trucks parked around, he knew that he hadn't missed it all. He jumped off his bicycle at the edge of the berm and walked it through people sitting there, some of them greeting him by name.

"Sulfuring," he said over his shoulder as he passed. "Sulfuring against the rot."

The ball field looked beautiful to him, the way the angled lines and bases and fences resolved the space into perfect sense. As he leaned the bike against the fence, he looked at the scoreboard over the right-field fence and saw that it was the bottom of the sixth inning, Milpitas leading five to three.

He grabbed his glove and began windmilling his right arm to warm it up. "Hey, Mr. McCarty," he said. "I'm here."

Mr. McCarty turned from the game. "Take a few warmup tosses with Sparky," he said. "I'll put you in when we take the field."

Sparky still had his shin guards on, and he let Louis sprint down the left-field foul line a ways before tossing him a ball. "About time you got here," he said.

"You know my dad, the vineyard comes first." Louis threw the ball back. "Bet you still had to milk your cows this morning at five."

"You got that right," Sparky said. "Dumb-ass animals."

They threw the ball back and forth a dozen times, Louis gradually moving from soft tosses to straight balls that smacked into Sparky's mitt. Then Sparky held the ball and waved Louis to his side.

"I got some news for you," he said. "Your brother's here."

"He is? Where?"

"In the stands, next to Nancy." He jerked his head to the right. "They been sitting together most of the game."

The batter at the plate struck out, and the Milpitas team jogged in from the field. Mr. McCarty clapped his hands, and Louis ran reluctantly out to his position before he had a chance to spot his brother.

It was only after he had taken his position in center field and thrown the ball with the left fielder to loosen his arm further that he began to search the crowd for Nancy and Gill. He looked carefully between pitches, beginning with the right-field line and working his gaze down through the benches behind the visitors' dugout.

He spotted Nancy sitting behind the home dugout. She waved at him when he looked her way, and pointed at the man sitting next to her. He was short and dark-haired, and even from center field, Louis could see that he had been injured. It looked as though half his face was smudged, out of focus in some way.

The man waved his hand in greeting. Louis saw Nancy lean over to talk to him, and then he saw her take a handful of popcorn from the bag on his knee. The way she took popcorn from his bag convinced Louis that it was his brother.

There was a grounder hit to shortstop, and Louis ran in a little ways, but the player was thrown out easily.

He took his position again and watched them between pitches. They looked perfectly at ease together, almost as though Gill were her steady. Louis found himself wishing that Gill was sitting beside someone else. He was glad his brother was here, but he didn't like to see him taking his place beside Nancy.

The San Natoma pitcher delivered a strike to the Milpitas player at the plate. Louis hoped that a ball would come his way, that he'd get a chance to do something spectacular. He wanted to shine, to make Gill proud of him, and he wanted Nancy to be watching him in the field, not leaning over to talk to his brother.

When she saw Louis warming up along the sidelines, Nancy grabbed Gill's arm. "There he is," she said.

She waved at Louis, but he went into the game before he saw them. Gill watched him lope onto the field with easy grace, throw the ball with other outfielders, spread his feet apart and bend at the waist and come back upright, supple as a blade of grass. He watched him crouch alertly, weight balanced between his feet, when the pitcher wound up. A younger version of himself, as he might have been but now would never be.

"Look!" Nancy said. "He sees us."

She waved at him, and Gill raised his hand as well. Louis, out in the field, waved once, then turned his head back toward the game.

Nancy leaned over to take some popcorn from the bag they were sharing. Gill couldn't remember ever sharing a bag of popcorn with a girl, simply and normally like this, when he was Louis's age.

Bill Finney circulated easily about the field, stopping and talking and scribbling notes in his spiral notebook, always making sure that he got the names right. Names sold papers. He only paid enough attention to the game to take down the important points, runs scored or moments of suspense. But he knew that Cap Andersen was keeping score, as he always did, and he could get that information from Cap after the game.

He noticed his daughter sitting next to Gilbert Tourneau, and he began to avoid that part of the crowd, began to avoid looking directly at them and risking eye contact. He felt guilty, having lied to her about Pascale, and awkward that the man now next to her was Pascale's son, the outcast son. He found himself wishing that Gill wasn't here, disturbing the story he was gathering, and he disliked himself for wishing that.

Through the innings, he glanced at them only from the side or the back, careful not to walk in front of the benches where they sat. He noticed her sitting especially tall, preening almost, and calling out to friends, introducing them to Gill. Gill was always perfectly polite, standing to say hello, and she chattered away, completely unembarrassed by the fact that she barely knew Gill, or that he was the only adult on the benches who wasn't wearing a coat and tie. Finney wondered whether anyone else recognized that Gill's work shirt was probably prison-issue. If he had asked her why she was sitting next to him, she would certainly have said with complete innocence that Gill was her steady's brother.

He looked over at them when Louis arrived to see if they had noticed, and Nancy was watching him. She met his eyes and waved him over, and he went as though he had been caught.

"Hi, Daddy," she said when he reached them. "Did you know Gill Tourneau before he left?"

"Of course." Finney leaned in to shake hands with Gill. "Are you enjoying the game?"

"Everybody asks me that," Gill said.

"Did you see Lou go in the game?" Nancy asked.

"Yes. I wonder why he was so late." Finney looked at Gill as though he might know, but Gill said nothing.

"Well," Finney said, "it's good to see you, Gilbert. Last time was when you were just leaving in 1917."

"Long time ago, Mr. Finney."

"Indeed," Finney said. "Well," he said. "I'll keep making my rounds."

Finney walked away, trying to walk normally as though he had just met any other friend of his daughter's, certain that he walked stiff and awkward, certain that every word he had said seemed stilted and insincere.

Louis saw the ball jump off the bat, and he ran easily back and to his right. It was hit well, but high. He turned and watched the ball grow larger and then stick in the well-worn pocket of his glove for the third out.

He ran the ball in, tossing it underhanded toward the pitcher's mound as he passed onto the infield dirt. Not spectacular, he thought, but not bad.

Mr. McCarty met him as he crossed the foul line. "You're batting in the seventh spot."

"Okay."

Mr. McCarty lowered his voice. "Did you see your brother? He's sitting next to Nancy."

"I saw," Louis nodded.

"Nobody else would have anything to do with him," he said. "You should go say hello."

Louis went to the low chain-link fence opposite where Gill and Nancy were sitting. "Gilbert, it's great you're back," he said.

Gill didn't reply right away. Louis tried to look at his scarred face normally, but the more he tried to look at him normally, the more he felt himself staring, and the more he felt Gill aware of his staring. Finally, he looked toward Nancy for help.

"Yes, we're all glad you're back," Nancy said.

"I'm not really back," Gill said. "I'm just in town for the game."

"Why were you so late?" Nancy demanded of Louis.

"I'll bet I know," Gill said. "Sulfuring."

"Oooooh, I can smell it," Nancy said.

"I know how the old man works," Gill said. "He coming?"

"I'm not sure," Louis said.

"You'll be all cleaned up for the dance, won't you, Lou?" Nancy asked.

"You bet I will."

Nancy turned to Gill. "Why don't you come to the dance too?"

"I don't think so."

"Why not? Say you'll come. Louis wants you to come too."

"You could come," Louis said.

"I wouldn't fit in," Gill said. "But I would like to see you after the game, Lou."

"Sure," Louis said. "Me too."

Back in the field, Louis kept looking for his mother and father to arrive. He began to think that his mother was wrong. If Gill was here, it meant that he wasn't still wandering, he was seeking them out. Louis began to foresee a reunion of sorts, this day, here, through this game. After a victory, Gill would seek him out to congratulate him. Their father would come, lay a hand on both their shoulders. They would all go together back up to the vineyard on the hill. And it would be as though the long years of separation had never happened.

But the eighth inning went by, and they didn't appear. Louis scanned the crowd between pitches, hoping to see his father loom up from behind, a head higher than anyone else standing. His search came up blank every time. He looked in at Gill and Nancy. Gill didn't seem to be concerned at all about whether their father showed up or not. He was simply listening to

Nancy, looking at the game from time to time. Nancy wasn't watching the game at all. When she wasn't talking to Gill, she was looking around and calling out to friends.

Louis didn't bat until the ninth inning, when there were already two outs. After Rick Mooney grounded to shortstop, Louis tossed one of his bats toward his teammates and stepped into the box. He recognized Sparky's voice encouraging him as he faced the Milpitas pitcher, and he wished he'd had batting practice in the morning. The Milpitas players were shouting for their pitcher to close it out, to put this game in the books. Louis took the first pitch, a strike on the outside corner, just to gauge the speed. When the umpire's right arm went up, the Milpitas players shouted approval.

"Pick your one," Mr. McCarty shouted.

The next pitch was inside, and Louis stepped back and let it go past, a ball. The pitcher seemed to have control, and Louis guessed the next ball would be outside corner. He tapped the plate with his bat and waited. When the pitcher let go of the ball, Louis could almost see it spin, almost see the red stitches on the ball blend into a small disk. He stepped into the pitch and rapped it between the first and second basemen and into right field for a single.

He took a turn at first base, then trotted back. He looked toward the benches, and he saw Gill clapping. Nancy had a surprised look on her face. He glanced around the rest of the crowd, but he didn't see his mother or father.

James Mallory, who had taken over as constable from Cap, was coaching first base, and he patted Louis's shoulder. "That's keeping it alive," he said.

Two pitches later, the game was over. Fred Garber, who worked at the Sorosis packing plant, had tried to tie the game with one swing and popped the ball up to second base. The Milpitas players jogged in from their positions, smiling and shouting, while the San Natoma players gathered in a circle on their side of the diamond.

"That's all right, boys." Mr. McCarty walked around them, slapping them on the back or shoulder, or patting them in a gentle way, tending them. "Good job. You played hard and you gave it your best."

Some of the crowd began to gather in the area around home plate to see the two teams greet. Nancy remained sitting and touched Gill on the arm.

"They do this every year," she said. "It's part of Fourth of July."

The Milpitas team formed itself along the first-base line, and the San

Natoma team did the same along the third-base line. The two coaches shook hands at home plate, then the players began to walk forward and they shook hands with each other as they passed, sometimes bragging or gibing at each other, or promising to win the next time, but with laughter and good humor.

The crowd kept up a quiet applause as the two teams walked. Bill Finney had his notepad out and was scribbling observations on the scene. A description of the teams greeting was always a satisfying ending to the article.

When Louis walked by home plate, Mr. McCarty touched him on the shoulder. "Wait here a moment, will you Lou?"

"Okay." Louis stepped out of the line and stood by his coach while the rest of the players walked by. In the stands, Nancy leaned forward, alert to something unusual happening, keen for discord.

When the teams had both passed, Mr. McCarty stepped forward and raised his hand to get everyone's attention. Normally there would be a group singing of "America the Beautiful," but most of the people present knew Mr. McCarty and were willing to listen.

"Well," he said, "it's been a beautiful Independence Day." He spoke nervously, in a high, reedy voice. "Even though San Natoma lost."

The crowd laughed good-naturedly. Mr. McCarty scratched his neck.

"And we've got fireworks, and a dance tonight too. So I hope you'll all be enjoying those."

Some people applauded lightly. Bill Finney walked up to the backstop with his notepad out, so that he could hear every word.

"I just wanted to say," Mr. McCarty said, "since it's the Fourth of July, we've got a veteran in the crowd, from the Great War, who never got a proper homecoming. And I wonder if we could ask him out here to home plate, and give him a round of applause." He took a couple of steps toward Gill. "Gilbert? You want to come out here for a second?"

Gill saw everyone's eyes on him, and he turned his gaze slowly around, holding up his damaged face like a flag.

Nancy pushed him in the shoulder. "Go on," she said.

At home plate, Louis began to clap. Both of the teams picked it up, and then the people in the crowd, and those sitting on the bench right next to Gill. Nancy began to clap as well.

"Go ahead," she said. "It's for you."

Gill rose up and walked toward home plate. He could hear a little hesitation in the applause when people saw the thick layers of scarring on his left cheek, a little tick between the claps and the muddy buzz of voices. He walked past one fat man wearing a rumpled striped shirt who was clapping and gawking at the same time.

At home plate, Mr. McCarty had his hand out, smiling and worried.

"I hope I did the right thing, Gill. Hope you don't mind."

Gill shook his hand. "You're a good person, Mr. McCarty."

"Look at everyone, Gill," Louis said.

Gill touched his left hand to his damaged left cheekbone, gazed dark-eyed at the people standing around the field. There were many who probably had known him before the war. Teachers of his, parents of schoolmates, the other growers from the area, merchants in town. Some of the boys and girls who had been in school with him were now, no doubt, the parents standing with that small blond boy, who held on to their hands and was staring solemnly at Gill. All joined now in an impromptu ceremony to welcome him home. And then, Gill thought, they could all go on with their lives, feeling good that they had been so generous.

"They're clapping for you," Louis said.

"They're clapping for themselves," Gill said quietly. "You're the only one might be clapping for me."

Mr. McCarty began to speak. "Gilbert Tourneau," he said, "was one of the first boys to sign up. He was a volunteer, because he believed in our country, and he was sent to France in 1918. He was wounded there, but now he's come home, and we should treasure him, just like we should treasure all our boys, all our sons who come home to us from far away."

Then Gill spotted Tourneau above the crowd, walking with Sophia. He had changed into a coat and tie, but some sulfur dust still clung to his beard. Gill saw him take in the scene, seeing his two sons together on a field of honor, a field that excluded him.

Their eyes met, and Louis hadn't yet noticed him. While he looked directly at his father, Gill suddenly put an arm around Louis's back and squeezed. Louis turned to Gill, his face suddenly glad and grateful at the embrace.

"Remember, I'd like to see you later," Gill said quietly.

Mr. McCarty finished his speech, and the crowd and the teams on the field again began to applaud politely.

"Louis!" Tourneau called, and his voice carried above the crowd. Louis looked up and saw his father standing next to his mother, saw him beckoning with his right hand. He looked at Gill confused.

"Louis! Come here!" Tourneau waved his younger son toward himself.

"Go ahead." Gill gave his half brother a little nudge. "I'll see you."

He watched Louis walk away from him. He saw his father smile, satisfied, then watched the three of them walk away.

Mr. McCarty waited helplessly. Then he quietly told Gill that he was sorry.

"You meant well, Mr. McCarty," Gill said.

Cap Andersen walked out to them on his wooden leg, carrying the scorebook, and when he was at their side, he began to sing.

Oh beautiful, for spacious skies
for amber waves of grain

The two teams joined in the song, and then the crowd did as well. This was the promised end to the afternoon, the end they had expected.

America, America
God shed his grace on thee

When the song was over, Mr. McCarty told Gill that he'd heard he was out of work, and said that there was a job for him at the Cash Store any time he wanted to put some hours in.

Gill said thanks. He might need some work.

As the teams left the field and the crowd dwindled, Bill Finney looked down at the open page in his notebook. It was blank. Again, he'd seen more than he would ever write.

TEN

Egypt

*I*n the low hills west of town, skid roads from the logging days cut across the land, rutted but still passable. High school students knew these roads, passed along the information from year to year, so that someone always located a dark, quiet place where they could go to smoke and drink, and couples could park undisturbed. The place was nicknamed Egypt. At times, the constable or some of the local ranchers would discover where it was and shut it down, but it never took long for someone to scout out a new dark place where they could gather, and to pass the word. Everyone knew, there was always an Egypt. For those who had graduated, it faded to a place of nostalgia, while for each new crop of students, it appeared daring and dangerous.

Nancy was thinking about Egypt while she was putting on her green eye shadow for the Fourth of July dance. After her last sister married, Nancy had a bedroom to herself, and she celebrated by spreading her things all over the shelves and never tidying up. In one corner of the room, there was a low vanity with a large round mirror above it, and she had filled the drawers with makeup kits and bottles of perfume, and taped publicity photos of Myrna Loy, and Clara Bow, and Theda Bara around the mirror's edge. She looked up at Theda Bara's face now before turning back to the mirror and thickening the green above her eyes.

Gladys knocked once and opened the door, bringing in a green dress on a hanger. "Nice and ironed," she said.

"Thanks, Mom." Nancy took the hem and held it by her face and looked at herself in the moon-shaped mirror. "Does it match?"

Glad bent her knees and looked at her daughter's eyes next to the dress. Nancy already had on thick mascara and dark kohl eyeliner. Now green eye shadow. Rouge and painted lips were next, no doubt. But she had learned from Nancy's older sisters that it was just a stage, and she didn't criticize.

"It looks fine," she said.

"Good." Nancy leaned back toward the mirror, again concentrating on her eyes.

Glad closed the bedroom door. In the living room, she found her husband placing a bookmark in the book he was reading.

"Is she still putting on makeup?" he asked.

"Helen and Emily went through the same thing," Glad said. "And they're both married to nice men."

"She could think about her education, and then marry a nice man."

"She brings home straight A's. You can't complain."

"Sometimes I wonder how." Finney opened up his book again.

Nancy heard her father through the door. He had been speaking loudly. She bit her lips as she carefully brushed on shadow. Her father didn't understand how hard it was for her, coming after older sisters who were so perfect, and so picture-pretty. She knew she didn't have the same looks that Helen or Emily did, she knew that she would never be popular like they were. She needed makeup, to hide the fact that her mouth was too wide for her face, and that her nose was a shade too long. And she needed to be smart, to get by when makeup wasn't enough.

When she finished with her face, she patted the spit curls that clung to each cheek, held down with sticky-gummy she'd mixed herself from ground flaxseed and water. Her hair was bobbed short, with bangs, and easy to arrange, but she wanted the curls to look right. Then she stood up and smoothed her slip over her hips.

She shimmied into the dress. It hung down to just below her knees, perfect for dancing, and she tried a few steps from the Varsity Drag, and then the Black Bottom, steps she and her friends had learned from the movies. At least the garçonne look suited her. Some of her friends had to wear tight brassieres to flatten themselves out, so that the dresses would hang straight from their shoulders to the low waist, but she didn't have to.

She picked up her silver compact. It had a tiny mirror inside, and a block of rouge, and under the rouge a place for nose powder. Finally she picked up her purse, small and silver-sequined, swinging from a chain. She looked inside one last time to see that the sheaths were still there, then snapped it shut. She wasn't sure when or if she would use them. She knew she was supposed to save herself, like her sisters had. But she didn't want to follow her sisters. She didn't want to put off gaining knowledge until she'd lost her freedom, and if that meant being a bad girl sometimes, she would be that, but be smart about it.

Chazzie's mother was picking her up and taking them both to the dance. But she knew Louis would be there soon after. She had seen how he had looked at her when she was sitting next to his brother. She liked that look. She knew he wouldn't want to think about her being there without him.

In the long twilight, Sparky waited for Louis outside the gate of his family's dairy. He was dressed for the dance, wearing ballooning pants with sharp creases and a loose coat, and his hair was slicked back with Stacomb. He was trying to look collegiate, as everybody was, and he was glad that he was going with Louis instead of using the family truck, which always kept a certain smell of sour milk.

Sparky leaned against the fender and lit a Camel and wondered about girls. Louis had a steady date, even though Nancy was kind of funny about it and told him all the time that she would never marry him. Not many other kids in their class had steadies. Sparky himself didn't, and sometimes he thought it was because he hated cows. He didn't know how to talk about anything except cows and baseball, and girls didn't want to talk much about baseball, which left cows and nothing. All he could say about cows was that he hated them and planned to go play baseball. Nobody was very impressed. It was confusing.

When Sparky saw the Buick's headlights approaching, he threw his cigarette down and stomped it out.

"Hey, Lou," he said as he opened the door.

"Watch out for those bottles," Louis said.

Sparky got into the seat and moved two dark green bottles down by his feet. "What you got?"

"Couple bottles of red wine." Louis let out the clutch and stepped on the gas. "And I got a flask of brandy in my pocket."

"Hot damn!" Sparky shouted. "Your dad going to notice?"

"Naw."

"How about the prohi agents?"

"If they catch it, we'll just call it shrinkage," Louis said.

"What's that?"

"Oh, wine gets absorbed into the wood of barrels, a few bottles break, some wine gets used to top off champagne. There's always a little less than the books say."

Louis drove along the center of the country road. There were no white lines, and the crowned blacktop fell off toward ditches on both sides.

"This is the first time I ever took something from the cellar without my father knowing about it," he said.

"He deserves it," Sparky said, "for dragging you off. He say why he did it?"

"I heard him talking with Mama, but they had the door closed, and the whole thing made me feel so shitty that I just wanted to leave. I didn't even ask if I could take the Buick."

"Have a swig of brandy. Cheer yourself up."

"Good idea." They both drank from the flask, and then Sparky hammered the cork back in with the palm of his hand.

"Better save some for Nancy," he said. "She'll think this is okay."

"You're right," Louis said. "She will."

Near the town square, they could hear the buzz of music and voices from the Oddfellows Hall. Radio dances had become popular in the past three years, and KQW from San Jose broadcast dance music every Saturday evening until the station signed off at midnight.

They parked in the dark lot behind the hall and walked into the bright sounds of singing and dancing. It was crowded inside, and people were trying to do the shimmy to the music, but there wasn't enough room for the loose-jointed kick steps of the dance. The girls wore straight, shiny dresses with bracelets around their wrists, and some had tied scarves around their heads, and most of the boys were wearing loose pants like Louis and Sparky, Oxford bags or cords, and they were all moving to King Oliver's band jazzing from the radio. Red, white, and blue crepe paper hung from walls and crisscrossed over the heads of the dancers in long, lazy arcs, and small American flags stood around the refreshments on the folding tables along one side of the room.

Louis looked around for Nancy, but he didn't spot her dancing. A number of people were crowding around the punch bowl, and Mr. Hogg, the realtor, stood by to guard it from being spiked, but she wasn't there either.

"Come on," he said to Sparky.

They found her and two other girls, Chazzie and Virginia, standing outside the hall around the corner from the back door, smoking. When Nancy saw Louis, she waved at him with her cigarette between her fingers.

"Hey, handsome," she said. She was smoking a Milos, a cigarette rolled in purple paper with a gold tip, and she wanted to make sure he noticed.

"Sorry I'm late," Louis said.

"Well, you missed the founding of our sorority," Nancy announced. "We're going to have a senior girls' sorority next year, called Smoke Skippa Schoola."

The girls all laughed, and Sparky brought out his pack of Camels. "I'll join the fraternity," he said.

"Are you going to have one, Lou?" Nancy asked.

"I don't like to smoke," he said.

"Oh, you've never even tried it," she said. "How do you know? You're just too good all the time," she said.

"I'm not too good all the time," he said.

"When haven't you been?" she asked.

"Tonight."

"Tonight?" She was pleased, but skeptical. "What did you do tonight?"

Louis hesitated. Everyone was looking at him.

"Go on," Sparky said.

Slowly, he slipped his hand into his pants pocket and brought out the flask of brandy.

The girls laughed and applauded. "Is it gin?" Chazzie asked.

"No," Sparky said. "But it's got a kick. And we've got two more bottles out in the car."

Louis uncorked the flask and passed it to Virginia. She took a drink and opened her eyes wide.

"My, my," she said.

Chazzie took a swallow and smacked her lips loudly. Then Nancy grabbed the flask, put her eyes on Louis, and drank twice as long as the other two girls.

"Hey, Nancy," Louis said. "Not so much all at once."

She took the flask down from her mouth and handed it to Sparky. She licked her lips.

"I'm going to be fun tonight," she said.

Inside, they joined in dancing to the long ribbon of songs from KQW, staying on the floor as one song faded and another began. Nancy danced with Louis, and Sparky was surprised to find himself in demand, being passed off between Chazzie and Virginia. The dance steps on the floor evolved one from another, Charleston, Collegiate, Black Bottom, Lindy Hop, prompted by a certain song, or by one couple suddenly changing and the others following their lead.

They left the hall once to smoke cigarettes and drink from Louis's flask in the dark away from the main door. Then they opened one of the bottles of red wine and drank from that as well, congratulating each other on getting a little tight, using that word for *drunk* because it sounded sophisticated.

When they returned to the dance floor, the radio announcer was reading off song titles and the names of the bands. Louis felt a little punch in the arm, and he turned around.

"Hey, Lou, what was the deal with your father at the game?"

It was Henry Messerschmidt, a short and skinny boy who wore glasses and whose parents, German immigrants, made him take piano lessons. Henry enjoyed needling the bigger boys in high school, protected by his own weak frame and the thick lenses that made his head look oddly oversized. None of the school's athletes would ever think of striking him.

"What do you mean, what was the deal?" Louis asked.

"Well, he took you away like you was six years old," Henry grinned. "Like you was still wearing short pants."

"No he didn't."

"Yeah," Henry said. "Waves his hand and away you go."

"Listen," Louis said. "If I went, it's because I wanted to."

"And leaving your brother standing there. You must have felt like a real jerk."

The music was beginning again. Louis turned toward Nancy to dance, but she stood with her arms folded, waiting to see how he would respond.

"I don't know," Henry said. "I always thought you lettermen were better at standing on your own two feet than the rest of us."

"I can stand on my own two feet."

"Handsome is as handsome does," Henry said in a singsong voice.

"At least I don't have to take piano lessons," Louis said.

"Oh," Henry said, "I'm so insulted."

He walked away grinning. Louis looked at Nancy, and he felt his shoulders sag. Everyone was dancing around them, and she was standing, a straight line across her face.

"You didn't leave because you wanted to," she said.

Someone turned up the radio, and Louis had to talk loud to make himself heard. "All right. So I didn't."

"Your dad's not always perfect, you know."

"You can say that again," Louis said.

"What?" Nancy leaned closer, held a theatrical hand up to her ear.

"I said I know. He's not perfect."

"I think that's the first time I've heard you say that."

"Let's go outside," Louis said. "It's quieter."

They walked out to the edge of the lot, where the darkness seemed to pause just before becoming complete. A cherry orchard stood beyond the cars, its fruit already gone to harvest, the columns of trees marching away and converging and disappearing. Nancy leaned against the fender of the car and lit a cigarette. Louis touched her hand as she took it down from her lips, and she passed it to him, and they spent some time in the quiet intimacy of a single cigarette, feeling the warmth from each other's lips on the paper.

Louis let the butt drop when they had finished. "He's only perfect in the vineyard. There, he's like God."

"And he thinks that carries over into the rest of life," Nancy said.

"There's the problem."

Nancy walked away from him, swinging her sequined purse. Louis could see her face when she turned back toward the hall, cheek and brow lit pale as the moon by the diffuse light, eyes dark and mysterious. The purse, silvery as a fish, winked and sparkled. He knew his father didn't approve of him going steady with Nancy, didn't think she was suitable. He liked that this evening. He liked taking bottles of wine from the cellar, asking no one's permission, and seeing the girl his father didn't think was the right one. He wanted to break rules for a change.

The purse spun and twinkled. "Get the bottle of wine," Nancy said, "will you Lou?"

He opened the back door of the car and grabbed the last half bottle by its neck. She took it from him with one hand and took a swallow, spilling a few drops onto her bare collarbone. From the hall, the dance music still mumbled.

She handed the bottle back to him. "I hate the name Nancy," she said. "It sounds so small town. I wish my name were Gloria. Or Diana. Or Cleopatra. I feel like a Cleopatra tonight."

"You don't need to be anybody but yourself," Louis said. "You're beautiful."

Nancy smiled, a wide lipstick smile. She felt a little drunk and wild, and she held up the silver purse, dangling it by its chain. "I've got something in here for you," she said.

"What is it?"

"Something your father wouldn't approve of. Mine either." She unsnapped the purse and held it up toward the dim light and mouthed it open.

He looked in and saw the packets of sheaths. He knew what they were, since a man on the baseball team had showed one off to all the younger players.

She snapped the purse shut again, clutched it to her chest. "What do you think?" she asked, suddenly a little shy.

He reached for the purse and took it from between her hands. Then he snapped it open himself.

"Do you want to go to Egypt?" he asked.

"I'm ready," she said. "We can't wait for our parents to give us permission to live. I want to know what it is."

ELEVEN ☀ *The Tree*

*A*fter the Fourth of July, Gill found four days' work in an onion field
leased by a Japanese farmer. Not many whites worked for wages on
Japanese farms, and Gill wouldn't even have heard of the job if Miguel
hadn't tipped him off. He worked a row with the farmer to his right, and the
farmer's eight-year-old son on his left, rooting out the bulbs one by one and
hacking off the greens. Midmorning, the farmer's wife brought out a new
baby nestled in a peach box, and left the box in the shade, and joined them
in the dirt. The baby cried while they worked, but the family ignored it.
Gill came back each day with clumps of mud dried to his hands and wrists,
smelling high of onion. Miguel kidded him when he returned, telling him
that picking prunes had made everyone else smell sweet, while he, Gill,
smelled more savory—*más sabroso.*

When the field was picked, he hitched back, carrying the cash he'd
earned in his jeans and a sackful of onions that the Japanese had said would
be graded out as too small. He arrived earlier than Miguel and the truck,
and he walked down the short spur to New Chicago. Ana was working—she
was always working—making tortillas so they would be hot and ready when
everyone came back. He watched her as he walked up, dressed in black,
tapping the dough with right fingers into left palm, placing a newly shaped
tortilla onto the hot ceramic *comal,* then called out to see her lift her head.

He gave her the sack of onions and all his earnings, half what he would
have made picking prunes. While he went to the water barrel and dipped out
a bucket to wash his hands, she opened the sack and pulled out an onion.

"*Qué bueno,*" she said, holding it to her nose and breathing in deeply.

"You're just trying to make me feel better," Gill said. "It's not much
money."

"The work we do never pays a lot of money," Ana said. "We get by."

Gill worked on the wartish lumps of mud on his hands, gradually softening them in the water and wearing them down. "If I had money," he said, "are there places to live in Milagro Park?"

"You don't need money to live there. Everyone there is poor."

"I wouldn't want to show up with nothing," Gill said. "I want to be able to come and help."

"You are a proud man," Ana said. "Too proud."

The next day, Gill rode in the truck toward San Natoma to take up Mr. McCarty's offer to work at the Cash Store. Nancy would be there, and it was clear she had Louis hooked, so he was bound to come around. And Gill was certain that Louis was a way past the booby traps and into the vineyard.

As the truck drove toward the highway, the truck bed swaying as the tires passed over bumps and cracks, Gill stood with one hand on a paling and waved at Ana until he could no longer see her.

In the blue of the morning, Louis walked behind his father into the center of a section of Cabernet. Tourneau swung his narrow spade as always, testing the soil every so often. Louis carried a small bucket containing a cloth bag attached to a broad-mouthed funnel, and a glass saccharometer protected in a metal case. Tourneau liked to test for sugar and acid twice a week in late July. Closer to harvest, he would test every day.

At the midpoint of the row, Tourneau planted his spade. "One hundred berries, Lou."

"Right." Louis began to ruffle the foliage of the vines, taking one hundred grapes from fifty vines. They had to come from the middles of bunches, never from the bunches most in the sun, never from the bunches deepest in leaf shade, never from the vines on the ends of the row. One hundred grapes from fifty vines, picked at random but aiming toward an average for that part of the vineyard.

While Louis added grapes to the small bucket, Tourneau moved behind him more slowly, picking out grapes himself and tasting them, chewing gently to burst the skin and free the juice without crushing the pips with their tannins, then spitting it all out and judging the change in sweetness between this day and three days ago. He couldn't yet guess when they would begin harvest. It was too soon for that. There could come a series of hot August days, unbroken by any ocean air, that would make the sugars spin up quickly and bring harvest early, or there could come a string of cool, overcast days, which would slow ripening. Best would be a steady moderate weather, which would allow the acids to drop and the sugars to climb, and allow the bunches simply to hang longer and the roots to feed more deeply in the stony slanted soil. Those conditions came rarely, and produced the finest vintages.

Louis came back with the grapes in the bucket, and Tourneau took them and emptied them into the cloth bag. Kneeling, he twisted the cloth between his strong hands, kneading it, making sure that the skin of every grape had burst, and watching the juice spill from the funnel end into the bucket. He squeezed the cloth patiently then, probing it, making sure that no single grape had escaped, pressing any he found between thumb and forefinger. Then he twisted the cloth tightly until all the pulp was pushed down into the wide end of the funnel, and the juice coming out dwindled from a thin trickle to a drip, and then stopped altogether.

Louis took the glass saccharometer from its metal case and drew out the thin, wandlike float, and Tourneau poured the juice into the long beaker. Then he took the float from Louis and let it slip into the juice and swirled it gently to rid it of any air bubbles that might throw off the reading. He held it level and let the float settle. Louis straightened up and watched standing, with his arms folded.

"Point zero six," Tourneau said. "Is that what you see, Lou?"

He offered the beaker. Louis knelt back down to take it, and he held it level and let the float steady, as his father had done.

"That's what I see," he said.

"That gives us a crude Balling of fifteen," Tourneau said. "Good for July."

"How do you keep those tables in your head?" Louis dumped out the juice and placed the glass beaker and wand back into the rubber molding inside the case.

"Experience." Tourneau slapped Louis on the shoulder. "Maybe if you spent less time with that girl, your head would clear and you'd start remembering them too."

They drove the wagon down into the Chardonnay acreage. Some of their workers were cultivating around the vines, clearing away the weeds that might be stealing nourishment from the soil around the short trunks, and others were tying up bearing vines over the trunks, making bell-shaped cages to protect the grapes from the sun and from birds.

The Balling for the Chardonnay was a little lower than for the Cabernet, as expected. The red wine grapes tended to ripen a little faster than the white wine grapes. While Tourneau wrote down the figure and the date in his vineyard log, Louis picked several grapes and tasted them, spitting out the single seeds found in Chardonnays.

"Higher than last year this time," Tourneau said, leafing through earlier pages.

"That's good."

"I wish we could measure acid right in the field, like we can sugars," Tourneau said. "Maybe when you go to Davis, you'll invent a way."

"It's too bad we don't have somebody to take the juice back to the winery while we go into the Pinot."

"There's nobody I would trust," Tourneau said. "Except you."

"Did you trust Gilbert when he was here?" Louis asked.

Tourneau looked up from the pages of the log.

"No," he said. "Gilbert was always more interested in being angry than in learning."

"Why was he angry?"

"No reason," Tourneau said. "No reason. I never asked him to do more work than I did myself."

"Well it's not fair," Louis said. "We're up here, and he's down there with nothing. And he was a hero."

"You mean in the war."

"Yes," Louis said. "He was a brave man."

"He chose to go to the war. He chose that."

Tourneau wrote three figures in the logbook and shut it.

"Right now, he's choosing to work somewhere else. I asked him to come home and he turned me down."

Tourneau picked up the beaker of Chardonnay juice and poured it into a clean bottle.

"I'm going to take this back to the cellar and measure for acid," he said. "I want you to take the sugars for Pinot, then bring the juice back to me. We'll get good ratios today for both the Chardonnay and the Pinot. Good? Then we can begin the third racking of last year's wine."

He handed the metal case over to Louis.

"You're the only one I would trust to do this. Not your grandfather. Never Gill. You. You're the one."

He walked back down the row to the wagon, rubbing the uncomfortable flesh above his liver, and climbed up behind Queenie. Before he snapped the reins, he turned back to Louis.

"Lou, don't go see him. He'll only lie to you."

Alone in the Pinot acreage, Louis again picked one hundred grapes, and wrung the juice through the funnel and poured it into the beaker, and placed the glass float into the juice. He twirled it carefully, just as he had seen his father do, to free it of any small air bubbles that might make it float too high.

He looked up toward the cellars, where he knew his father would be measuring the acid of the Chardonnay, neutralizing it drop by drop with an alkali solution until he reached the end point. He thought he should have said something more, something stronger, but he couldn't think of anything that would have moved his father.

He looked again at the beaker, the float balanced and measuring.

In the late afternoons, while Nancy was wiping down the soda fountain and ringing out the cash drawer, she watched for the moment Gill finished sweeping up and peeled off his store apron and ran his hands through his hair. At that moment, he seemed to shift from an employee at McCarty's Cash Store to the independent man with no plans and no fixed address, the darker brother she found herself thinking about. She liked to leave at the same time as him, so that she could walk with him down to the road where he hitched back to New Chicago. Sometimes she had to hurry if she wanted to walk with him. He would never wait for her, and always treated it as a matter of chance that they walked in the same direction at the same time. She felt herself at a disadvantage with him, a different feeling than she had with Louis. Gill obviously didn't need her. But she enjoyed the savor of that different feeling, being less in control. When she walked with him, she could imagine that she had the love of both Louis and Gill—one brother safe and dependable, the other smaller, more taut, more risky.

Gill had been working at the Cash Store for three weeks. He'd shown up one morning and asked Mr. McCarty if he was serious about giving him a job. Soon he was loading and unloading bulk items for both suppliers and customers, sweeping up the store, sorting mail into the slots behind the counter, and making deliveries several times a day. Nancy gave him free sodas and malts and tried to talk with him, but he would never sit at the counter—that's for paying customers, he said. He walked with her to the road leading north, but he always laughed off Nancy's questions about where he had been, how long he thought he could live in New Chicago, what he was going to do with himself. One day at a time, he said. His answers only made her want to know more, though she had the feeling he knew that, and enjoyed her curiosity.

Louis stopped picking her up at the Cash Store. He said it didn't have anything to do with Gill, didn't have anything to do with his father. He was just working long hours now. She didn't believe him, but she let him pick her up at home when they had a date. On Fridays, she waited for him out in the print shop with her father. She didn't like waiting for him in the house, because her mother embarrassed her. Her mother always made such a fuss over Louis, wanted him to sit down and chat for a bit, offered him cookies. She always asked him what his plans for the future were, even though he had already told her he intended to go to UC-Davis. It was worst when she asked him how his family was. As though she hadn't seen or registered the fact that Louis's half brother was not welcomed by his father. It was torture listening to her, and Nancy couldn't wait to pry Louis away, though he always had to stay long enough to seem polite. She had lost her virginity only four weeks ago, but when she saw Louis with her mother, it no longer seemed part of a great adventure.

It was better in the print shop, sitting and reading while her father worked on the Linotype, or helping him out by feeding papers into the Buffalo folder, as she had done when she was twelve. When she wasn't helping, he left her alone and didn't ask about her makeup, or the hat she was wearing. And when Lou came, her father didn't ask him awful questions that could be only half answered.

That Friday, she was sitting in an old platform rocker that had been banished to the print shop, reading *Sister Carrie* while her father clacked away at the Linotype. Her father had called it a ponderous book, but worthwhile. Nancy was reading it like a guidebook for small-town girls who end up in the big city. She thought that Carrie was sometimes dumb, even though she seemed to come out on top, and she made mental notes of Carrie's various mistakes.

While his daughter read, Bill Finney was typesetting the week's events, knowing that he would write nothing about Gilbert Tourneau working at the Cash Store. Nearly everyone in town had mentioned it to him, and everyone had an opinion. Some believed that Paul Tourneau had told Gill never to set foot on the vineyard, and that he was a terrible father. Others thought that Gill was a troublemaker—hadn't he made trouble on Jacobsen's ranch?—and it gave them the willies to look at his face. Most people thought that Mr. McCarty was a saint for giving Gill work, though a couple wondered if Gill wouldn't end up robbing the till and taking off in the delivery truck.

Finney thought that if Gill was in town, it was because he had some unfinished business with his father. Tourneau would always be blind to his son's hurt, because to see it would be to see his own part in it. He thought that when Tourneau saw his son honored, however late and improvised the ceremony was, it had only made him want to guard his hilltop vineyard more jealously. And Gill was going to lash out against him in some way.

He continued to work the big square keys of the Linotype, laying out half the news. If the story happened as he foresaw, he would print none of it.

When Nancy heard Lou's car pull up, she marked her place in the book, stood up, and smoothed her skirt. She enjoyed the feeling of wearing just knickers underneath. It was impossible to believe that girls had been wearing corsets just ten years ago, and she was glad that her older sisters had already made clear to her mother what proper dress was, that lisle stockings weren't acceptable when everybody was wearing silk.

Louis knocked, and Nancy opened the heavy, timbered door for him, and they hugged quickly.

The clacking from the Linotype stopped, and Mr. Finney sat back and pushed his glasses up his forehead. "Just the person I was looking for," he said. "I've got an inch of column left to fill. Tell me how the vintage looks, and I'll put it in. How many weeks until crush?"

"About three for the reds," Louis said. "Later in September for the whites."

Finney bent down to the keyboard and typed rapidly. Then he looked up again. "And the grapes will be . . ."

"Fine, as long as we don't get any cool weather to slow things down."

"Perfect." He put his glasses back down and typed out several more lines, then raised his right hand with a flourish.

"What movie are you going to see?" he asked.

Louis looked at Nancy.

"There's a new Clara Bow playing," she said. "*The Daring Years.*"

"Sounds like a movie with heart interest," Finney said.

"I hope so." Nancy tugged at Louis's hand. "We've got to go, Daddy."

"Have a good time." He bent again over the keyboard.

Outside, Nancy grabbed Louis by the hair at the back of his head and kissed him.

"Let's just go riding," she said.

The sunset was coming a little earlier every day now, the Coast Range casting its blue shadow over the western Santa Clara Valley. They passed Joey's gas station on their way through town. It was quiet and empty, and the green enameled pumps still seemed to give off a polished glow in the pale light.

"Go show yourself the ropes," she said, and stuck her tongue out. She looked at Louis for approval, and he smiled, but he didn't turn his head.

"Did you bring some wine?" Nancy asked.

"I do every time, don't I?"

"Then what are we waiting for?" She found the unlabeled green bottle under the seat and opened it with a corkscrew from the glove compartment. She took a drink and handed it to him, but he said he'd wait. They passed by a large dry yard along the San Natoma–Los Gatos road, where the fresh-picked prunes were laid out to let the sun bake the moisture out of them, and the air they drove through was sugared and sweet. As they passed, men were wheeling stacks of trays out onto the yard.

"It smells so good here," Nancy said.

"That's a lot of work." Louis shook his head. "Doesn't look like as much fun as crushing grapes."

"Prunes aren't as much fun as wine, either," Nancy said.

"Must be on their third picking," Louis said. "We'll pick up some of their workers for grapes."

"Stop being a grape grower for a while, will you?" Nancy said. "Just try and enjoy the moment."

"Okay," Louis said.

"Here." She pushed the bottle at him again, and he drank from it while keeping his left hand on the wheel. Then he handed it back.

"That's better," she said. "Let's go straight to Egypt."

In the backseat, Nancy made Louis lie down while she rolled down her stockings and hiked up her skirt. She was always in a hurry, as though she had to make sure again that it was really happening, as though sex were a forbidden language she had to prove to herself she could still speak. Louis was quiet throughout, until he told her that it had happened. Then they got out of the car on different sides and straightened themselves up.

Usually, they got back into the backseat and held each other, but on this night Nancy lit one of her violet-scented cigarettes and walked out under the full and rounded night sky, into the loud cricket song that surrounded them.

Louis came around to her side of the car. "What's the matter?" he asked at last.

"That's just what you would ask," she muttered.

"What?"

"Nothing," she said. "A little bored, I guess."

"I love you," he offered.

She laughed. "That's just what you would say."

She walked back to the car and sat down against the tire, and she motioned Louis over. He came and leaned back between her legs, his head resting against her waist, and she began to play with his hair. She ran her hands through it, thick and black and curly, and she wrapped bits around her index finger and tugged, not enough to cause pain, just enough to let him feel it.

"What if I don't want to be in love?" she said. "What if I don't want to get married and end up living in San Natoma? What if I don't want to end up like those movies with heart interest that they play every week? Does that make everything wrong?"

"I don't know," Louis said. "I just want to do what's right."

"What's right," Nancy repeated. She looked past him, looked at Egypt. She saw a wide spot in an old rutted road, nothing but weeds beaten down by cars and farm trucks nosing in for a moment's privacy.

In the weeks following the Fourth of July, Sophia began to see signs everywhere that something was changing. Her father had stopped coming to the vineyard house for dinner, had said he wouldn't set foot there, said he would rather stay in his damp cabin. Her son was gone many evenings, absent from her in a way he never had been before. Her presence no longer moved him, and when he hugged her, his arms felt cool and watery, as though his body was already elsewhere. Her husband spent late nights in the cellars after a full day in the vineyards, searching for perfection. He swore he would make a wine that could age for twelve years or more, so that when Prohibition finally ended he could present it to the world, finished and flawless. Gill's strong absence was at the center of all these changes, she was sure.

In the evenings, when Louis was gone and she was alone with her husband in the echoing house, she began to want him in bed as she hadn't for many years. She surprised him one night by taking his hand and leading him into their bedroom. Soon, she wanted him every night, beginning things herself if he didn't. Tourneau was pleased and grateful at her sudden change. She understood what he thought—that her new desire came from wanting to heal things after Gill's refusal. She wasn't sure, though she knew her desire was a sign, like the others.

When several weeks had passed, and Gill hadn't seen Louis come in to the Cash Store, he asked Nancy to take a turn around the town square with him after work. He'd noticed the way she hurried to walk with him. And if Louis wasn't coming to see him on his own, he needed Nancy to reel him in.

Nancy said yes right away, as though she'd been hoping for him to ask her all along, and they walked through one of the four openings in the low wall around the square and strolled on the broad circular path, among the chestnuts and Italian stone pines. He walked on her left side, hiding the scarred side of his face from her. He always did that. It was a habit he'd grown comfortable with.

"So where's that brother of mine?" Gill asked. "Why doesn't he come around?"

Nancy made a face. "He *says* he's busy at the vineyard. That's why he never gets down into town before evening."

"Racking, I bet."

"If it's not racking, it will be something else. Seems like there's always something."

"And you don't like that," Gill said.

"A girl doesn't like to be number two."

"Everything comes in second to the vineyard," Gill said.

They walked through shade and blades of sunlight, the only two people in the square. Around them, traffic began to buzz as shops closed for the day. Nancy ran her fingers through her hair, and Gill noticed her breasts rise taut against the fabric of her blouse.

"I like walking in the square," she said. "Nobody ever does. And it seems like you could have some green secret here, right in the middle of everything, and nobody would even know it."

"You're too young to have secrets."

"Oh," she said, "you don't *know* that."

"So tell me a secret."

"If I tell you one," she said, "you have to tell me one."

"Okay," he said. "Deal."

Nancy smoothed her dress over her hips. "Was there an Egypt when you grew up here?" she asked.

"Of course. Egypt goes way back."

"My secret is I've been to Egypt. With Louis."

She smiled at him, a strange conspiratorial smile, pleased to let him know that she broke the rules.

He smiled back at her, pretended to be impressed. "So what's it like there with my brother?"

"Okay," she said.

"Just okay?"

"Well I wasn't really sure what to expect," she said. "But I wanted to find out."

"That's the problem with Egypt," Gill said. "When you first go there, it's exciting. But pretty soon, you realize it's the oldest place in the world."

"That's *it*," Nancy said. "That's exactly what I've been feeling."

Gill nodded understandingly.

"And Louis doesn't help," she went on. "He's scared of it, because we're doing something wrong. I'll tell you a secret about Louis."

"Okay."

"The real reason he doesn't come by the Cash Store is because you're there. His father told him not to see you."

"Did he say that to you?"

"No," she said. "But I can tell."

"And he's afraid to cross the old man."

"He's not like you." Nancy put on her conspiratorial smile again. "Now you have to tell me a secret."

Gill thought about what would impress Nancy. "I once ran a still for a famous bootlegger. I can't tell you his name, but you've heard of him. He's in the paper all the time. And his right-hand man is a tough customer who was called Big Boy."

"Was it Joe Parente?" Nancy asked. "I read about him."

"Much bigger than Joe Parente."

"Was it Hans Stittmater?"

"You read a lot, don't you?"

"All the time."

"Bigger than either of those. And I guarantee you've seen his name in the paper. And Big Boy would just as soon kill you as look at you."

"Wow," Nancy said.

"Tell you what." Gill had been waiting for a chance to say this, and now, when she seemed so young, was the right time. "Why don't you bring Louis out to see me in New Chicago? Maybe I can get him to loosen up a little. Or make him a little jealous."

"Should I? I can get him to do what I want him to."

"I'll bet you can."

"Okay. I'll do it."

The afternoon shade was creeping toward the square, and Nancy leaned closer to Gill. "Can I tell you one more secret?" she asked

"Sure."

She whispered. "I like your face. It makes you different."

Late Friday evening, Louis drove slowly along the rutted trace into New Chicago, with Nancy by his side. Before him, he saw the fire pit blazing, and the light from the flames painted the two crooked houses with a lurid reddish cast, tilting cutouts against the featureless black background. Several dark figures squatted around the fire, and he watched them rise as the twin beams of his headlights probed toward them. He wondered if his brother could really feel at home here, and he was suddenly sure he had done the right thing in coming. Coming to Gill's rescue.

Nancy had been at him all night to go to New Chicago. She said she was tired of doing the same thing all the time, she wanted to do something different. And she asked him how he felt, knowing his brother was living with some pickers while he was high and mighty up at the vineyard. They met up with Sparky and Chazzie to drink wine and talk, then drove around aimlessly. She didn't want to go to Egypt, said she felt old there. She wanted him to go see his brother, and asked him if he was afraid to go because of his father. Was that the only reason he wouldn't go?

After one bottle was empty and another open, Louis turned the car toward New Chicago. He had wanted to see Gill since he'd left him at the ball field. He was growing more tired of his father bullying him about Nancy, about where he would go to school and how long he would apprentice, bullying him into sharing his every ambition. He didn't want to believe what his father said about Gill's lying speech. With the wine and Nancy's hectoring talk, he found it easy to go against what his father had told him. And now, seeing the dark men rise and face him, he wanted to find Gill among them and bring him out.

At the campfire, Gill was the first one who saw the headlights. He stood up, and Miguel rose beside him, and they watched the pointed lights probe toward them.

"Not police?" Miguel asked. There was always a possibility that the law would decide to evict them from the abandoned houses, and he'd had enough trouble with police during harvest that he was always a little fearful.

"Don't worry," Gill said. "I think I know who it is."

The car stopped at a short distance from the fire, and the engine fell silent. Gill smiled when he saw Louis and Nancy step out onto the dirt. The light of the fire and the lanterns was dim, but he recognized them in their youthfulness. Nancy was slender and narrow, and hadn't yet grown into her body, and Louis, despite his broad shoulders, had slim, boyish hips. They stepped from the car at the same time, but Louis went immediately over to her side in a way that seemed courtly and caring. Nancy touched his arm, and Gill saw him reach back into the car and bring out a bottle.

"Friends of yours, *güero*?" Miguel asked.

"My brother and his girl," Gill said. "I've been waiting for them."

"Gill?" Louis called.

"Come on in, brother," Gill said. "Come into the light."

"I wanted to see you," Louis said.

"Here I am." He smiled at Nancy. "Hi, beautiful," he said.

"Hi, handsome," she answered.

"Don't just stand there," Gill said. "Come on, sit down."

He took Louis by the elbow and sat him down next to Miguel. Nancy came and sat down next to Louis, simply and naturally, though she saw that she was the only woman sitting down, that Ana and Rosarita were standing apart.

"*Te presento* Miguel," Gill said. "And Javier. And Frank." Gill remained on his feet as he spoke, took the bottle from Louis and held it against the firelight to see if it was finished bright. He tilted it back for a quick swallow, then passed it to Miguel.

"You didn't bring the best wine," he said.

"The best is way in the back in the cellar . . ."

"You can't get back there?"

"Yes," Louis said, "I can get back there."

"I'm glad you came, Louis. I've been thinking about you. Every day I look up into those hills, and it's like I can see what's going on. You're checking sugars every day, and the Balling on the Pinot in the southeast block, where it's sunny, is the highest. And you're overhauling the crusher, and cleaning the barrels, and going over the harvest wagons, replacing anything that's worn in the tack. You're probably banging together some shooks to make boxes. And you're just going to have time to rack last year's still wine for the third time before the crush. Am I right?"

"You're right," Louis said.

Miguel passed the bottle to Javier, who took it and drank until the wine spilled from the corners of his mouth. Miguel snatched it away from him. Javier swallowed and belched loudly, then stood up and beat his chest with his fist. Then he opened his mouth in a hollow smile toward Louis and Nancy and nodded his head. Louis could see he was missing his two front teeth.

"Javier was dropped on his head as a baby," Gill said to Louis. "He's a little simple."

"Oh," Louis said.

"Hell for picking prunes, though. Like a machine."

Miguel, with a smile, passed the bottle over to Louis, who hesitated a moment without drinking. Nancy took the bottle from his hands and swallowed from it, and smiled like she had taken a dare.

"There's a girl who knows how to drink," Gill said.

"That's right," Nancy said.

Gill was still on his feet, still pacing. "Frank," he said, "Louis was playing in the baseball game I went to see. He's a star."

"Really?" Francisco had been sitting on the side of the ring opposite Louis and Nancy, sitting shyly with his head lowered and peeking at them, like someone much younger than he was. Now he unbent himself, tall and stick thin, and stood up. Louis stood up as well to shake hands with him. Francisco was almost as tall as Louis, but he kept his head bent and his shoulders curving down, so that he didn't seem tall.

"What position do you play?" he asked, pronouncing his English very carefully.

"Center field," Lou said. "And my best friend is a catcher."

"I play too," Francisco said. He looked around him, timid but proud. "I'm going to try out for junior varsity in high school next year."

"That's great," Louis said. "What spot do you play?"

"He plays catcher too," Miguel said. "Catcher of prunes. He is the champion prune catcher of all time."

"I play first base," Francisco said resentfully.

"Don't believe him." Miguel stood up and took the bottle from Gill. "He only plays first base in his dreams."

"I *do*," Francisco said.

"*Ni en sueños.* You are a prune picker," Miguel said. "Now sit down. *Siéntate.*"

Francisco kicked at the ground and sat down. Miguel turned to Louis. "You are the son of the *patrón* of the grapes, no?"

"At Beau Pays," Louis said.

"When you pick?"

"Crush is in three weeks."

"Hey," Nancy said.

"You still need pickers?"

"Sure," Louis said.

"Hey," Nancy said again.

"Yes, Nancy," Gill answered her.

"How come none of them are sitting around the fire?" She pointed toward Ana and Rosarita.

"I don't know," Gill said. "Why don't you ask them?"

"All right," Nancy said. "I will."

She walked over to the two women. Gill nudged his brother. "She's pretty, eh?"

"Yes." Louis felt himself blushing. "I think she is."

Nancy held out her hand to Rosarita. She guessed Rosarita was about a year younger than she was. "Hi. My name is Nancy."

Rosarita took her hand, not looking her in the face. "My name is Rosarita."

Nancy smiled. "Why don't you come over by the fire with the rest of us? Drink some wine with us. It's good."

Ana stepped forward. The smallpox scars on her cheeks were small specks of shadow, cast across her face. "Ah, *señorita*. We do not do so."

"Why not?"

"It's very well for you to do as you please," Ana said. "But for us, a girl who drinks wine is known for that."

"Who will know?" Nancy asked. "It's just one night."

"Her father will know. And I, her aunt, will know. And she will know herself. It is enough."

"It's a new age for women," Nancy said. "We're free now. We can vote."

"It's a new age for you, not for us. I am sorry." Ana spread her hands before her, empty palms up, to show she had nothing to offer. "You know nothing about us. Nothing."

Gill, at the fireside, asked Louis about the vineyard, drew out the details of how the various sections were ripening, what blends they might be using for champagne, what wine was still in oak and what had been bottled. Louis found that Gill could talk about the vineyard and winery as though he had never been away, as though they had been working together on that year's crop. Soon they were sharing stories about how hard it was to work under the eye of Paul Tourneau. If a task were done flawlessly, it barely merited comment, since that was only as things were meant to be. But if any errors crept in, then you'd hear about it for days. While they talked, Louis began to think that Gill knew more about how he felt toward his father than anyone else ever could.

"I can hear the old man," Gill was saying. *"You've got to drive the work, or else the work will drive you."*

"Right," Louis laughed. "Dead on."

"He's something," Gill said. "But I have to admit, he knows every single thing about that vineyard."

"You know quite a bit yourself."

Gill took a sip from the bottle and passed it over to Miguel. "Sure. I even wanted to start my own vineyard once. Over at Ojo de la Montaña."

"You must miss it sometimes," Louis said.

"Yeah." Gill knew where Louis was heading.

"So why don't you come back?" Louis asked. "It would be better than here."

"What's wrong with here?" Miguel asked. "We live here every year."

"Nothing's *wrong* with here," Louis said. "I don't mean anything's wrong with living here."

"You are mistaken," Miguel said. "Everything is wrong with here."

Gill put up his hand, and Miguel nodded. He had made his point.

"So why don't I come back?" Gill asked.

"Sure," Louis said. "Papa would let you."

"He would? Well that's mighty white of him." Gill nodded his head toward the women. "Here comes your girl."

Nancy came to the fireside with a frown on her face. "Light me a cigarette, Lou."

"What's the matter?" Gill asked. "Didn't find any 'new women' over there?"

She snatched the cigarette from Louis and took a drag. "They're a couple of wet blankets," she said.

"You've got to understand what's going on," Gill said. "Rosarita there, when she gets back to Milagro Park, is going to have her *quinceañera*. You know what that is?"

"I don't think I care," Nancy said.

"When a girl turns fifteen, they have a party for her, and she dresses in white, like a bride. And they have a cake, white like a wedding cake. But on top of the cake is not a bride and a groom, but a little statue of a young girl, also dressed in white. See," he said, "Ana is trying to protect her. It's important that a young girl can feel pure for her *quinceañera*."

"So I'm not pure enough for her?" Nancy demanded.

"Do you want to be?" Gill asked.

"No," Nancy said, sounding a little drunk. She laughed, pleased with herself for saying it. "That's what I don't want to be."

"Good." Gill handed her the bottle. "Now have another drink of wine and don't get bent out of shape."

She took the bottle and drank. "Almost empty."

Gill took it from her and finished it and held it neck down, so that a couple of drops fell from the glass rim. "Another dead soldier," he said.

"Now what do we do?" Nancy asked.

"Go get some more." Gill looked at Louis.

"We could do that," Louis said. "Do you want to go up to Beau Pays tonight?"

"I was hoping to hear those words," Gill said. "And I kind of wanted to hear them from you."

"Sounds fun!" Nancy said.

Louis looked across the fire at Francisco, sitting bent and embracing his thin knees. "Good luck with baseball, Frank," he said.

Francisco looked up and his brown eyes gladdened.

Gill walked away from the circle to the crooked porch, where Ana and Rosarita sat. "*Nos vemos, Ana*," he said. "In Milagro Park."

"I hope so," she said.

"I'll be there for Rosa's *quniceañera*," he said. "And see her dance with her father, all dressed in white."

He took one of Ana's hands between both of his own, held it for a moment and felt it warm.

"*Vaya con dios*," she said.

He walked to the car, followed by Javier's incoherent mutterings.

Nancy was talking as the car tunneled into the night, talking about herself and her plans to go away to college after high school and avoid the fate of her older sisters. She never mentioned Louis's name when she talked about her plans—she only mentioned the wide world, the world wide and new. Gill kept her talking about herself with comments of interest and murmurs of approval, but Louis could tell he was only half paying attention to her. As the miles passed, he could feel his brother at his back, leaning forward, could feel his brother's heart beating behind him.

They slowed through the quiet town square, shadowy with tall trees, and turned southwest on the road up to the vineyard.

"I know this road," Gill said. "I could drive it blindfolded, even now, even after ten years."

"Where have you been in the past ten years, Gill?" Louis kept his eyes ahead as the headlights picked out the dim trees curving around the road-bed. "How have you kept yourself?"

"Yeah," Nancy said brightly. "You never really told me."

"Oh," Gill said, "lots of places."

Louis could tell his brother was smiling in that tight way he had, the smile stretching from the smooth half of his face across to the injured half of his face.

"Come on," Nancy said, "you have to do better than that."

"Well," Gill said, "where do you think I've been?"

"I don't know," Louis said. The road was snaking up the hill now, and the land sloped steeply away to the right, down into the ravine. "This is going to sound a little crazy, but sometimes I thought you couldn't be too far away, that you must be hiding up in the redwoods, up above the vineyard. And I'd go up there sometimes and say 'Gilbert . . .' And wait for an answer."

"Good thing the old man didn't catch you," Gill said.

"I was just a little kid," Louis said.

"But you missed me a little bit."

"Yeah, sometimes."

"I can guess when. Maybe when Paul Tourneau was a little tough on you."

Nancy said, "You still haven't told us where you were, what you did."

Gill laughed. "I was hiding up in the redwoods, and I heard Lou call my name every time, but I never dared show myself."

"Oh, come on," Nancy said.

Gill laughed again.

The road changed to gravel, small bits chunking up into the wheel wells and against the mud flaps, and Louis slowed the car's speed. When the road jogged toward the ravine, Gill looked sharply out the window.

"Do you still call that the killing tree?" he asked.

"Where Mr. McCarty's two sons died," Louis said. "Awful sad."

"Yeah." Gill settled back down in his seat. "So the road still isn't paved all the way up. But you've got telephone, electricity, right?"

"Sure. The lines run right alongside the road."

"That's good." He looked toward the bank sloping up from the road, saw the lines strung from poles and trees. "When the McCarty boys died, there was no way to let anyone know. We just brought the two bodies down in the back of a truck and parked outside the Cash Store."

"Yuck," Nancy said. "Just in the back of the truck? Yuck."

"That was the only way we had to do it," Gill said. "I was young at the time, just happened to be in the truck when we were coming down the hill and found the accident. But I still remember being parked there, and a crowd gathering around, and Mr. McCarty refusing to come out of the store, like he was hiding and his sons wouldn't be dead as long as he stayed in the store. It was Paul Tourneau who finally went in, and found him back by the sacks of beans, and walked him out."

They climbed deep into the hills, the road high above the creek bed, carved into the side of the steep drainage. When Louis turned the car up away from the creek, the road changed to dirt and curved up the thick rounded finger of land that began to broaden and flatten as they neared the vineyard. Louis brought the car to a stop, set the brake, and got out.

"What's up?" Gill asked.

"Tripwire alarm," Louis said. "Hooked up to a dry cell battery. I don't want to wake anyone up."

Gill nodded, looked carefully at the tree where Louis unhooked the alarm.

When they came to the last curve before the winery house, Louis cut off the headlights. He explained that the lights would shine right into the house if he left them on, that he didn't want to stir anyone. And if they saw the lights on, in the house or in the winery, they couldn't go in.

As they drove in darkness, a whispering hush of leaves surrounded them. The road was passing between blocks of vines, the foliage reaching tall above the roof of the car on both sides, grapes growing heavy and dark in the hidden middle of each living plant. Then the land cleared, and they saw the house was dark.

Louis moved the car quietly to the winery building and cut the engine. They got out of the car silently. The three-story building, set against the hillside, loomed over them like a large blank face. Nancy whispered to Louis to light her a cigarette, but Louis said no, she couldn't smoke inside the winery, it was bad for the wine. They stood there for a moment, looking up at the dark brow of the building. Then Gill walked up to the barn-style door and swung it open. It creaked once, and Louis froze. But Gill pushed it open a bit wider.

"Come in," he said in a loud whisper.

Gill reached to the right as he came in the door, and he found the candles and the candleholders on a shelf built into the wall, just as they had been ten years earlier. The matches were kept handy in a tin dispenser nailed to the wall, the same tin dispenser he remembered. He lit a candle and looked around as Louis was lighting candles for Nancy and himself.

"No kerosene lamps in the cellar," Louis said. "The wine is breathing. It could breathe in the smell."

"No electricity?" Nancy asked.

"There's some lights," Louis said. "But we don't want to use them now."

Gill stepped toward the cooperage, where the wine had been stored before its third racking. There were deep rows of one-hundred-and-seventy-gallon puncheons lying on their sides with a wooden stopper poking out of each, stacked two high with narrow corridors lacing between them and ending at an earthen wall. Gill looked up to the heavy twelve-inch beams of the ceilings, and the braces below the redwood fermenting tanks. Above them on the third floor were the stemmer and the crusher where the grapes would be delivered. All designed so that gravity worked to help the transformation of grapes into wine.

He walked down one of the corridors, the puncheons rising twelve feet high on either side of him, and ran his hands over the barrelheads. They were smooth ovals, lustrous and dark, but he could still trace the path of the adze that had shaped them. The hoops were bronze, and the staves and barrelheads were oak from Limoges.

He rapped one barrelhead square with his knuckles, and the barrel resonated with sound, the tone of a deep gong.

"Let me try that," Nancy said. She hammered her fist on the next barrel, which gave off a slightly higher tone, then ran down to the next and hammered on it as well.

"I'm an orchestra," she said.

"You know how somebody could ruin wine in these barrels?" Gill asked aloud. "All you'd have to do would be take some rusty nails, rusty is better, and drive one into each barrel in some inconspicuous spot. Just let that taint of metal get into the wine. And it would drive Paul Tourneau crazy."

He paused, looked at the expression on Louis's face. Then he laughed. "Come on, I want to look at the cellar books."

Gill placed his candle on the long workbench opposite the tiers of barrels and pulled down the cellar book for 1916, the last year he had worked through harvest. He began to flip pages until he came across his own writing. "Look," he said, running his fingers along the inked lines. "I worked on every single barrel that year." He closed the book and put it back. "At least he didn't erase me from the cellar books."

"Of course not," Louis said.

Nancy came up behind Louis. "My hand hurts," she said.

Gill ran his fingers across the leather spines of the cellar books until he came to the one for 1899. He laid it open on the bench and looked at Louis. "You recognize this writing?"

Louis bent over the pages that glowed upon the dark scarred wood of the workbench, and he saw a shaky handwriting in large disconnected letters across the page.

"It's in French," he said.

"Recognize it?" Gill asked again.

"No," Louis said.

"It's Grandfather's writing." He looked at the uneven lines, describing the tasting of a young wine from that year. "My grandfather, not yours. My mother's father. This is the last cellar book he wrote in. He died the next year, the year I was born. I used to come in here sometimes and look at this book when Paul Tourneau wasn't around."

"Are we going to have some champagne?" Nancy asked. "My hand really hurts."

"Sure." Gill slapped the book shut and put it back on the shelf, and he took three tasting glasses from a closed cabinet above the bench. "Let's get a bottle of the best. That's what we're here for."

He walked toward the sliding door leading back into the cellars, where the wines aged in bottles. But Louis ran after him and touched his arm.

"I have to turn off the tear gas," he said.

"Oh." Gill smiled. "Right. Forgot myself."

He watched as Louis found a small key hanging hidden behind one of the thick pillars, and then went down a narrow corridor between the puncheons and unlocked a padlock holding down a lever. Louis pulled the lever out and down, and left the padlock open and hanging from it.

"Okay," he said.

Gill slid back the door, and the three of them entered the cave by candlelight.

"My God," said Nancy.

The racks of bottles, resting on their sides in the dark, rose from the floor to the ceiling, more than twelve feet high, and stretched back into the side of the mountain, beyond the range of their poor candles, seeming infinite. The walls of bottles reached high on both sides of them, each wall redoubled many times over on either side, wide to right and left and deep ahead of them into a curving darkness.

"How many bottles of wine does your father have back here?" Nancy asked. "A million?"

"I really don't know," Louis said. They were walking forward quietly, speaking in hushed tones, though no sound they spoke in here would ever be heard in the house. It was cool in the cave, and dry, and the height of the ceiling and the tall green glass walls made them like children venturing into a giant's world, cupping their candles with their hands.

They passed by riddling racks, empty now, where champagne bottles were turned and canted to urge the yeast cells down the neck of the bottle, and cast-iron corking machines that could force six corks at once into the slender bottles with one pull on a lever. Gill noted the equipment as they crept by, either remembering his work with it, or remarking on its newness. When they came to where the champagne was cellared, the bottles were thicker and heavier, and the dimples in the bottle bottoms were deeper.

He handed glasses to Louis and Nancy, put his on an upended barrel along with his candle, and grabbed a bottle of champagne from the rack. The bottle wasn't labeled and there was no foil over the cork. Gill simply untwisted the wire agraffe and shot the cork up into the darkness. As the wine bubbled up, he let it spill into his glass, then poured some into Louis's and Nancy's glasses.

"Champagne to our real friends," he said. "Real pain to our sham friends." His voice was small under the vaulted ceiling, disappeared quickly beyond the puddle of light given off by their three candles. They touched glasses, but the chink of the toast was tiny.

"What would you do, Nancy," Gill asked, "if you owned all this? If all this were yours?"

"I'd take a bath in champagne." Nancy spun around with her glass like a dancer. "Every day around sunset, I'd open a bottle of champagne and drink in the taste of harvest time, September in California, when it seems like life will never end."

"How about that, Louis?" Gill asked. "This all really will be yours one day. What are you going to do?"

"I never wanted it to be all mine," Louis said. "I never wanted you gone."

"No?"

"Of course not."

"Maybe not when you were five years old," Gill said. "But how about now, when you know what it means to be favorite son."

"No," Louis said.

"I can't believe Paul Tourneau hasn't told you how bad I am. He has, hasn't he?"

Louis looked away.

"What did he tell you?"

"He said that everything you'd say would be a lie."

Gill laughed. "Then he's the father of lies, isn't he?"

"Is that why we came up here?" Nancy asked. "So that you two could talk? I thought we came up to drink and have fun."

She walked over to Gill, a little jaunty, stood right in front of him and looked in his eyes. She took his chin in her two hands, her hands open like wings along each side of his jawline. She studied him, as though about to kiss him. Then she dropped her hands to his shoulders.

"Let's dance," she said.

"To what?"

"I'll hum."

She began to hum some Gershwin quietly, and she led him in one slow circle around the cool concrete floor, her feet shuffling a bit from drink. Gill stopped and took her hands from his shoulders.

"Why don't you open another bottle of champagne," Gill said.

She bunched her lips and turned away and wandered back among the tall dark walls of bottles.

Gill looked at Louis, looked at his smooth young face whitish and drawn in the candlelight. It wasn't possible to hate him, wasn't possible to resent him. Everything would be simpler if Louis were more like Bull Jacobsen and he could find pleasure in taking something away from him.

They heard the pop of a champagne cork from back in the cellar, and Nancy giggled.

"Don't you want to come back, Gill?" Louis asked. "I'm sure we could find some way to put the past behind us."

Another champagne cork popped from within the stored bottles.

"She's trying to get your attention," Gill said. "She's a little tight."

"I know."

"She thinks she's special, doesn't she?"

"Yes, I guess so."

"Well, you're such a good-looking guy, you'll have lots of girlfriends," Gill said. "You'll always be the handsome one."

"Gill, I want to help you." There was a pleading note in Louis's voice. "I feel guilty every day I think of you down in New Chicago."

"There's a sentiment Paul Tourneau never had trouble with," Gill said. "Did you ever hear how my mother died?"

Nancy's voice came from between bottles. "I'm getting all wet," she said.

"I just heard she died from heart troubles," Louis said.

"Heart troubles." Gill clapped Louis on the shoulder. "Come on. There's one more stop I want to make tonight."

He picked up his candle and an unopened bottle and began walking back out of the cellars, past the endless aisles of bottles, paying no attention to them now. Louis found Nancy and took her by the hand.

"Where are we going?" she asked.

"I don't know." He turned to see Gill's candle, hesitating in the darkness ahead.

"What if I don't want to?"

"Do it for me."

Gill's candle began to move again.

"Don't pull on my hand," Nancy said. "It hurts."

Gill walked out of the cellar and past the cooperage, and then he blew out his candle and replaced it on the small shelf. He stepped out into the moonlight, and he heard the whispers of grape leaves all around him. Above and below him, the vineyard blocks were broad in leaf and heavy with grapes, the grapes no longer swelling larger now, but instead changing and sugaring and softening. He took a few steps so that he could look up to the blocks above the winery, and the leafy tops of the vines reflected the pale moonlight in serried rows, spreading over the entire hillside like a rumpled blanket, until reaching the dark edge of the tall trees.

"It's so beautiful here," he said. "And I'll never live here again."

He heard Louis and Nancy behind him, and then he began to walk the path he remembered in his dreams, walking as though he were a boy again. He knew the path perfectly well. He walked up through the blocks of grapes, and then skirted the uncleared land to where he had seen his mother's moth-wing-colored gown move in stutters and hesitation in the light of the bonfire.

Then he was before it, the oak tree where his mother had died, still standing, seemingly unchanged in the ten years since he had seen it. Ten years, not a long span of time in the life of an oak. The leaves of the oak were silvered by the moonlight, all touching and overlapping above the trunk like a single rippled sheet. And he saw her now, pale and lovely, like an angel draped along the branches. And he saw that other tree, the one in no-man's-land that had burst and left him forever carrying the marks of the wounded.

He opened the bottle of wine, shot the cork out into the full foliage that hid the ripening grapes, and drank. Then he put it down and walked up to the trunk of the oak and laid his hand against its bark, ridged and rough in sections, and smooth between. Amid the roots, he found a jagged rock, and he began to trace his initials into the tree bark with the edge of it, smoothly at first, and then deeper, chopping into the bark as though to open an edge he could peel back like skin.

Nancy and Louis crashed to a halt behind him, and he heard Nancy say, "What are we doing here?"

"I don't know," Louis said.

Gill ignored them. He chunked the rough curve of a G into the bark.

"Well I'm not going to just stand here," Nancy said.

"Gill?" Louis called. "What are you doing?"

"You can stay if you want," Nancy said. "I'm going."

"Wait just a second," Louis said.

"You want me to walk home? Fine, I'll walk home."

Nancy grabbed the open bottle and began to walk away. Louis hesitated, looked up at his brother at the tree, then ran after Nancy and grabbed her around the waist.

"Let me go." She jerked herself free.

For a moment, there was a still quiet between them, with a wet little chunk coming from the tree, wet-sounding like a kiss. Then they heard another sound, pushing through the vineyard, approaching them. It was the large sound of a body, pushing though the vines, and Louis could see the glow of a lantern waving in their direction.

"Shit," he whispered. "It's my father."

"I don't care," Nancy said in a normal voice.

"I left the winery unlocked, and we've taken bottles out of bond. Oh, shit."

"I don't care," Nancy said loudly. "I'm ready to go, and I'm going to go."

Louis snatched the bottle out of her hands and threw it up into the uncleared land. The light was almost on them, and the sound was tall and dark.

"Papa?" he called.

"Lou? Is that you?"

Augusto Corvo came around the last row of vines, holding a lantern in his left hand, and his cavalry pistol in his right hand.

"Grandpa," Louis said in relief.

"You two are out late," Corvo lowered the cavalry pistol. "And you left the winery open."

"I know."

Corvo looked keenly around them, looked up at the oak tree above them.

"Gill was here. Wasn't he?"

Louis and Nancy turned to look. Gill had gone, vanished, as though he had disappeared into the tree. The oak stood alone now, silvery and bleeding a little from its fresh-scarred bark. They hadn't even heard him leave.

"Where did he go?" Louis asked stupidly.

Corvo looked at the tree. "Poor boy," he said.

"Gilbert!" Louis called.

"Lou," Nancy said, "I'm still going."

"Gill!"

"Lou. I'm leaving."

"Just a second, Nancy."

He put his hand on her shoulder, but she shoved it away.

"Don't touch me," she said.

"Poor boy." Corvo shook his head.

TWELVE

The Crush

*T*he wind shift came in late August that year, a shift to the north that was chill at first, but heralded the ripening Indian summer weather. The Pacific High, a pool of still, warm air, edged eastward toward the continent, and the winds spilling clockwise around it would first blow away the coastal fogs. Then, as the high pressure lapped over the coast, temperatures would rise in all the inland valleys. Under a steady heating sun, the fully formed grapes could fill rapidly with sugar and arrive at their peak in days.

Winegrowers call harvest time the crush. As the days of still, hot air arrived, Tourneau and Louis checked sugar and acid every day, and Tourneau had some tents set up for pickers on a flat piece of land half a mile from the winery, and spread a canopy over a large outdoor grill and oven. Since the 'teens, as more transients than locals came to pick grapes, Tourneau had found that providing a place to sleep on the grounds kept workers on through the end of the crush. When they accepted a place to stay and the food and light worker's wine he provided, they accepted a bond, an obligation to the vineyard.

He sent Louis out to gather a picking crew, now that prunes were ending, saying it was one of the jobs of a harvest manager. "You'll be doing more and more here, every year," he said. "Your grandfather will be doing less. And it will give you a chance to practice your Spanish."

Louis hadn't seen Gill after that last moment, when he was carving his initials into the tree. He had looked for him the day after, calling his name in the wood as he had done when a young boy, but there was no answer. He went by the Cash Store, and also went by the orchard where the Familia Pulido was working, spying out the window for a short white man working with a group of Mexicans. Once, he drove back to New Chicago during the day and parked at a distance. He saw one woman, dressed in black, working around the fire pit. He stayed for a time, as though he could conjure up his brother through watching, but the woman remained alone.

He hadn't seen Nancy after that night either. She'd been silent during the drive down the hill after Gill disappeared, and when he had asked her when they were going to see each other again, she'd said, "When you grow some brains" and then ran into her house. She hadn't been home anytime he'd called during the past three weeks, and he figured she had her mother answering the phone for her. He knew she had her mother wrapped around her little finger.

Louis turned the truck off toward New Chicago while assembling a crew and drove through the warm, still air. The dirt track to the tilting and sinking houses was clear now, compacted by the Pulido truck, and the weeds grew high and yellow alongside. But the Pulidos would be moving on soon, back to Southern California after the seasons of harvest, abandoning once again the already abandoned city. And the track would grow green and empty with winter.

Louis left the truck in the same place he had parked two weeks earlier, with Nancy. He saw Miguel stand up near the fire circle, and Francisco and Javier, but he didn't see the two women, Ana and Rosarita, and he didn't see Gill.

"I know why you have come," Miguel said. He was wearing a clean linen shirt tucked into his jeans, and his hair was slicked back, and his face shiny and pleased.

"Yeah?" Louis looked past him and scanned the camp, looking for some sign that Gill was still there.

"You want us to pick your grapes, no?"

"That's right," Louis said. "Like we spoke about."

"We just finished prunes," Miguel said. He hooked his thumbs inside his belt and rocked back and forth on his heels. "The owner there, Jacobsen, gave us a big bonus for staying through the whole harvest. You giving a bonus?"

"We give a bonus, if you stay through."

"What kind of grapes, don Luis? Mataro? Alicante?"

Louis shook his head. "We grow better grapes than that. Pinot, Cabernet, Chardonnay. We'll be picking the Pinot first."

"Better for you," Miguel smiled. "Not better for us. Alicante grows four, five tons an acre. Easy to fill up boxes. Make money fast. Pinot, one ton an acre. Slow."

Louis looked over to one of the old houses. At a window on the second floor, he saw Ana, dressed in black. She was looking down at him.

"What if I told you that an Alicante vineyard wanted us?"

"We pay a nickel more a box than other vineyards, so long as the fruit is perfect."

"We just got a big bonus." Miguel turned and walked back into the circle, and Louis followed him. "We are going to a dance tonight, at the Palm Gardens Ballroom in San Jose. They have a Mexican dance every couple of weeks."

"That's good," Louis said. "You'll have a good time."

"You think so?" Miguel stood by Francisco and clapped him on the shoulder. "Last time we went to a dance, this one was dancing with a woman who was almost black from working under the sun, who had hands rough as bricks from picking fruit off the ground. And he asked her what she did, and she said she worked in an office. And she asked him what he did, and you know what he said?"

Francisco looked down and wiped some dirt from his shoes. Louis waited, silent.

"He said he was going to start college next year." Miguel paused for a moment, then laughed. "Yes, they have a good time, lying to each other. Maybe this time he'll say he is a baseball player."

Francisco looked at his father resentfully.

"Okay, don Luis," Miguel said. "We will be at your vineyard Monday, before sunrise."

"All of you?" Louis said.

"All of us. Me, Francisco, Javier, Rosarita, Ana. All of us."

Javier moaned and stood up suddenly, and Miguel took his arm.

"It's all right," he said. "You better go now, don Luis. We'll see you on Monday."

"Okay." Louis turned and saw Ana, still framed by the window, raise her black-sleeved arm and wave at him slowly. He walked back to the truck through the blanketing heat of a late, false summer, the September heat that marked summer's end.

 Gladys Finney liked to think of herself as the happy angel of her daughters' lives, hovering over their shoulders, shepherding them safely through the dating years as their confidante and advisor, and finally seeing them safely into the arms of a man who would take care of them. She had done this successfully with her first two daughters, and she planned to do the same with her third daughter, even though her husband spoiled her some and claimed that she was different. Glad had seen her daughters stop dating certain boys, of course, and she thought that what had happened with Nancy was no different. For the past three weeks, she had answered the phone, and if it was Louis Tourneau, she told him that Nancy wasn't in. Glad was a little worried that Nancy had stayed home on Friday and Saturday nights, being more of a bookworm than she normally was, holing up and reading things her father gave her. But she thought it would pass.

This Friday, Nancy was going to the movies with just a couple of her girlfriends from school, and Glad was comforted to see her again in front of her round mirror in her bedroom, putting rouge on her cheeks. She walked into the room and looked over Nancy's shoulder at her face in the mirror.

"You look nice," she told Nancy. "You've been so pale lately."

Nancy made a face at herself. "I don't think I look nice. I think I'm just covering things up."

"Oh, no. Makeup just enhances your *natural* beauty."

"If I had any to enhance." She stretched her mouth tall into an elongated O and applied some lipstick. Then she blotted her lips several times on tissue paper. "I'm just hiding what I really look like."

"Did he make you feel like that?" Glad sat down on the edge of the bed near Nancy. "What did he say to you?"

"Nothing, Mother."

Glad didn't believe her daughter. "Yes he did. What did he say to make you feel ugly?"

"Nothing. It's just the way I am."

"Now listen here. When boys want to make girls feel cheap, they tell them that they're not pretty. And then they try to take advantage of them. Did he try to take advantage of you?"

"No."

"Hmm." She looked at Nancy, who turned away to the mirror. "If he did . . . I'm not doubting your word, but if he did, then you're much better off without him. That only means he doesn't really care for you as a person."

"He didn't do that, Mom."

"I always thought of him as a nice boy."

"He is nice. He's the nicest boy in the world."

"Then why don't you want to see him?"

Nancy looked back at the mirror and pressed her lips together, then opened them with a puffing sound.

"I just don't," she said.

"Someday, you'll meet someone *really* nice. And you'll know he's the right one, because he makes you feel just as nice. I know. I saw everything your big sisters went through."

Glad patted her daughter briskly on the shoulder.

"What movie are you going to see?"

"Lillian Gish. *The Wind.*"

Later that evening, Bill Finney was working with slugs of finished type, assembling them onto the big galley plates of the offset press. Birthdays, weddings, family reunions, obituaries, ads from the stores, the real estate agents, the bank. The life of the town, laid down in comprehensible lines, in the definitive snap of the Hoe press.

Or half the life of the town, he told himself. The half that would be welcomed by his readers, by his advertisers.

When he heard the door open, he thought it might be Nancy, home early from the movies. But from the sound of the first footstep on the poured-concrete floor, he knew it was someone else. He knew precisely the sound of Nancy's movements.

He peered around the large plates of the Hoe and saw Louis Tourneau, standing uncertainly at the doorway, one hand still on the door handle.

"Come on in, Lou."

He stood up, and the young man walked diffidently forward.

"Nancy's not here," Finney said. "If that's what you're thinking."

"I didn't expect she would be," Louis said.

"But you were hoping."

"Maybe a little."

Finney sat down at the keyboard of the Linotype. "Tell me something about the crush, Lou. I'll put you in the paper."

Louis walked to his side. "We'll probably start picking on Monday, Tuesday the latest. My father said he knew it would come on fast once the wind shifted."

"Grapes are sugaring right up?"

"Yeah." Louis looked away. "Did you know that a bunch of red wine grapes doesn't change color all at once?"

Finney looked up at him, interested. "No, I didn't know that."

"They start turning from green to red from the stem end of the bunch, like the color is bleeding down into the grapes from the mother vine, seeping down and changing them one by one. It's slow at first, when the weather is cool and foggy. Then, when it gets warmer, it speeds up, and they turn from green, to reddish, to almost black. Right down to the last berry at the very apex of the bunch. Then you know that crush isn't too far away."

"Hmmm." Finney was typing slowly and thoughtfully as Louis spoke. "And that's what happened this year."

"Yeah."

"Thanks, Lou. I'll put that in."

"Okay." Louis stood silently, watching Finney type, not making any motion to leave. When the bell above the keyboard dinged at the end of a line, Finney turned his chair to face him.

"I am sorry that Nancy doesn't want to see you now, Lou. She tells me she's going to get straight A's this year, so she can go to college. And she doesn't want to just go to San Jose Teachers, she wants to go to Cal. Maybe it's just that. Summer's over, she wants to concentrate on school."

"Maybe." Louis frowned, looked away. "Mr. Finney, have you heard anything about where Gill might be?"

Finney shook his head. "He stopped showing up at the Cash Store about three weeks ago. Nobody in town has seen him. Pat McCarty's upset about it. He thinks he did something wrong."

"I went to New Chicago. He wasn't there either. Nancy hasn't heard anything, has she?"

"He was gone for ten years, Lou. Maybe he's gone back to wherever he was."

"I just can't believe that."

"I wish I could help."

Louis shrugged. "Sorry to have bothered you."

"No bother." Finney stood up. "If you ever want to talk again, stop on by."

"Okay. Thanks."

"After the crush, maybe."

When the door shut behind Louis, Finney went back to the press, but he did not immediately begin to fix the slugs of type. He thought that Louis wanted the sweet and well-ordered world, the kind world he described in his paper week by week. Louis wanted the world in accord with his wishes for it. Everybody did. Gill did too, probably, wherever he was.

Marco and Carlo ran out from between the rows of vines and onto the plat where the harvesters' tents had been set up. It was late in the dusty and yellow Sunday afternoon, and already smoke rose from the large outdoor kitchen, and men and women were walking about, anxious for the following morning when they could begin making money again. The two boys paused and searched through the people. Each boy had half a dozen dead birds hanging from a string on his belt. The string ran through the throat of the birds and out their mouthing beaks, and a little dried blood stuck to the throat feathers, and their eyes were open and flat black. They had some grackles on the strings, with black iridescent head feathers, and brownish cowbirds, and spotted starlings with dark beaks, all stiffening at their sides.

Then Marco spotted Paul Tourneau, wearing his broad straw hat and swinging the spade he carried like a walking stick. He punched his brother in the arm.

"There he is," he whooped.

They ran to where Tourneau stood with Louis, fumbling their strings of birds loose from their belts.

"Look, Mr. Tourneau," they said together.

Tourneau smiled down at them, running his hand through his tangled black beard. "How did you get them?"

"Slingshots!"

"Good." He pointed at the dead birds with a thick, blunt finger. "Now you won't be eating my grapes."

As the boys watched, he dipped his hand into a pocket and brought out two nickels and gave them each one.

"Now hang these birds from the fence posts around the southeast block, where we're starting tomorrow. A good warning for the other birds, eh?"

He patted them each on the shoulder.

"*Allez, les braves hommes.*"

They watched the two boys scurry away. The birds would be strung to fence posts by their necks, facing outward like dead sentinels. They would hang through autumn, growing light and dry as straw, until the twine finally wore through and they fell, severed, at the edge of the vineyard.

"You never would kill birds for me," Tourneau said to Louis.

"I never liked to," Louis said.

"No rabbits either. A nickel for every rabbit, and you would never kill a one for me."

"I never liked to see them dead once I'd seen them alive."

"They want to eat the same grapes that keep all of us," Tourneau said. "You, your mother, me, all these pickers for the next few weeks. I'd see them all dead if it meant that I'd make the finest wine in California."

He looked over the vineyard and began talking about which blocks of grapes they would be picking, and on which days, if the weather held. A few white clouds hovered over the Santa Clara Valley, and Tourneau drew his blunt squarish hands over the eastern sky, as though tracing a map of the vineyard onto the scattered clouds. In three weeks, he thought, they could get the berries off, each block picked as its sugar was peaking, and the fruit crushed and into the fermenters.

"You did well assembling a picking crew, Louis," he said. "You worked hard."

Louis looked south in the direction of the tree where he had last seen Gill. A dead cowbird would now be hanging on a fence post opposite that tree.

"Thanks, Papa," he said.

Tourneau paused. "You're not seeing that Nancy anymore, the daughter of the newspaperman."

"No," Louis said. "I'm not."

"Tell you what," Tourneau said. "After the crush, we'll go down to Goosetown together. How does that sound?"

"I don't know, Papa."

"This is your harvest as much as mine," Tourneau said. "You'll deserve some reward. And in Goosetown, you'll forget all about that little girl. Even a sensitive boy who won't kill rabbits can forget things in Goosetown."

"Okay, Papa," Louis said. "We'll go."

He looked at the sky, saw the lines traced across it by his father's hands.

The hills to the east were black and featureless, but the crests of the hills were etched clearly against a pale, predawn yellow. Tourneau stood tall in the back of one of the tray wagons, and the picking crew waited on the ground at the edge of the southeast block. They were edgy and jumpy, ready to start. There were some young people from Italian families who would start school late, and a few fruit tramps who had no fixed address and who would be heading south once walnuts were in. More than half were Mexican families like the Pulidos, who had been living in the States since war broke out in Mexico the previous decade. The pickers all carried the serpette, a harvesting knife with a short wooden handle and a sharp, crescent-shaped blade. Some pickers swiped their serpettes against small whetstones as they waited, and others looped a string from the knife's handle around their wrists, so that it would stay handy while they were parting the leafy branches with both hands.

Although it was cool in the dawn, most of the picking crew wore broad straw hats against the hot sun that was coming, and many wore neckerchiefs above their collars to keep their necks from sunburn. They wore overalls or double-kneed jeans, since some of the picking would be kneeling work, and they wore long-sleeved plaid or denim shirts, sleeves rolled up over the elbow.

When it grew light enough to see, Tourneau held up two clusters of grapes. "This one," he held up his right hand, "is the way the grapes should look. If you see any grapes that have raisined up, or have been sucked dry by bees, knock them off." He demonstrated by using his thumb to push off a grape with a slightly puckered skin.

"If you see a cluster like this, don't pick it." He held up his left hand and showed a cluster with some graying blotches of bunch rot, a cluster that the sulfur had missed on some wet morning during the summer.

There were harvest boxes waiting at the head of each row, and Louis had already assigned rows to the various groups. The upper limb of the sun had not yet broken over the ridge, but it was growing light enough to tell good clusters of grapes from bad ones.

"Try not to let the skin of the grapes break when they drop into the box," Tourneau said. "All right. *Allez. Bonne vendange.*"

The pickers all took off at a quick trot, chattering and clapping their hands together to get feeling in them, and within seconds they were rustling aside leaves and slicing through grape stems. The clusters began to fall softly into boxes scraped close to the trunks of the grapevines, guided down gently by each picker's cradling left hand. Up and down the rows of vines, the same rustle and muffled kiss of grapes falling on other swelling grapes was heard.

Louis handled the reins of Queenie, hauling one of the tray wagons, while Augusto Corvo drove the other behind Prince. They kept the wagons moving slowly up and down the allées, and pickers trotted out with full boxes, placed them on the still moving wagons, and picked up an empty box from the head of the row. The whole section of the vineyard seemed to be in motion, leaves brushed up and away, grapes falling into boxes, pickers moving the harvest boxes into place under the vines and chattering across the rows to each other, teasing anyone who fell behind as they worked their way across.

Just after sunrise, Louis's wagon was filled with boxes mounded with black grapes, and he turned the wagon toward the cellar. Angelo, one of the full-time men, stopped picking and climbed up beside him. Louis gave the reins a short snap over Queenie's hindquarters, and she picked up her pace, knowing the way.

The unloading area, behind the third level of the winery building, was flat and sheltered by oak trees. Paul Tourneau began taking the boxes from the wagon bed even before the wagon came to a complete halt. Louis and Angelo jumped down to help, and together they stacked the boxes where the oak trees would shade them, so the grapes would not cook in the sun before they were crushed. Then Louis and Angelo climbed back behind the horse and headed down the hill to the section being picked. Louis looked back to see his father plucking stray leaves out of the boxes and lifting clusters to inspect them.

In the section, the initial chatter and banter had slowed down, the pickers saving their breath for work, and a spirit of quiet earnestness had settled in over the vines. The sun was up now, and the air at ground level was heating steadily. Francisco and Miguel were working down adjacent rows, both picking grapes into buckets they then emptied into boxes chalked with a large P. There were spiderwebs crossing the dark insides of the leafy vines, and they had to brush them aside with their arms and the serpette to reach the clusters hanging there. Once, as Francisco was bringing out a cluster, a gob of web clung to his arm and spun itself up across his nose and mouth, and he dropped the grapes and began spitting and slapping at himself. Miguel laughed.

"The spiders want the grapes too. And the bees." Miguel was one of those who always worked with his sleeves rolled down, no matter how hot it was, to lessen the chance for bee stings and spider bites.

Francisco spit once more, then picked up the cluster he had dropped. "Should I put it in the bucket?"

"Knock off any that have broken skin," Miguel said. "They are paying us well for prime fruit."

As Louis drove Queenie along at a walking pace, Francisco picked up a full box and trotted out to the wagon. The box weighed over fifty pounds, and carrying it made the veins on his arms stand out. Louis smiled when he heaved it onto the wagon bed and snatched two empty boxes off the end.

"Good job, Frank," he said, while keeping the wagon rolling slowly ahead.

Francisco trotted back down the row to the vine he had been working on and dropped the boxes nearby. Miguel looked up.

"What did your friend say to you?" he asked.

"That I was doing a good job."

"Ha ha. His job is easier." They both looked up and saw Augusto and Louis standing in the wagons that were passing up and down the allées, seeming to float upon an unbroken layer of grape leaves, like barges on a river.

As the day warmed toward noon, the vineyard began to hum with bees, grown accustomed to sucking the sweet grape juice from the fruit pecked open by birds. The pickers simply tried to pick around them without bothering them, though some said that every picker owed the harvest at least one sting. Francisco, when he grew hungry, ate from a cluster of grapes, though they still tasted a little sour to him.

He made a face at his father. "Are they sure these grapes are ripe?"

"These are for champagne. That's why they get picked early. Champagne that you and I will never taste. So eat now."

Francisco ate some more grapes, not picking them off one by one but holding the whole bunch up to his mouth and biting down, and chewing, and spitting out the pips and the rubbery skins. As he took another bite, he watched his father crouch down and reach to the center of some canes with both hands, the left spreading the leaves apart and reaching in to the fruit, the right holding the knife.

Then Miguel jerked back.

"*Chingada madre,*" he cursed.

He held up both his hands, open like claws near his chest. From his right hand dangled the serpette, and the hand was sticky with grape juice, and a fresh bee sting reddened at the base of this thumb. His left hand was bleeding, gashed in the palm by the jerking serpette.

He grimaced at his left hand. The blood was bright and shocking. It oozed out along the length of the cut and dripped down his wrist.

Francisco looked for a second, then turned and ran to the end of the row.

"Don Luis!" he called "*¡Patrón!*"

Louis reined in Queenie where she was and saw Francisco jumping and shouting. He grabbed the small first-aid kit, war surplus in a green metal box, and ran to where Francisco pointed.

Miguel was standing, waiting for him, his arm held out like a torch, and he had broken out in a sudden sweat.

"It doesn't hurt," he said furiously.

"Do you need a doctor?" Louis was down on one knee, flipping open the metal clasps on the kit and looking up at the angry, bleeding man standing straight and braced.

"No," Miguel shouted. "It doesn't hurt. No doctor."

Louis squeezed some ointment from a metal tube onto a gauze pad and pressed it onto the cut to stop the bleeding, holding Miguel's hand flat between both of his own. Francisco stood by watching, his long thin arms dangling by his sides, and Miguel turned to him.

"What are you waiting for? Are you making any money standing there?"

"No," Francisco said.

"Then get back to work."

Francisco looked at Louis, who was reaching down into the kit for a roll of gauze.

"Now," Miguel said. "*Ándale.*"

Louis wrapped gauze around the pad to hold it in place, figure-eighting it around the thumb and across the palm. "Are you sure you don't need a doctor?" he asked.

Miguel jerked his hand away and looked at it closely, thin-lipped and frowning.

"It's pretty deep," Louis said.

"It's just my left hand," Miguel said. "Go back to your wagon. Let me get back to work."

Other pickers were calling for the wagon, calling for more boxes, and Louis closed up the first-aid kit and trotted back to where Queenie stood with her head down. Francisco, back at his vine, was cutting grape stems but also glancing secretly at his father to judge how he really was.

Miguel flexed his hand, and his mouth tightened. "It will be stiff tomorrow," he said to himself. Then he picked up the cluster of grapes he had dropped, knocked off a few grapes that had shattered, and laid it in the bucket.

In the early afternoon, enough grapes had been picked for the first crush. Any grapes picked later would come to the winery sun-warmed and add too much heat to the fermentation. They would be left in boxes to cool overnight, and crushed the next morning.

Paul Tourneau gathered some of the full-time men to help, and Monsignor Roig i Verdaguer had come to give a blessing. They stood in a large semicircle under the oak tree shade behind the third floor of the winery. Louis and Angelo held wooden paddles and waited by the crusher, a large bin draped with a wire mesh screen. At the bottom of the bin, two grooved hardwood rollers would turn against each other, rotating at different rates to crush the thick-skinned grapes but leave the bitter pips whole. An opening at the lower end of the bin allowed the juice, along with the pulp and skins—the must—to drain down into the winery itself.

Tourneau picked up a box of grapes, and then lifted it easily above his head while the men and women laughed and applauded.

"When I am too weak to lift the first box of grapes," he said, "then Louis will be master here."

"Not for many years," someone shouted.

The monsignor cleared his throat, and Tourneau put down the box.

"Where is Sophia?" he asked.

"Here I am." She came into the semicircle dressed in blue and holding a silver platter with a bottle of wine and two glasses, which she placed on a table near the crusher. Tourneau pulled the cork on the bottle and poured two glasses half full.

The monsignor lifted one glass up, the crystal globe filled with a dark red wine, dense and heavy. And he smiled while those gathered lowered their heads.

"I always begin with a poem," he said.

Back of the wine is the Vintner,
And back through the years, his Skill—
And back of it all are the Vines in the Sun
And the Rain
And the Master's Will.

"This is a happy time." He spoke in a deep and resonant voice. "When the grape begins its journey to become wine. A journey mysterious in some ways, like our life's journey. But one which ends in a great change, for some of these grapes will become the holy wine of sacrament. Like our own lives will end in knowing and loving God.

"May God's blessings be upon this harvest, upon the toilers in the field and the workers in the winery, and upon Paul Tourneau and his family, who through the years use their skill to bring the mysterious liquid, the blood of our Lord, to life again. In the name of the Father, and the Son, and the Holy Spirit, amen."

The gathered people murmured "Amen," and then they lifted their heads. Paul Tourneau picked up the other glass and touched it to the monsignor's glass, and they drank. Then he put down the glass and raised the first box of grapes high over his head and crashed the fruit into the crusher. Some of the fruit split and sprayed grape juice sparkling into the air.

Louis and Angelo attacked the grapes on the mesh with their wooden paddles, mashing and spreading them against the mesh until the individual berries dropped from the stems and fell into the rollers below. Another man turned a hand crank that moved the rollers, splitting the skins of those grapes that had not been split by being pushed through the sieve. Another box was emptied onto the wire, and then another, crashing down and dropping some fruit directly down into the trough, while Louis and Angelo kept their long-handled tools scraping the grapes free from their stems and breaking most of them into skin and juice and pulp. When the screen grew crowded with stems, Louis called for a halt and shoveled the brown and twisted stems onto a large canvas tarpaulin laid out to the side. They would be plowed back into the vineyard during the winter.

Louis kept track in his head while he worked. Forty boxes equaled about a ton, and a ton of grapes would fill a one-hundred-and-seventy-gallon puncheon. Flies buzzed around the mesh and in Louis's eyes, attracted by the fruit sugar and the sweat that fell from his face, and small, bothersome yellow jackets hovered above the grapes.

"You ready for a break?" Johnny, one of the men carting over boxes, offered to take his paddle.

Inside the winery building, it was dark and cool and fragrant, as the fresh juice and bluish skins and pulp spilled down from the crusher outside. It all fell from a wooden chute into a basket press, a tall cylinder of wooden slats with a thick disk that could be ratcheted down onto the must as needed. One man stood on a ladder and directed the must around the porcelain-covered base of the press, distributing it evenly with a long wooden stick. Free-run juice, the most delicate and flavorful juice obtained without pressing, was already seeping between the slats and pouring out through a spout at the bottom of the press and into a puncheon. Tourneau stood by the spout and dipped a small beaker into the spill now and then and held it to the light. The juice was coming out almost clear, with a faint tinge of salmon color to it.

Then the crushed grapes stopped flowing down the chute, and the man on the ladder scraped the last bits of pulp.

"Ha," Tourneau said. "The first day's crush is over." The free-run juice was still pouring, but more slowly.

"Should I begin pressing?" The man on the ladder had stepped down and was fitting the long oaken handle into the ratchet at the top of the basket press. The handle curved down so that it could be grasped at shoulder level.

"Wait for Louis." Tourneau looked up and saw the upper door let in some slanted sunshine. He blinked, and then saw his son coming down the stairs.

Louis joined Tourneau at the base of the basket press and took a sip of the free-run juice in the beaker. He swirled it around in his mouth. Berries, cherries, violets, and a tang that came from the fruit picked before the sugars had peaked, before the acids had fallen.

He nodded at his father. "That's what we want for the sparkling wine."

"Just a light pressing now." Tourneau smiled at his son. "To make it the color of a partridge's eye."

Louis joined the other worker at the press handle, and they walked it back and forth. In one direction, it moved the wooden disk down the long central screw. In the other, it clacked back on its ratchet, loudly marking their steps. As the disk pressed down onto the mass of pulp and skin, juice began to flow again out the spout, and it grew harder to work the long handle. After every turn, Louis looked at his father, waiting for the signal to stop. Tourneau held the beaker against a candle, not tasting now. The salmon tinge had deepened slightly.

"Almost perfect, now. Give it five more turns."

They clacked the handle back, and put their weight into moving it forward. The fresh grape juice spilled out. They clacked the handle back again. Louis suddenly saw the entire vineyard in motion, all at the same time; pickers on their knees in the fields, cutting clusters into buckets and pouring the buckets into boxes. His grandfather, standing with the reins in his hands while Prince walked serenely up and down the allées and boxes were slapped onto the wagon bed. John and Angelo, emptying box after box onto the wire mesh above the crusher, himself using the paddle to separate the berries from their stems, and the juice and must falling in the gravity-flow design down into the basket press. For this moment, changing the living fruit into living wine.

"Good!" Tourneau said. He held the beaker up to the light. "Louis. Come taste and see."

Louis jumped down from the basket press. And somewhere, his brother stood apart, exiled, and Louis felt him watching them all with his half-scarred face.

The spill from the spout had slowed, and once it stopped the grapes would be pressed into a different puncheon for some other, less-fine wine.

Louis took the beaker from his father, saw the candle turn roseate through the glass, and tasted.

"It's good," Tourneau said. "It's good."

THIRTEEN

The Garden of the World

*T*he crush continued into the first week of October. Block by block, the grapes ripened, as Tourneau had foreseen. The whites for still wine reached twenty-two degrees Brix, and then the blacks broke through twenty-three. The picking crews moved in with their chalk-marked harvest boxes and serpettes, making money steadily, and the grapes were gotten off and hauled to the winery. Each block was crushed in turn, directed into different fermenting tanks, and a dose of starter yeast was added to begin the process that turned grape juice into wine.

Unlike other years, Louis chose not to go to school while the crush was on. Tourneau had said he could go, but Louis decided to stay for every step of the process, and his father was pleased to let him. Before sunrise, he helped with the crush of the previous afternoon's picking, the grapes that would have been too hot to start into fermentation. Then, after directing the picking crew what block to begin on, he returned to the winery to do measurements on the wine in fermentation. On each tank, the variety and the date picked and the Brix were marked in chalk: pinot noir, octo. 1, 23.2. Twice a day, the Brix and the temperature of the tank were chalked on the wood below, the sugar numbers falling as the alcohol was rising, and the temperature watched carefully. The yeast worked best between sixty-five and eighty degrees.

The tanks fermenting red wine also had to be punched down several times a day. Louis climbed a stepladder to the rim of each tank in turn, holding a long pole with a wooden disk pegged to the end, and he peeled back the muslin covering the opening. The red wine was fermenting with its skins, and the carbon dioxide from the yeast pushed the skins up into a textured magenta crust, the *chapeau*, crowning over the wine and holding heat in. When Louis first pushed the disk down into the crust, it gave a little but did not crack. He laid his weight onto the pole end, and then the disk broke through the grape skins, and the new-making wine geysered up through the hole he'd made. He had to work his way around the tank, moving the step-ladder and expanding that initial crack until all the skins were once more mixed in with the wine. His father had told him that in the old days in Burgundy, a man would strip naked and jump into a tank and simply cling to the edge and thrash his legs until the *chapeau* was broken up.

Louis helped with hauling grapes and crushing the morning's picking. He measured sugars and acid to determine where the next day's picking would take place. He pumped wines in the winery from fermenting tanks to barrels for aging, and helped shovel out the pomace from the basket press into a tank to make piquette, and clean the press and the crusher for different grape varieties. Then he worked again into the evening, measuring and testing the various lots, talking over with his father which should be used for the blended reds, which could be used for pure Pinot noir or Cabernet, which wines might age into great wines and which simply good wines.

When the Pinot noir for still wine came in, he began to sleep out in the winery, eating with the pickers at the outdoor kitchen, staying away from the house. He set up a cot on the same floor as the big fermenting tanks, near enough to an open window that the carbon dioxide wasn't a threat. The air inside the winery then was jammy, dark, ripe, like the smell of ripe fruit that has been sitting in the sun mixed with the smell of forest after a warm rain. Before he went to bed each night, he made a final check of the fermenting tanks, laying his hand high against the wood planks. The wood was warmed from the inside, heated by the fermenting wine, and he could hear the fermentation as well. It sounded like the buzzing of a swarm of bees, restless and changing.

When he had felt all the tanks, sure that none were heating too much, he lay down to sleep, surrounded by the rich, ripe air. He'd given himself wholly to the work of the vineyard, even though he found no joy in it now. He thought Gill belonged there with him, and in his brother's absence, he felt better if he gave up other pleasures for the life his brother was denied.

Gill knew that after the last day of picking and crushing grapes, everyone would gather around the outdoor kitchen to drink and celebrate, and that everyone would be drunk and asleep by midnight. He had told Mr. Beckwourth that it would be the right time to take some trucks up the hill, catch everyone by surprise, load up with champagne. Gill had been keeping an eye on the harvest, driving up above the vineyard, parking the car he'd been loaned, and passing through the redwoods that skirted the cleared land. He knew from his years of work what order the various blocks would be picked in, and he knew that the last to be picked would be the highest and steepest section, where the grapes took longest to ripen.

He was watching on the day when the pickers moved into that block, complaining good-naturedly that it was more fit for goats than for grapes. The boxes full of picked clusters had to be carried out to a slatboard sled with thick wooden runners and strapped down before one of the horses could haul them to the winery, and the empty boxes had to be strapped to the sled again to be dragged back up to the pickers. Gill watched the pickers move through the rows, plunging their hands into the hot cage of foliage to slice through the stem and then guide the cluster down into a box. They were working fast, but he knew that they would not finish until the next day.

When he saw Louis walking back up the hill beside Queenie, and Paul Tourneau walking along the other side of the horse, he took a step back into the green shade, even though he knew he was too far away to be spotted. Louis and Tourneau brought the horse to a halt, Louis patting her on the shoulder, and then they each began to carry empty boxes down to the pickers.

Gill held his breath, touching the papery bark of a second-growth redwood beside him. He watched his father come back to the horse with a cluster of grapes in his hand, pick off several, chew them. When Louis came back, Tourneau offered him the cluster, and Louis in turn picked off several. They walked up and down the allée, chewing slowly together, with their hands in the pockets of their overalls. Then they both turned their heads and spit out the skins and seeds at the same time, moving their heads with the same quick jerk. If Gill hadn't already known, it would have been enough to see their bodies spin and gesture together to know them as father and son.

He watched from the green uplands until the sled was loaded again, watched them walk down the hill together with the harvest.

The following day, as the final rows were picked, Paul Tourneau brought two fresh-slaughtered pigs to the outdoor kitchen and left them for the women. He told them that the pigs had given their lives for the happiness of man, and now they had to make sure that their sacrifice was not in vain.

Then he walked to the flat area behind the winery and found Augusto with Prince and a sled of boxes being unloaded, to wait overnight before being crushed.

"Another year, Augusto!" he said. "Another vintage."

Augusto pulled a broad red handkerchief out of his pocket and wiped the sweat off his forehead. "Another year gone," he said, and coughed.

"Not gone, *mon vieux*. Bottled, or in barrels."

"Gone," Augusto croaked, then coughed again.

"Oh, you are just too old to see the future. This vintage will be drunk after Prohibition has passed, perfect in, say, seven years."

"I won't be around to see it," Augusto said. "After working every day on this hillside. Working as hard as you do."

"Then take a rest, old man." Tourneau took the halter of Prince and led him around.

He walked beside the tall horse, patting it on its muscled shoulder bright with sweat, and they both turned up the hill toward the last block, leaving old Augusto coughing behind them.

The sled runners bumped and dragged over the dried clods of earth left after harrowing. Tourneau looked up and saw Louis at the very last row, against the uncleared land, strapping down full boxes of grapes, and he raised his hand.

"The pigs are spitted!" He brought Prince to a halt beside Queenie, and a picker came out with a box of grapes and laid it on the empty sled. "Tonight," Tourneau said to the picker, "*carnitas y chicharrones.*"

"*Bueno.*" The picker grinned and took an empty box back down the row.

Louis stood up, his load secured to the sled. "You and Prince should bring down the last of it."

Tourneau moved beside him and they looked out over the acres of vineyard that fell off below them. "I'm glad you haven't started back to school yet," Tourneau said. "So that you could be here now. It's grand, isn't it?"

"Yes," Louis said. "It's grand."

Beyond the acres of vineyard, and the three-story winery butted up against the hillside, the broad Santa Clara Valley rolled out before them, now freshly harvested of plums, and cherries, and apricots, and pears, and grapes.

In the early evening, Gill waited at the rendezvous spot, listening to the ceaseless cricket song. They had agreed to meet at a wide waste area on a logging road, a place where redwood logs had been skidded by oxen, then loaded onto wagons hauled by five-horse teams into town. This place had been Egypt once, when Gill was Louis's age, though Gill had never been one of the popular boys who brought a girl up.

When the headlights cut through the thin trees, Gill leaned forward, into the beams of light as though they brought a strong and blinding wind. There was the Dodge, followed by three large trucks with high-sided frames over the truck beds that could be covered with canvas. The Dodge aimed right at Gill, trucks rumbling behind it, then veered off and stopped. The doors of the vehicles opened with squeaks and groans, and eight men stepped out, all dressed in dark pants and coats.

Mr. Beckwourth walked forward from the Dodge. In the dark, Gill could see his face widen.

"So, tonight's the night at last, Mr. Tourneau."

Gill nodded. "You coming along?"

"I'll leave that to the heavy guys and meet you at our warehouse in Campbell. The police are good there."

"So who's in charge?" Gill looked toward the men standing beside the trucks. Some were leaning against fenders and lighting cigarettes.

"You drive with Sailor Jack."

A tall man with long limbs raised his hand.

Gill scowled and pointed to the last truck. "What's he doing here?"

"Hey Big Boy," Beckwourth said. "Your old pal wants to say hello."

Big Boy had been standing inconspicuously on the far side of one truck, trying not to call attention to himself. He shambled up, wearing a slouch cap, and he grinned sheepishly.

"Hi, Gill."

He put out his hand, but Gill ignored it.

"What's he doing here?" Gill asked again.

"This is business," Mr. Beckwourth said. "I know he set you up once, but that's over with. He's here because he still owes me money, and because he's a hell of a driver in the dark. Sees like a cat, don't you Big Boy."

Big Boy grinned and nodded.

"He's just dumb enough to let some floozie take his money and smash up my car." Mr. Beckwourth slapped him on the back and walked over to talk with Sailor Jack.

Gill stared off to the east, past where Big Boy stood. He felt Beckwourth had been giving him the needle as well, since Lupita had taken as much from him as she had from Big Boy.

"Sorry, Gill," Big Boy said. "But things didn't turn out so good for me either."

"Listen," Gill said, "you ever hear where she ended up?"

"Shit, no," Big Boy said. "She blew us both off. You don't still think about her, do you?"

"I've got other things to think about."

"You got another girl?"

Gill looked sideways at Big Boy. "If I did, I wouldn't tell *you*."

Big Boy laughed as though Gill had told the best joke in the world, laughed as though they really were old pals again. He offered Gill a smoke, and Gill took it, and they lit up and looked to the east together.

As they stood there, the moon began to rise from behind the eastern hills, smooth as eggshells, the upper limb curving between two rounded hilltops. One day past full, it would be high overhead at midnight, still high some hours later when they would be starting back down the hill.

The roasted pork was laid out on a massive oak block, cut into chunks and covered by the crisped skin of the pig, a yard-long stretch of tan crackling. Sophia stood behind the oak block holding a cleaver, and whenever the supply of pork ran low, she took up a fresh slab and chopped it with a quick hammering beat, then shoved it sideways with the blade under the crackling. "*Carnitas, carnitas,*" one of the other women in the outdoor kitchen called. They were making tortillas with a light pat of fingers into the palm of the hand, and seasoning the air with chile peppers and beans.

The pickers who filed up always bowed their heads to Sophia, because she was the wife of the *patrón*. She smiled at them, to try to show that she was not so distant from them. But they remained grave and reticent while they piled some pork on a tortilla, and perhaps broke off a piece of crackling. They relaxed when they left her table and went to the barrel to draw a glass of wine.

When the sun fell behind the western hills, Sophia realized that Louis hadn't come to eat. He had grown even more distant in the past weeks. He wasn't going on dates now, but she saw him seldom. He had been sleeping in the winery, eating in the field, withdrawing from everything except work.

In the firelight, Miguel held out his hand to Ana. She gently unwrapped the bandage, and she sucked in her breath when she saw the cut. It was open and red, the edges puckered toward each other but not quite joined. Ana massaged the flesh of the palm gently. She believed touch helped bring things together. Then she picked up a small bottle of Mercurochrome to keep the cut from infection, and she painted it up and down while Miguel's face tightened at the sting.

"Don't eat any *chicharrones* with that hand," she said as she wrapped fresh gauze over the cut. "Don't get any grease on it."

They both sat and watched as people gathered in groups around the food or the barrel, all content that they had made good money and the harvest was in. Two men had taken out guitars and were bringing them into tune with each other, plucking the E string together and touching the pearly knobs while bending their heads down. The young were adding wood to the fire.

"When are we going home?" Ana asked.

"To Pátzcuaro? I don't know."

"*Tonto.*" Ana tapped him on the shoulder.

They both saw Francisco and Rosarita carrying a long branch the width of a thigh to the fire.

"They should be in school," Ana said.

"They should be picking walnuts next week."

"Let somebody else pick walnuts this year. We should go home and find some work, and they should be in school."

"You think they can school themselves out of picking fruit." Miguel smiled with half his mouth.

"I don't know," Ana said. "I hope so."

"They won't school themselves out of being Mexican, in this land where people don't love us."

Ana shrugged her shoulders. "If I said to you, *hermano,* give up your Mexican citizenship, become a citizen of this country where we live, you would say no, of course not."

"Of course not," Miguel said. "I will never be a citizen of any country but Mexico."

"No matter how long you stay."

"Of course not."

"But they *will* be citizens," Ana said. "They will. And you have to allow it to happen."

She sighed.

"I don't know how things will come together. They never did for my husband. He was always at odds with the world."

"Or the world was at odds with him," Miguel said.

"But maybe it doesn't have to be that way for our children."

The fire was growing higher, and the guitarists were satisfied that the guitars were in tune.

Miguel said, "Do you hope that Gilberto will come? To Milagro Park?"

"It's the last thing he said to me," Ana said. "I'm only thirty-two."

Sophia stepped through the door beside the crusher that led down into the winery, carrying a cone of tortilla and pork wrapped in some newspaper. The steps down to the second floor were narrow and unlit. Lone electric bulbs threw up huge areas of shadow around the massive tanks and barrels, and the space inside the winery seemed dark and enormous, the limiting walls and ceilings visible only as an indeterminate blackness. She could hear the rolling buzz of fermentation coming from the big tanks, already beginning in the fresh-crushed grapes, and the air was thick with smells.

She walked down the stairs with care, stopped at the bottom of one of the twenty-thousand-gallon fermentation tanks that stood four times as tall as she was. She noticed a plank hanging over the edge of the tank.

"Louis?" she called.

She heard her son scuttle over to the side, and then his face appeared over the edge of the tank. He was wearing a leather apron and holding the dial of the long thermometer in his fist.

"I'll be right down," he said.

He disappeared from view again, and she heard his voice over the low rumble speaking some temperatures to himself. Then she watched him scale down the ladder holding the thermometer and carefully finding each rung with the sole of the big fireman's boots he was wearing.

She opened her mouth to speak when he reached the ground, but he held up a finger and told her to wait. Then he picked up a piece of chalk and marked the time, the temperature, and the Brix in neat columns on the face of the redwood.

"There," he said.

"I brought you something to eat," she said.

"Thanks, Mama." He took the wrapped food from her and picked out some pieces of pork to eat as he walked down to some large casks resting on their sides.

"Topping off on harvest night." She followed and watched him step onto a footstool beside the first cask.

"Has to be done." A bung wrapped in cheesecloth was snugged into a hole at the top of the cask, and as he loosened it, the carbon dioxide whooshed up and shot a little splash of new wine onto the darkened wood.

"Of course," Sophia said. "But you could also dance. Eat, drink, sing. Praise the harvest and our blessings."

"I don't have time for that." He smelled the bunghole, then looked down into it. The wine was a bit below the top of the cask.

"If you don't watch out," she said, "you'll end up more like your father than your father."

"That's what he wants, isn't it?"

Louis retrieved a jug of wine from the floor and poured until wine lapped at the edges of the opening. He could hear his father's voice saying that air was an enemy to wine.

"Gill's gone. And I'm here. And I'm going to carry on the work. And it doesn't matter much what else I lose along the way."

"Don't punish yourself." Sophia handed some fresh cheesecloth to her son and touched his hand briefly before she let go. "I have a feeling everything is going to come together in the end."

He wrapped the cheesecloth around the bung and tapped it in gently, so that the wine overflowed but did not splash.

"Okay, Mama," he said. "I'll finish this row of casks, then I'll come out for the music."

Just past midnight, the three truck engines rumbled alive in the logged-over flats, warming up as the moon rose high, and the waiting men threw down their cigarettes and clustered around the truck cabs before climbing up. Gill had counted several with Thompson submachine guns, pistol-gripped with round cartridges carrying a hundred rounds, and almost everybody carried a Colt .45, the new fully automatic version that held fourteen rounds. Sailor Jack took out his pistol, thumbed a button to release the cartridge and peered at it, then slapped it back in with a satisfying click. He holstered the gun under his shoulder and told Gill to climb into the lead truck next to Big Boy, who was driving.

Sailor Jack climbed up beside Gill and shut the door.

"Let's get underway," he said.

Big Boy pushed the truck into gear, and it began to roll forward, stiff and bouncy on its springs with no load. The other two trucks followed, leaving behind them a cold cloud of dust to settle on the empty field.

They passed through Crossroads, careful to stay under the speed limit and spaced far enough apart so that they wouldn't appear to be a convoy. Gill sat wedged between Big Boy and Sailor Jack, and Sailor Jack leaned away from him, as though to keep him at a distance. His eyes were never still, darting ahead to check for police, over to Gill, to Big Boy driving, then into the mirror to see if the other trucks were far enough behind. He patted his pistol under his coat and asked Gill again and again about the setup, the alarm systems, how to turn off the tear gas, what the building was like, whether he had really gone all the way back to where the wine was stored.

"No shotgun traps, you're sure."

"Just the tear gas," Gill said.

"Maybe they got some rifles up there?"

"Sure."

"They'd be stupid to throw down on us. But a shotgun trap don't know it's stupid to throw down on somebody carrying a Tommy."

"It was only a few weeks ago I was up there, and there was just the tear gas."

"With your brother, eh?"

Sailor Jack leaned back to observe Gill, darted his eyes forward, then turned them back to Gill.

"You like your brother?"

"Half brother," Gill said. "Until last July, I hadn't seen him for ten years."

"Did you like him when you saw him?"

"He's just a kid."

"Hmm." Sailor Jack patted his gun. "So how does it feel to be knocking over your old man's place?"

Big Boy peered over the steering wheel and lifted a hip to let out a loud fart. Then he spoke across Gill to Sailor Jack. "You can trust Gill. He's good. He hates his old man."

"Yeah?" Sailor Jack said to Big Boy. "But isn't family still family?"

"Don't be saying who I hate or don't hate," Gill said.

"No," Big Boy said. "He's wanted to knock over his father for a long time. He blames him for his face."

Sailor Jack laughed. "Hell, we can all do that. We all can blame our old man for the face we're wearing."

"Quit fucking with me," Gill said. "If I'm here, it's just because I'm getting back some of what's mine."

Sailor Jack patted his gun, checked the rearview mirror. "I just have trouble trusting somebody who's knocking over his own flesh and blood. It's more complicated than I like."

Gill sat back against the truck seat, looked straight ahead. He saw San Natoma ahead of him, the quiet brick storefronts washed with pale waning moonlight.

The fire of harvest's end was lowering, and Sophia was in Paul Tourneau's arms, being danced slowly around the circle. Only one guitar was playing now, a slow song that repeated a simple chord progression over and over. Most of the workers had gone to sleep long ago, filled with food and wine after a long last day's work, but she knew Tourneau always stayed up until the end, to have the last dance of the night with her.

After she'd left Louis in the winery, she went to the vineyard house to change her clothes. She took off the pants and blouse she'd worn to serve food, and put on a long skirt bound at the waist with a red sash, and a white blouse trimmed with lace, and she took the time to bind a few grape leaves into her hair. When Tourneau saw her approach the fire, he took off the accordion and bounded to her side, and brought her in on his arm to laughter and applause. He danced with her then, and several times during the evening she caught his eye and he took off his accordion to dance with her again.

Louis appeared briefly, and she made him dance with her as well. She knew she hadn't really moved him. He still felt distant in her arms. But at least he'd come out of the winery.

Now at the end of the evening, Tourneau had lifted her up again, and with the music slowly plucked from the guitar they turned around the fire one last time before coming to a halt. They both gazed up the hill at the rows of vines, ragged and picked, brokenly reflecting the moonlight. And she massaged his lower back with the flat of her hand, in a way she knew he would recognize, in a way that would leave no doubt that she wanted him.

Once the truck passed by the sharp turn and the killing tree, Gill told Big Boy to slow it down, and he looked carefully through the windows of the truck, to sight the tree where the tripwire alarm was hidden.

When he felt they were getting close, he held up his hand.

"Stop here."

Big Boy stopped the truck and left the headlamps on. Sailor Jack let Gill out and stood a little back from him, and Gill heard him pat his pistol. Men from the other trucks also got out and stretched their legs, and two of them lit kerosene lamps.

Gill got down on his hands and knees and crawled forward, so that he wouldn't accidentally set off the alarm. Within a dozen yards, he found it: strong black twine stretched across the road, invisible even in daytime.

"Got it," he said.

Sailor Jack waved up one of the men carrying a lantern. Together, they traced the twine to the spring switch and the dry cell batteries on the side of the road.

"Easy pickin's," Sailor Jack said. He waved Gill back and watched as the man with the lamp disconnected the batteries. When he gave the thumbs-up, Sailor Jack kicked through the trip wire. The spring switch snapped shut, but only silence followed.

"Now," he asked Gill, "where's the phone line?"

"Right up there in the trees," Gill said.

Sailor Jack grabbed bolt cutters and walked up the bank. He looked for a moment to distinguish the electrical line from the phone line, then snapped the phone line in two. Gill watched everyone checking their weapons again in the headlights. He was the only one without a gun of some kind. Then they attached the kerosene lamps, still lit, to the rear of the first two trucks. All the headlamps were cut and everyone climbed back aboard. Gill sat again next to Big Boy, who was blinking and waiting for his eyes to adjust to the moonlight.

"Good to go?" Sailor Jack asked.

"Couple minutes," Big Boy said.

Gill looked out at the gravel road, skull-colored.

Big Boy blinked slowly. Then he put the truck in gear, and the convoy started slowly up the road, the back two trucks guided by dim kerosene lanterns swinging before them.

On the verandah of the vineyard house, Paul Tourneau sat down heavily in one of the broad wooden chairs and looked toward the *chaine d'or*. He had left Sophia in bed and come out wearing just trousers and a shirt, to savor one last breath of harvest night. All the fruit was off, crushed, the year's work now in casks, or fermenting in the big tanks. Safe, from rot or insects or birds or disease or weather.

The hills of the *chaine d'or* were smoothed by the moon's pale light, untouched, virgin and distant. As he looked, he pressed his hand against his belly, probing the swelling and tenderness of the right side. He manipulated himself slowly, finding just the point that hurt most, pushing on it, confirming the pain for himself. He found himself doing this often after making love with Sophia, leaving his wife who was still so young and beautiful and seeking out that weakest spot in himself—but only when alone, when no one else could see.

He ran his hand over his belly, pushed in again to feel the hurt.

Then he heard a rumbling from down the hill. He stood and peered out from the middle of the verandah, but he couldn't see anything move.

"Sophia," he called back into the house.

The rumbling grew closer as she joined him, her hair loose, wearing a nightgown with a shawl around her shoulders. She turned her head toward the noise. "What could it be?"

"Go back into the bedroom," he said. "Lock the door."

She went inside, and Tourneau watched until he saw something moving on the road, coming closer. Then he walked to the gun closet in the back hallway, pulled out a shotgun, broke it to see that both barrels were loaded, and snapped it together.

As he stepped onto the verandah, headlights suddenly cut on, blinding him, and he heard the truck doors break open and the sounds of men and metal.

He shaded his eyes. Three pairs of headlights glared at him, all facing straight on to the house. The doors of the trucks were open, and gun barrels poked around each one, aiming at his chest.

"Drop the gun, Pops," one voice called.

Tourneau lowered the barrel of the shotgun.

"Drop it. And hands up."

He laid the gun down on the porch and raised his hands slowly.

"Now tell her to come out. So she won't get hurt."

Tourneau stared into the lights, saying nothing.

"Don't go simple on us," the voice said.

"Hey, Papa," another voice said. "It will be easier if she just comes out with her hands up."

Tourneau leaned toward the voices. Then he saw, walking toward him, a dark man, limned by headlights.

"Gilbert," he said.

"Hi, Papa." Gill knelt and picked up the shotgun. He looked at his father, massive and helpless, with his hands in the air. "I've been waiting for this a long time. Maybe you have too, in your own way."

"Gill," Tourneau whispered. "You know where the rifles are. Run inside, get Sophia, save her. Call the police and run away."

"Ha ha." Gill touched his father's chest with the barrel of the shotgun, just above the heart, tapped him there twice. Then he turned to the doorway.

"Sophia. Come on out. You won't be hurt. We didn't come for that."

"Don't come out, Sophia. Call for help."

Sophia appeared at the doorway, turned her face away from the headlights so that her long black hair fell over one shoulder. "I wondered if you'd come," she said. "For harvest."

"Here I am," Gill said. "Is Lou in the house?"

"Don't say anything," Tourneau said.

"The phone line's dead," she said to Tourneau. "He can't call for help." She turned to Gill. "No, he's sleeping in the winery again."

Gill waved at the trucks. "All clear. Let's go."

The men at the trucks came out from cover and began walking toward the porch, no longer aiming their guns but still holding them ready. Sailor Jack came beside the three of them. "Where's the kid?" he asked.

"In the winery," Gill pointed toward the tall, dark building beyond the house. "He's probably asleep, and he won't have a gun."

"Maybe."

Sailor Jack took the shotgun out of Gill's hands.

"You won't need this," he said.

They marched Tourneau and Sophia with them over to the winery, warning them to be quiet.

Big Boy walked beside Sailor Jack. He'd taken off his coat, and his shoulder holster rode at an awkward angle over the folds of flesh.

"So, he don't hate his brother, eh?" Sailor Jack asked.

"Not like he hates his father," Big Boy said. "Least I don't remember him saying much."

"Okay, Gill, show us that you're good. Just bring him out quiet, like a lamb."

"I'll be right back, asshole," Gill said.

Sailor Jack chuckled and patted his holster.

Inside the cellars for the second time in ten years, Gill breathed in the rich fruited scent of fermenting wine. The smell of every harvest. The smell of completed work, the smell of being able to go back to school with his father's niggard blessing.

He reached for a candle to the right and lit it, then walked up the stairway to the second floor, where the big fermenting tanks stood.

He walked carefully around the tanks, one hand holding the candle, the other passing along the tall redwood staves, warmed now by the fermentation within. The candle seemed too tiny to throw even a shadow among the massive tanks. It simply lit a small globe of light that faltered and died a few feet from the flame.

On the far side of the last tank, closest to the window, he found his brother on a cot. Louis was sleeping the sleep of the young, deep after hard work. Gill could hear him breathing, the breath blending with the buzz of fermentation. He knelt beside the cot, brought the candle closer to his brother's face. It was smooth in profile, like a polished medallion, hairless and full-lipped and deep-lidded. Both like and unlike his face. It was a fuller and fleshier version of the smooth side of Gill's face, younger and unlined.

Gently, he said, "Louis."

Louis stirred, perhaps saw the inside of a dream, then settled again. His pupils moved under his eyelids.

Slightly louder. "Louis."

Louis turned onto his back, his face full and open, his mouth parted with breathing. Then he rose up, as though his upper body were suddenly weightless, and kissed his brother on the cheek.

"Jesus!" Gill jumped back, embarrassed and ashamed.

Louis shook his head and his eyes wakened.

"It's you," Louis said.

"Hi, brother," Gill said.

Louis sat up in the cot. "I knew you'd come back."

"You did?"

"Or I hoped so at least."

Louis pulled on a shirt and overalls, and then sat down to put on some shoes. He paused to look up at his brother, standing silently.

"You haven't told Papa yet. Have you." It was more statement than question.

"Told him what?"

"That you want to come back."

"No," Gill said. "I haven't told him."

Louis stood up and walked to the wall switch. The electric lights came on in the winery, single bulbs dangling over the walkways and at the tops of stairs.

"Well, I'll tell him," Louis said. "He'll just have to let the past be the past. Because this is the way it's supposed to be, all of us, working together."

He picked up a wine thief, a slender glass tube for tasting samples, and handed it to Gill.

"Come on, I'll give you a taste of the Pinot we already have in the puncheons."

Gill remained standing where he was. "Is that the way it's supposed to be?"

Louis stopped. "Of course. It's the only way that's fair."

"Shit," Gill said.

"What?"

"Nothing. You're a better person than I am, that's all."

"What are you talking about, Gill?"

"Listen, we'll taste the Pinot in a little while. Let's go back to the house and try to talk to Papa now, okay?"

"Okay," Louis said. "I'll tell him. I swear I will."

They walked between the tall fermenting tanks, and Louis described the state of the wine in each one, pointing out the columns of chalked figures on the side for Gill's approval. He was especially proud of the last Cabernet they had harvested, with the Brix a shade over twenty-five, the kind of perfect fruit you dream of. Gill nodded to all this, agreed, gave his blessing. While they were going down the stairs to the ground floor, Louis said that he had broken up with Nancy.

"We both decided we weren't right for each other," Louis said.

"Good," Gill said. "She was a bitch."

"No, she wasn't," Louis said.

Gill stopped at the bottom of the stair and waited for Louis.

"She wasn't?" he asked.

"Well"—Louis joined Gill—"maybe she was. I don't know."

"You're still a little stuck on her, aren't you?"

"I want her to be happy. I worry about her."

Gill put his hand on Louis's shoulder. "You went the limit with her, right?"

"A few times."

"And you feel responsible for her." Gill nodded. "You can care about somebody years afterward, even if you've just been chasing around like me."

"Yeah?"

"You'll carry a load of regrets around, no matter who tells who it's over."

"So what should I do?" Louis asked.

"Nothing."

Gill put his arm around his brother's shoulder and began walking with him toward the door.

"You'll just have to learn to live with regret."

He let him walk a little ahead.

As soon as Louis swung open the winery door, he was seized and thrown facedown on the hard-packed ground. He tried to get up, but someone had a knee in his back, and he heard his mother shouting at him not to fight, they had guns, and his brother yelling that there was no need to be so rough.

He lay still then, cheek against the earth, and he felt the knee on his back relax, and a hand patting him down for weapons. There were dark shoes and dark legs standing all around.

He rose up suddenly, tried to throw off the man bestriding him, but a quick gun barrel rapped the side of his head, printing his cheekbone with blood.

"I said go easy," Gill said. "Look, he's not packing, and he's lying still."

The man over Louis nodded and stood up, and Sailor Jack smiled.

"I like to get the fight out of them before they start," he said. "Can he get up?"

"I can get up," Louis said. He stood and looked at Gill, then walked over to join Sophia and Tourneau, standing surrounded by men with guns. Gill didn't meet his look, gazed at the dark ground between them.

One man was left outside the winery, and the rest shuffled inside. Tourneau, Sophia, and Louis were herded to one side, and Big Boy stood behind them with a .45 in his hand. Sailor Jack came in front of Tourneau, looked at him, then looked at the massive fermenting tanks, the double rows of puncheons aging wine. He gestured around him.

"This must be your whole life's work. But for us, this is only one night's work. We're just here to pick up a load of champagne. Let us do our one night's work, and we'll leave your life's work alone. Deal?"

Louis looked over at his father, saw the small hard eyes. He knew his father would never say a single word to acquiesce. Even if they were to take everything, he would never let it be with his permission.

"No deal?" Sailor Jack asked. "Let me ask, are there any booby traps in the winery? Anything to keep us from going in and loading up?"

Tourneau said nothing. Sailor Jack looked back to the cave opening, where the vaults of wine were carved into the mountainside.

"Okay, Gill," he said. "Show us that you're good."

Gill walked over to the large wooden pillar, reached around it, and pulled the small key from the nail. He held the key up, showed it to his father.

"The key to the kingdom," he said.

Tourneau turned and stared at Louis.

Louis looked down. "I'm sorry, Papa," he said.

Gill went to the shutoff lever for the tear gas, hidden behind another pillar, unlocked it, and pulled it out and down.

"Okay," he said, "let's load up."

"Just a second." Sailor Jack turned back to Tourneau. "Are there any other traps besides the tear gas?"

"No." Tourneau looked at him hatefully.

"No shotgun traps? Nothing?"

"No. Nothing."

"Good," Sailor Jack said. "Because just to make sure, we're going to have your son walk us back to the champagne."

"Go ahead," Tourneau said. "Take him."

Two men cut Louis out from the group and pushed him toward the cave opening. They walked some ten steps behind him, carrying their Tommy guns at their sides by the pistol grip, ready but not aimed.

"Just walk nice and slow all the way to the back," one said.

Louis could hear his own footsteps as he walked on, hear the footsteps of the two men who shadowed him. The cave was lit now by widely spaced electric lights, but the walls of bottles still seemed broad and unending, still curved beyond sight into the side of the mountain.

The men behind were whistling and laughing at the number of bottles, but Louis heard only voices in his head.

Go ahead.

Take him.

Live with regret.

Go ahead.

Live with regret.

When they reached the end of the cellars, deep into the cave where the champagne was kept, one of the men said, "I wish we had a dozen trucks, and a couple dozen men."

"I worked hard on this wine," Louis said.

"Well good for you, sonny," the man said.

Back in the winery, Sailor Jack made Sophia and Tourneau sit on the floor with their backs to the wall. Tourneau watched the opening into the cellars, wondering if he would hear a gunshot, wondering if he had sent his son to be executed. When he saw Louis emerge, he sagged against the wall and took Sophia's hand in his.

The men made Louis sit against the wall as well, and Tourneau leaned over and whispered quietly, "I should have gone. I shouldn't have let them take you."

"It's all my fault," Louis said. "I brought Gill up to the winery."

"It's not your fault," Tourneau said.

Sailor Jack told Big Boy to stand guard over the three prisoners, since he was too fat to be much good in loading the trucks. He cursed when he heard that the champagne was at the far end of the cave, but then he shrugged. There was plenty of night left.

Gill showed the men how to pack the champagne into boxes, and they began rolling it out to the waiting trucks on dollies. He avoided looking at where Big Boy stood, with his pistol drawn, over Louis and Sophia and his father. He felt their eyes on him, every time he walked past behind a pile of boxes, especially Louis's. So he watched the floor carefully where he was wheeling the dolly, making sure that no cracks or bumps would cause him to drop something.

When the first truck was piled high with boxes of champagne, two men stayed outside to cover it with a dirty white tarp. The others began to load the second truck. All the men worked in silence now, quiet and earnest. They had shucked their coats, hanging them on the truck doors and rear-view mirrors, and they worked in white shirts, suspenders and neckties, some with their shoulder holsters flat to their ribs. They perspired slightly under their arms, and now that everything was secure, they worked as efficiently as warehousemen loading stock.

After the second truck was loaded, one man asked Sailor Jack if they could open a couple of bottles and have a drink. Sailor Jack shook his head.

"Drink on your own time," he said. "This is business."

Inside, Big Boy grew bored standing guard. He watched the other men file past with the dollies, and he thought about how much money was going to be made tonight. And he wouldn't get a cent of it. He would be free and clear with Mr. Beckwourth for the car that bitch Lupita had wrecked, and that was it. Everyone would be making money hand over fist except him.

He soured further when he saw Gill walk by, rolling a dolly like he was one of the guys. He had never really liked Gill. There was always something stuck up about him that irked Big Boy. Gill had deserved to be set up, for not trusting Big Boy to divvy up the money right. Now Big Boy was more irritated that Gill would come out of this night all to the good, while he would be flat broke.

He looked down at the three people he was guarding, sitting against the wall with their feet out straight. The old man looked the most sullen, so he kicked at the sole of his shoe.

"Hey," he said. "Did you know that I used to run a still with your kid?"

Tourneau looked up at him. "Is that so?"

"Sure." Big Boy waved his gun around. "Near Coyote. Rye whiskey. Good stuff, too. I got him into the business."

"Yes?" Tourneau suddenly pictured his oldest son in the hills east of the Santa Clara, fermenting grains and distilling them. "So why didn't he stay with that?"

"He couldn't be happy with it. Fact is, Gill's never been happy in his life." Big Boy laughed. "He always wanted your winery. You know why?"

"Tell me."

"Because he thought you owed him, big time. So how about it?" Big Boy kicked the sole of Tourneau's shoe again. "Do you owe him?"

"No. He owes me."

"I knew you'd say that," Big Boy grinned. "But if he'd never met me, he never would have done it. In fact if it weren't for me, we wouldn't all be here tonight. You might say I was the spark that lit the fuse."

"You're proud of yourself," Tourneau stated.

"Mister?" Louis asked. "When Gill came back to this side of the valley, did he always mean to rob us?"

Big Boy pursed his thick lips, stroked his chin. Then he smiled, wide and fleshy, dimpling his fat cheeks. He smiled like a butcher with a sharp cleaver in his hands, and he lifted his chin slightly to speak, to speak with great and fat satisfaction.

A gunshot, proud and blooming, echoed through the winery.

The men wheeling dollies froze, then crouched and drew their pistols. They looked around, unsure where the gunfire had come from.

The gun fired again, from the second story near the fermentation tanks.

Big Boy spread his arms wide, as though to embrace the three sitting on the floor before him. Then he brought his hands to his heart, one hand still holding the .45, and fell to his knees. He slowly opened his mouth, and a mush of blood grew from between his lips.

On the second floor, Augusto Corvo cackled.

"Got me one, dead as an Indian!" He danced around with his cavalry pistol.

The men began to fire up at Augusto. He took cover behind the massive fermenting tanks as bullets ripped splintered pieces from the redwood staves. When the gunshots quieted, he poked around the tank and took one quick shot, which led to another round of gunfire.

While shots crossed the winery, Tourneau stood up and grabbed the .45 from Big Boy's hand, then pushed him over with his foot. The big man toppled softly to one side and wheezed.

He looked across the winery floor. Nobody was watching them, but there were six men with pistols between them and the door that led outside. They couldn't escape that way.

He waited until there was another exchange, and all the men were looking up to the second level. Then he gestured with the gun. Louis helped Sophia up, and they ran, crouching, into the wine cellar. Tourneau followed them with the gun in his hand. One man noticed him as he disappeared into the cave mouth, but too late to turn and aim.

"Take your mother to the back, all the way," Tourneau said. "I'll hold them off."

Outside, near the trucks, Sailor Jack heard the shots and took up a Tommy gun. He turned to Gill, standing beside him. "I thought you said we were good."

"I thought we were," Gill said.

"Come on."

Sailor Jack made Gill walk through the door first. Inside, a man told them what had happened, and they heard Augusto talking about fighting off the Indians, keeping the land free.

"Who is it?" Sailor Jack asked.

"The grandfather," Gill said.

"Alone?"

"He's just a crazy old man."

"Crazy old man with a horse pistol."

Sailor Jack had several men distract Augusto with a scattering of gunfire, and he climbed the stairway up to the second floor, carrying his gun by its pistol grip.

"Augusto!" Gill called. "Throw down your gun. Give yourself up."

"Gilbert?" Augusto's voice floated out. "Is that you?"

"Give yourself up. Or they'll get you."

"But I've got them on the run, boy."

Gill watched Sailor Jack reach the near side of one of the fermentation tanks and begin to inch his way around the dark side, then disappear.

"On the run!"

The Tommy gun spattered out of the dark and cut off the voice, and the rapid crack of bullets reverberated throughout the winery.

Then the bullets ceased. An echoing silence settled into the dim space, like a low hum, broken only by Sailor Jack's slow footsteps coming back down the stair.

"Big Boy's iced," one man said.

"Well, fuck a duck." Sailor Jack walked over to the fallen body, nudged it with his foot, looked at the eyes, glazed and surprised, and the ribbon of blood that covered the chin.

"I thought this was going to be neat and clean," he said. "Where's the three of them?"

"Ran into the cave. I think the old man took Big Boy's .45."

Sailor Jack shook his head wearily. "We've got another half truck to load. He's making things hard on us."

He sighed as he reloaded his Tommy gun with a fresh hundred-round canister, and he looked at Gill.

"Come on, Gill. Show us that you're good."

They entered the cave together, walking carefully, listening for a sound that would give away Tourneau. Sailor Jack frowned. The tall walls of bottles divided the cave into narrow aisles and passages, poorly lit alcoves and blind alleys. It was like a maze of liquid walls, filled with shadows and ambushes.

They walked down one left-hand passage, paused at each opening that gave way to other aisles and listened for breathing. It was so dark at the very ends of the aisles that Paul Tourneau could have been standing still there, still as a hangman, and they would not have seen him. Once, Sailor Jack pointed his gun to shoot, then realized that all he had seen was a misplaced bottle, breaking the solid line.

They reached the end of the passage, and Sailor Jack breathed deeply. "I don't like this," he whispered. "Where could they be hiding?"

"Anywhere," Gill whispered back. "And he knows every nook and cranny of this cellar."

They backed out to the main way and walked down to another breach that opened into the labyrinth of aging wine. The walls of bottles were nearly ceiling high, stacks of dusty, dimpled bottles, bottom side out, with a number stenciled under each section. The passage ended in darkness, and the aisles that opened up on either side of it would also end in darkness.

"I don't like this," Sailor Jack repeated.

"Let me go ahead," Gill said. "Maybe I can call him out."

"You're not packing."

"Maybe better that way."

"Okay," Sailor Jack whispered. "I'll be behind you if he fires."

Gill stepped forward into the passage, paused at the first aisles, then moved forward. He could hear his footsteps on the concrete floor, but he made no attempt to muffle them.

"Papa?" he called. "I don't have a gun."

There was no answer. Gill walked farther, looked left and right.

"Papa, it will be safe for you if you come out with your hands up."

He walked farther into the maze, sure that his father was lurking somewhere nearby, waiting for him.

"They just want wine. They don't want to hurt anyone."

As he peered down one aisle, he paused. He could hear breathing. It wasn't a blind alley, like the others. It opened onto a little alcove with a table, and a cabinet holding some glasses.

Gill waited, standing half in the aisle. Finally he saw movement. His father's eyes, reflecting the dim light, shining darkly. The large beard, the large bearish shoulders. The metallic glint off the gun in his hands.

"I could have killed you by now," Tourneau said.

"Why didn't you?" Gill asked.

"You're my son, damn it. Have you forgotten?"

"You know, I always loved the night when harvest was finally complete," Gill said. "When all the fruit was off, and crushed and warm in the fermenters. And people were happy and dancing. Especially if the moon was full and the night warm. Like tonight."

"Is that why you've come back tonight, like a thief?"

"Wherever I was in the world, I never felt at home there. There was only here. It was always harvest, always warm. And you, always standing in my way."

"And I'm still here," Tourneau said. "Protecting my wine."

"But it's not your wine. That's what you never understood."

"My wine," Tourneau said. "Mine."

He lifted his pistol and aimed above and to the right of Gill's head and squeezed the trigger. The gunshot shattered a bottle and sprayed wine and shards of glass into the air.

Then Sailor Jack was crouching beside Gill, firing toward the sound of the shot. Glass cracked and red wine poured onto the floor as the bullets crashed through the walls and down the aisle.

The echoes died, and Gill and Sailor Jack looked down the aisle where Tourneau had stood. It was empty and deserted, but deeper within the aisles they heard glass crunching, and the gurgle of wine bleeding from smashed bottles.

"I think I got him," Sailor Jack said. "But where did he go?"

A bullet ripped past Sailor Jack's head, coming from somewhere through the walls of bottles.

"Shit." Sailor Jack backed up, staying low to the ground, and Gill backed up with him.

"Get out." Tourneau's voice, a snarl of pain, seemed to come from all around them. "Get out."

"Let's beat it." Sailor Jack scrambled back to the main way. Then, spitefully, he emptied his Tommy gun back among the champagne bottles, making them explode as the pressure from the wine burst the glass apart.

"Let's see how that bites him."

They sprinted back into the winery, and Sailor Jack pointed to the door. "Haul ass. I'm not losing another man in this death trap."

"Only two and a half trucks?" one asked.

"They'll be happy if we get it there," Sailor Jack said. "Let's move it."

The men began to holster their guns, pick up their coats and hats and put them on, buttoning up neatly. Two men picked up Big Boy, swaying him between them, to be lashed to the bed of the half-empty truck.

Sailor Jack stood by the door, waving his men through, telling them to hurry up, counting them off. Gill stood unmoving in the midst of the empty-ing room. When the last of the men was out the door, Sailor Jack paused and looked at Gill.

"You coming?" he asked.

Gill shook his head. "It's blood money now."

"It was always blood money for you, half-face," Sailor Jack said. "But suit yourself."

The door slammed shut, then bounced open again, and outside the truck engines roared to life after one brief burst of gunfire. Gill turned and saw Louis peeking out from the mouth of the cave.

"Let's check on your grandfather first," Gill said.

He began to climb the stairs, but before he'd gone up three steps, Louis pulled him back down by his collar. Gill fell to his back, and Louis was on top of him, throwing wild punches at the side of his head and crying.

Gill covered up, protected his face and temples with his forearms, and Louis stopped in less than a minute. He sat back and wiped the snot from his nose.

"Come on," Gill said again. "Let's check on your grandfather first."

They found him leaning against the big fermenting tank, his cheek against the planks of wood, as though still enjoying the warmth of the grapes turn-ing to wine, as though listening to the buzzing change. He wasn't breathing, and his old cavalry pistol had dropped by his feet.

"That's what I was afraid of," Gill said.

"I'm going to go get Papa," Louis said.

"Good." Gill hoisted Augusto's body over his shoulder and began to walk with him down the stairs. Sophia waited at the bottom, and as Gill walked past, he felt a tug on Augusto's arms. Not as violent a tug as the one he gave to his mother so many years ago, when he tried to pull her from his father's back, but still needy and forceful.

He paused and looked behind him, and saw Sophia lifting Augusto's hands to her face, kissing them, breathing over them with her head bent. Then she lowered the hands and followed Louis into the cellars.

Outside, the three trucks were gone. The gibbous moon cast a bone-colored light on the circular track left in the dust. Gill slow-walked to the farm truck and the Buick and found the tires shot out on both.

"We'll have to use the wagon," he said to himself.

The wagon rested near the corral, still stained with the sugary juice that had oozed from the fresh-picked grapes in harvest boxes. It smelled sweet as Gill dropped Augusto over the side and heard his head knock against the wood. He reached into the wagon bed and placed Augusto's hands over his chest, touched his face so that it turned upward, and brushed his eyelids closed.

In the cellar, Louis found his father sitting in the shadows with his back against a wall of bottles, holding his left upper arm with his right hand. The pistol rested in his lap.

"I'm hit, Lou," Tourneau said. "Are they gone?"

"They're gone."

"Did they get away with the champagne?"

"A lot, but not as much as they wanted."

"Good." Tourneau squeezed his eyes shut in pain, then opened them and blinked several times. "We're in trouble, Lou. We need to sell that champagne."

"Grandpa's dead," Louis said.

"Ah." Tourneau sighed. He saw Sophia appear at the end of the aisle, quiet in the dim light. "Augusto," he said.

"I kissed his hands good-bye," she said.

"Well. Come help me up."

Louis knelt by his father's side and draped his father's unhurt arm over his shoulder. They staggered upright together. Tourneau's right leg was bleeding, and he tried to hop forward on his left leg while leaning on Louis. They made several steps, tilting back and forth against the bottles.

"I'm going to try to put some weight on it," Tourneau said.

"The bone might be cracked," Sophia said.

Tourneau slowly lowered his right foot to the floor, rested his heel down, then took a quick step forward.

He yelled, fell against Louis, and they both went to the floor. Louis tried to brace himself against his father's bulk to cushion his fall.

"Christ almighty," Tourneau said, panting.

"I'm going to go get Gill," Louis said.

"Why is he still here?" Tourneau said.

"I'll be right back."

He returned with Gill a minute later. Tourneau was again sitting on the floor gripping his left arm, while Sophia was stanching the bleeding at his leg.

Tourneau shook his head at Gill, and his black beard brushed his chest. "I didn't want to see you again."

"You won't, after tonight."

Gill knelt down on one side and Louis on the other, and they lifted Tourneau to his feet. Tourneau's left arm, his wounded one, rested on Gill's shoulders, and the blood oozed down and mixed with Augusto's that already marred his shirt.

They walked slowly out of the labyrinth of bottled wine, the two half brothers supporting their father, Sophia walking several steps ahead with her head bowed, as though leading a procession. Outside, Gill directed them toward the wagon. Sophia lowered the tailgate and saw the soles of her father's boots facing her, the slick leather shining dully in the moonlight.

She gasped, and Tourneau looked up from between his two sons and stopped still.

"I'm not ready for the charnel wagon." He glared at Gill. "Maybe I'll outlive you both."

"The truck's shot up," Gill said, while Louis remained silent. "We've got to get you down the hill."

Tourneau swung his large head over to Louis. Then he shook himself free from his two sons, hopped forward on his good leg, and backed himself into the wagon bed.

"I'll ride sitting up, at least," he said.

Tourneau sat stoically while they hitched up the horses. Sophia climbed into the wagon bed and knelt next to him, Augusto's body to the other side. Then Louis took the reins, and Gill climbed into the seat beside him, and they started down the hill.

As the wagon jolted over the uneven road, Tourneau groaned despite himself, and his face grayed in the falling moonlight. Sophia wiped the perspiration that dotted his forehead in the cool air while she kept pressure on his wounded leg to slow the bleeding. One hump slanted across the road, and the wagon rocked unevenly left and right as the wheels passed over it one at a time, and he cried out.

Louis turned around. "We'll get you there as soon as we can."

Tourneau groaned deeply and shook his head.

By the time they reached the sharp turn at the killing tree, Tourneau was semiconscious, muttering when the wagon bed jostled him. Sophia tried to cushion his ride, molding her body against his, but Louis kept the speed up as fast as was safe in the dim light, and the ride was roughened.

He turned to Gill as they rounded the turn. "How bad do you think he is?"

"I didn't see any bones coming through," Gill said. "The doctor will patch him up."

They rode a little ways in the creaking sound of the wagon joints, and the tread of the horses, and their low snorts and breathings. Then Louis turned to Gill again.

"What are you going to do now?"

"Hop off the wagon at the bottom of the hill. Find a way out of town before I get spotted and hauled in."

"Let me ask you, Gill. Were you always planning on robbing the vineyard when you came back?"

"I wanted to get back something that was mine," Gill said. "Something taken away from me a long time ago."

Behind them, in the wagon bed, Sophia had begun to quietly sing a lullaby, a soothing song for Tourneau.

"That's not the same as robbery, is it? And when I got it, I was going to go someplace new and good, and start over."

He looked over his shoulder at Sophia. She was stretching her hands out, touching both her dead father and her wounded husband, and the shawl draped over her shoulders and arms enlarged her embrace, so that it seemed she could encompass all of them.

"Now that's gone. And I can never come back here."

The wagon creaked over a rocky patch.

"I remember another trip down this hill," Gill said. "Did you get around to asking how my mother died?"

"No," Louis said.

"You find somebody who knows the story to tell you sometime. You'll never hear it from your father."

Sophia's song changed into a hymn, soft yet sweetly audible above the road noise and the hushed groans.

Near town, Louis pulled up on the reins. "Dr. Appleton's to the left," he said.

Gill nodded and hopped off the wagon. Sophia stroked Tourneau's forehead and cast her dark eyes across the two brothers. "I'll pray for you," she said to Gill.

"Thanks for that."

"Send us a card now and then," Louis said. "Don't say where you're living, just let us know that you're well."

"You'd better head to the doctor's," Gill said.

He turned southeast, where a false dawn hovered over the hills.

"Wait."

Louis jumped off the wagon and began to unbutton his shirt.

"You've got bloodstains all over your shoulders," he said. "Here. Take this. Maybe it will help you not get caught."

Gill paused, looked at Louis offering his shirt to him at the end of an outstretched hand. His smooth young face looked wistful.

Gill took off his own shirt and dropped it in the ditch beside the road. Then he took Louis's between his arms and draped it around his neck, and reached out, and brushed the tips of his fingers across his brother's cheek.

"Thanks," Gill said.

Louis climbed back into the wagon seat and gave the reins a shake. The horses started forward, and he gave the right rein an extra snap to make Prince step up and turn the wagon to the left.

Then Louis and Sophia both turned to look after Gill. He walked in the opposite direction, advancing slowly into the pale uncertain light, and he was pulling his brother's shirt over his arms. For a moment, he had both arms raised in the air, and the shirt floated about him, expanding in the breeze like a sail.

FOURTEEN

Epilogue

In the fall of 1928, that splendid year on the edge of the Great Depression, Louis never returned to school. Tourneau was laid up in bed with his wounded leg and arm, and Louis had to see the new wine through fermentation, dosed with sulfur, into aging barrels. He trekked between the winery and the house and told his father everything that was going on with the wine, then listened to a long list of orders and instructions. Whenever he came in to see his father, he found him sitting up, with his broad back against the headboard, tense and alert. It was as though Tourneau didn't exist until Louis was with him, talking about the winery. At times, he held Louis with him, talking about unrelated matters, even after he had just given him an urgent task. He complained about his doctors, how long they had told him to stay in bed, a numbness at the fingertips of his left hand, the graveyard stew and other thin food for sick people that Sophia made for him. Louis answered with short, discouraging sentences, and when his father finally trailed off, he trudged back to the winery.

It was Sophia who told Louis that he should not think about returning to school that year. Soon after the robbery, she announced that she was going to have a baby, and she spoke of her pregnancy as though it were a miracle, as though the coming child would repair all damage. She grew lively and animated, nursing her husband. She wore white and spoke excitedly of the times they were living in, and the time to come. Once, when Louis left his father, she drew him into the kitchen. A pot of chicken soup was on the range, and a bed tray was readied with buttered bread and a glass of milk.

"We'll all have to sacrifice," she said. "All of us. But you'll see. It will make us magnificent. We will stay up here on this hillside, and live on water and air if we have to."

Louis looked at her, his eyes flat and tired. "Doesn't he want me to go to college anymore?"

"Of course he does."

Sophia took her son's face in her hands and kissed his cheek.

"He would never ask this of you."

She kissed his forehead.

"Tell him it was your idea. Your idea to skip school this year. Your idea to sacrifice. Tell him."

She put her arms around him and hugged him to her, then she kissed his cheek again.

"It will mean more to him if he knows it was your idea," she said. "It will restore him. He'll eat the food I bring him. He'll sleep well, tonight and every night. Tell him. Go back and tell him now, and see how it makes you feel."

She hugged Louis once more and released him, and he walked slowly back to the room where his father lay. He already felt this new child as a burden.

On that morning when his brother left for the last time, Louis had driven the wagon past the green town square and McCarty's Cash Store, where a couple of boys with bicycles were waiting to pick up their bundles of the weekly newspaper to deliver. The boys stared from under their broad, short-brimmed caps at the strange wagon clipping briskly by, the shawled woman kneeling in the wagon bed and singing a hymn, the driver wearing just an undershirt, the dull moaning sound. Louis looked back at the two boys, lowered his head and hid his face. He snapped the reins to ask the horses to step up.

Dr. Appleton's office was in a small white house on Lumber Street, formerly a private home, and Louis had to run next door to the doctor's two-story Victorian to wake him. The doctor took one look at Augusto Corvo and shook his head, and he and Louis walked Tourneau into the examining room, followed by Sophia. They laid him down on a flat, white-sheeted hospital bed, and the doctor began cutting through the clothing to expose the bullet wounds.

"Lay out your grandfather in the next room," Doctor Appleton said. "I'll have to make out a death certificate for him."

Louis picked up his grandfather from the back of the wagon and carried him in, holding him in his flexed arms before him like a lover would. He placed him on a hospital bed in the next room, arranged his hands peacefully over his chest, made sure his eyes were closed. He peeked in to where his father lay and saw his mother hovering near the doctor, speaking in a low, insistent voice.

Outside, Louis was passed by a boy on a bicycle, carrying the *San Natoma Star* rubber-banded into tight rolls in a big canvas bag that hung over his shoulders and had pouches front and back. He walked to the Cash Store, where Bill Finney had just finished handing out the news to all his delivery boys, and told him he had a story for the paper.

Finney took a pencil from behind his ear and a pad of paper from his hip pocket. "What's up?"

Louis looked up and down the quiet, empty street.

"Can we go to your print shop and talk?"

"Sure." Finney put away the pencil and paper. "Need a ride?"

"I'll take the wagon."

Finney drove at a slow pace and allowed Louis to follow him closely. He pulled up outside the converted barn and they walked together through the print shop to the back office. Finney sat down in one of the comfortable leather chairs and motioned for Louis to sit in the other one, but Louis first threw the dead bolt on the door.

"So we don't get disturbed," he said.

"Okay," Finney said.

Louis paced back and forth, then sat on the very edge of his chair. He breathed deeply. "Mr. Finney, can you tell me how Gilbert's mother died?"

Finney stood up and took a pipe from a pipe stand on his desk. He filled it with tobacco from a large tin and tamped it down. "How much do you know?" he asked.

"Nothing," Louis said. "I know nothing."

"Okay." Finney sat down and lit his pipe.

He told Louis everything he had learned over the years, and the ways he had learned it. He repeated the old gossip about why Tourneau had married Pascale, without love and simply to gain the land, and the rumors of his neglect of her afterward. He discussed the tales he had heard, that he thought came from some of the migrant laborers: that she had appeared to them as an angel both before and after her death, that she had died and then her body had risen, that she had flown in a white glow the night that she died. Some claimed that they had heard her put a curse on the vineyard. It seemed clear that she had died in a tree and was found gazing toward the vineyard when it was being cleared during the phylloxera outbreak. He'd heard that from enough people that it didn't seem made up. It also seemed pretty clear that Paul Tourneau hadn't stopped work even one day because of her death, and in fact had a big fiesta two days later to celebrate clearing the field of diseased roots.

"If Paul thought he was at fault at all in Pascale's death, he never admitted it. He's always had a certain ruthlessness, and that let him do what he needed to do for that vineyard. But I think Gill always blamed him. Gill was damaged, long before he was injured in the war. And every time Paul looked at Gill, he saw something from the past he'd just as soon forget. He probably didn't mind letting him go off to war and away from Beau Pays."

"I remember cake," Louis said. "And shaking hands with him."

"You tell me," Finney said, "what Gill might not have forgiven or forgotten, even after so many years."

Louis sat with his head in his hands, looking straight before him.

There was a tapping on the door, and Nancy's voice came through it.

"Papa? Is Louis in there? I saw the wagon."

Louis didn't move at the sound of her voice. She rattled the door. "Papa, I can smell your pipe. What's wrong?"

Finney looked a question at Louis, but he didn't move. The door stopped rattling. A few seconds later, there was a tapping at the side window.

"Louis." Nancy's face appeared between her cupped hands, pressed at the window. "What happened? What's wrong?"

"What's wrong, Louis?" Finney asked.

Louis looked up. The tapping at the window continued.

Later that day, Miguel and Ana were seated in the cab of the Hudson, driving southeast. In the back of the truck, they had piled high the mattresses, and pillows, and sheets, and canvas bags of clothes that they had lived with for the past four months. Francisco and Rosarita lay back against the mattresses, watching the blue sky unfurl behind them as the truck tires whined down the road, and Javier stood up in the truck bed, holding one of the stakes to support himself.

They had seen the signs of the robbery when they and the other pickers had broken camp—the open door of the winery, the truck shot up, the stone silence of the house—but it gave them no reason to wait. They had been paid for their labor, and there were no more paydays coming from Beau Pays. All the families and young single men were packing and making ready to chase the next harvest, the next payday, in apples or walnuts or almonds. And there were some grapes still to be picked, it was said, farther north in Napa and Sonoma.

The Hudson headed in the opposite direction, away from the unfinished harvests. Ana had finally convinced Miguel that this year, the children should not start school a month and a half late and then never catch up. They should have a chance, in high school, to see if they could finish, maybe learn to type, maybe really be able to work in an office. And Miguel gave in. He would *hacerle la lucha* while they went to school, look for work laying pipe, or in the brickyards or paper mills. If nothing else, he could probably catch on in the sanatorium. He stated with bitter certainty that the children would grow up to think they were better than their parents, but Ana told him no, that they would think him the best of fathers.

They drove through San Jose, stopping once for gas at Pirelli's Associated Gas Station, and then continued south toward Coyote, and Morgan Hill, and Gilroy. They passed through cherry and pear and prunes, orchards that they or their friends had worked in over the years, now looking ragged and ready for pruning.

"How much money did we make?" Miguel asked.

"I haven't counted," Ana said. "A lot, if you can keep the truck from breaking down."

"I'll keep the truck from breaking down," Miguel said. He smiled as he kept his hands on the wheel.

"Are we going to come again next year, to New Chicago?" Ana asked.

"Do you have a better idea?"

"No," Ana said. "I just hope something will change someday."

South of Gilroy, in the shadow of a locust tree, they saw a small man stand up and put his thumb out.

"Stop for him," she said. "Stop for that one."

"That *bolillo*?"

"He looks sad," Ana said. "Forlorn."

"Everyone is forlorn."

"If we don't pick him up, who will?"

Without reply, Miguel downshifted the Hudson, stopped to carry one more with them on the road home.

In the spring of 1929, Tourneau was forced to graft over half the vineyard to *pagadebito* grapes, the debt-payers, Alicante Bouschet and Mataro. They both yielded four times as much per acre as Pinot, and home winemakers liked them for the color and abundance of their juice. With Hoover's election, Prohibition was likely to continue another four years. Tourneau couldn't sell enough fine still wines to the Church to pay the mortgages, and much of the champagne that he could have sold as medicinal had been stolen. Although he had always sworn not to graft over his vines, the bank refused to roll over his debt unless he increased his yield. Albert Jackson, of the Bank of Italy, had lines of credit out to many grape growers in the Valley, and he knew what others were doing to stay in business. Tourneau had no choice, and hoped only that grape prices would rebound just as the grafts began to bear.

Tourneau could do little of the work himself. He needed a cane to walk, and his left hand was not strong. But every morning around ten, he walked carefully down to see the grafting continue, to watch his son carry on the work, carry out his vision.

Louis grew used to his father's daily visits. He watched him struggle over the turned, uneven dirt of the allées, hopping and cursing and planting his cane as he advanced. At first Louis had run to assist him, but his father had shaken him off and told him to get back to work.

Louis chewed Copenhagen while grafting. He liked to hold the new scion, a tapered cutting with two buds, in his mouth while making the cuts, and the chewing tobacco kept his mouth moist. He studied the vine before him, planted in the year his father's first wife died, and chose a section of smooth, straight grain. He sawed at the top of the straight section, toppling off the six living spurs, and then with a splitting tool and a hammer, split the trunk straight across the pith to a depth of a little over an inch. He used the wedge on the edge of the splitting tool to keep the cut open, and inserted the scion at one edge of the trunk. He needed the cambium of the scion, the thin living layer of wood just under the bark, to be in contact with the cambium of the trunk.

He cut another scion, placed it in his mouth, and inserted it at the other edge of the cut. Then he withdrew the wedge and tied raffia around the top of the trunk. Whichever of the two scions proved more vigorous would be trained up, and the other cut off.

When he looked up, Tourneau was standing crookedly over him, leaning on his cane.

"Every time we cut off a vine, it's like we're cutting off one of my own limbs," Tourneau said.

Louis nodded, scooted down to the next vine, and studied it for a place to cut. The straighter the grain, the easier it was to fit in the scion.

"*Pagadebito*," Tourneau continued, "*pagadebito*. But whose debts are we paying? Think, every cut you make, Gilbert's hand is behind it."

Louis placed the curving saw blade where he had chosen and began to work it back and forth.

At the end of the day, Louis went up to the edge of the redwoods, above the cleared land, as he had done when he was young and Gill was missing. In San Natoma, the prune orchards were blossoming. The town would be holding its annual Blossom Festival that weekend, with fireworks, dances, concerts, to celebrate the return of springtime, the promise of harvest held in the cup of each flower.

In the past, Louis had enjoyed this time of year, the seemingly eternal sense of freshness and renewal in the stainless white crowns of flowers that were everywhere in the valley. He had enjoyed the prayers and songs giving thanks, to God, for living in a blessed place. Now, he wondered how many of those orchards concealed old and bitter debts beneath the entirely human dreams that had given shape to them.

He looked up at the somber redwoods that had never answered his questions. Looked down at the thousands of acres of fruit trees, whitened with blossoms above the sketchy black trunks, that unfolded across the valley floor like the pages of a book.

"They're not my debts," he said. "They're not my debts."

In the valley below, the town prepared a celebration.

ACKNOWLEDGMENTS

The town of San Natoma, featured in this novel, has much in common historically and geographically with Saratoga, California, the town where my mother grew up. In key aspects, however, San Natoma is a creation of my imagination. The characters and events are fictional, and are not intended to represent actual people or events.

I did research for this book at the Bancroft Library at UC-Berkeley, the Napa Valley Wine Library in St. Helena, the Sonoma County Wine Library in Healdsburg, and the California History Center at De Anza College. I would like to thank the wonderful reference librarians at those institutions, especially Lisa Christiansen at the California History Center. I would also like to extend special thanks to Dave Muret of the Santa Lucia Highlands Winegrowers for a fine afternoon discussing grape growing and winemaking.

This manuscript was read and aided by many friends and fellow writers. I'd like to thank Dorothy Solomon, Pam Carlquist, Kristen Rogers, Ron Molen, and Kay Cook, who saw drafts of the early chapters. Thanks also go to Valerie Cohen, who reads true, and to Alan Winnikoff and Alison Bond. A final push from Margaret Dalrymple at University of Nevada Press was most necessary and appreciated.

While writing and revising this book, I enjoyed the support of the Department of English and the College of Arts and Sciences at Bowling Green State University, and I'd like to thank especially Kristine Blair and Wendell Mayo. And finally, my thanks to Kimberly, who has seen me high and low.